Christmas, Alabama

Christmas, Alabama

A novel

Susan Sands

TULE
PUBLISHING

Dear Reader,

I want to thank my parents, Linda and Ray Noel, who continue to be my biggest cheerleaders. As I watch them struggle with my dad's dementia, I see and feel their joy as I realize my publishing dreams. My dad still asks every time I see him, "Sue, how are your books doing?" He struggles to know what day it is and how to walk sometimes, but so far, he hasn't failed to ask about my writing. My mom still reads every book I write as it's written. I wish everyone had parents like mine.

Thanks to the amazing Tule publishing team. They never disappoint. We are lucky authors to work with such talented people.

Love to my husband, Doug, who hasn't seen as many home cooked meals as he'd like this year. To Kevin, Cameron, and Reagan: I appreciate the adults you've become while Mom has spent the last few years at her computer most of the time.

Special thanks goes out to my lifelong pal, Rennie Longlois Clifton, for hawking my books in our hometown! She's spent much time hand-selling these stories, and I so appreciate it!!

This book was a delight to write. I've never attempted a Christmas story before, and I so loved dressing Ministry, Alabama up for the holidays!

I hope you enjoy the return of Ministry's ensemble cast throughout *Christmas, Alabama*! I created a snowy, cozy, fun story with all our favorite characters as they pop in and make an appearance, while I introduced a new and wonderful couple in Rachel and Nick.

Please let me know what you think!!
All the Best!
Susan Sands

Chapter One

R ACHEL PRUDHOMME ABSORBED more truth through the lens of her camera than words, true or not, could speak. Eyes didn't lie. Expressions caught off guard didn't lie.

The bride wore an exquisite white, off-the-shoulder beaded gown, and the groom, a sharply-tailored black tux. Their smiles were radiant. The wedding party smiled, and their families, despite a few obvious squabbles, smiled too.

But something was off. It wasn't obvious, and Rachel might have missed it had she not zoomed in on her subjects—the bride and groom—through the viewfinder. They weren't the dreamy, happy couple they appeared to be. There was a tightness around the eyes and mouth of the groom. A sadness behind the smile of the bride.

Yet, everyone was participating in this expensive and very public lie, and all were smiling their way through the photos and poses. Or maybe it wasn't quite a lie, but more of an imbalance. Vows were made and cake was cut amidst the flowers and music. The band played and the guests danced.

Maybe nobody knew anything was amiss, or if they did, they pretended they didn't.

Rachel had learned the hard way that this was none of her concern. Maybe they'd had a fight over the cost of the wedding, or the destination of the honeymoon. Or, perhaps he'd waited too long to propose. Whatever was at play here, weddings brought out the stress and inner beast in everyone, all while they smiled and played the parts of the happiest people on the planet for their families and friends. The photos were the key to remembrance. This was a Thanksgiving wedding. The food was heavy, harvest fare. The flowers were deep shades of crimson, linen and champagne, and golds. The greenery was heavy and dark. The autumnal tones, spicy cinnamon candles, combined with the cool temperature outside set the stage for rich, lasting memories.

So, Rachel would do her job to cement the memories for this couple, hopefully, a lifetime's worth. The stress, the fight, or whatever had happened prior to the ceremony wouldn't carry through when they looked at their wedding photos in ten years if Rachel did her job well. The photos made the re-remembering pure perfection.

"Hey, Rach, could we get a shot of Grandma Jean with the garter on her leg?" the bride asked, her smile bright.

The alcohol was clearly doing its job now. "Sure." Rachel followed the bride to where the elderly lady was perched on the best man's knee, skirt hiked. "Okay, Grandma Jean. Show us some leg!"

Everyone laughed, and all was well. Rachel wondered for a moment if she'd imagined the earlier angst. Not likely, but she continued snapping photos until the "happy" couple was tucked into the getaway car and celebrated out the drive.

Rachel took a few more shots of lingering guests who asked to have their picture taken, and then, after they finally trickled out the door, she took refuge in the large, renovated kitchen of The Evangeline House, the most popular venue in Ministry, Alabama for all the goings-on in town.

"That one lasted a while. I thought we were going to have to shoo them like flies out the door," Miss Maureen, the owner said. She was sipping tea on a barstool, her sensible black flats kicked off on the floor.

"Once the bar was shut down and the band packed up, you'd have thought they might have gotten the message," Rachel said.

Miss Maureen laughed. "You never know how late weddings will go. It often depends how young the crowd is and how much alcohol they consume. Did you get some good shots?"

Rachel nodded. "They were all very photogenic. No major catastrophes."

"They were out-of-towners from Huntsville, so I don't know the family. They seemed pleased with everything. Paid their bill, said thank you, and left."

"Seems like there was something underlying with that couple, don't you think?" Rachel asked.

Miss Maureen laughed. "Oh, honey, I've been doing this for more years than I can count, and there's always more there than meets the eye. I quit trying to figure people out ages ago. I'll leave that up to your sister."

Rachel smiled. Her sister, Sabine, was the town's clinical therapist, and she was continuously booked up. "Must be hard knowing all the town's secrets."

"She bears it well, all things considered. So, how are you settling in here? Are the people of Ministry treating you well?" Miss Maureen had a shrewd and sharp eye.

Rachel had put her feet up on a chair, feeling comfortable here in this place with this woman who was her sister's mother-in-law. Sabine had married Miss Maureen's son, Ben, who was now the mayor of Ministry, last year. Rachel had moved here to be near her mother and sister after some chaotic years flitting around as a freelance photographer.

"I'm doing pretty well; thanks for asking. It's not exactly an open society here. So, I expect it will take some time to feel like a native."

Miss Maureen laughed. "A native? The best you can expect as a lovely single woman is open hostility from the other single women and their mommas until you find a man and get yourself off the market."

Rachel snorted. "Yeah. I've noticed. There aren't a lot of unattached men around here that have all the desired qualities." Like a decent job and most of their teeth.

"So, the race is *on* when one does come along. Better be

careful not to get caught in the fray when it happens." Miss Maureen rolled her eyes. "Those women will be on him like a pack of rabid *dawgs*, I tell you.

Rachel loved the accents here. She had her own slight drawl, she supposed, but it was more indicative of her upbringing in Louisiana. "I appreciate the fair warning, but I'm not on a major man hunt at the moment. Life has been exciting enough lately without bringing that into the mix. I'll let the others go after the bachelors, should they pop up."

The older woman waved her hand like she was swatting a fly. "It'll happen when it happens, sweetheart, and you'll be in the thick of it before you know it."

Rachel smiled. This tiny town wasn't so bad. She'd enjoyed getting to know people, mostly her sister's husband's people, the Laroux family. Heck, they seemed to make up half the town. Coming from New Orleans, this slow, slow, way of life was a bit of a culture shock.

"Well, I'd better get moving. I've got lots of editing to do on these shots. They'll want them yesterday if they're anything like every other bride and groom I've ever photographed."

"Alright, darling. I'll see you at Thanksgiving dinner Thursday."

"I'll be there. Thanks again for including me."

"Nonsense. You're family; we wouldn't have it any other way."

"MINISTRY, ALABAMA? ARE you kidding?" Dr. Nicholas Sullivan couldn't believe what he'd just heard.

"Nick, it's a favor to the new VP of operations—to me. Yours is the only contract up for renewal in the next few months. And it would merely be through the first of the year." His administrator's tone had taken on a near-whine.

"I'm a trauma surgeon at one of the largest hospitals in Atlanta. How does this happen?" Nick asked aloud, maybe to himself as much as his admin.

"There isn't anyone else willing, for any amount of money. They're all married with families and time left on their very specific contracts. You're the one we can leverage—and bargain with. The company is willing to make it worth your while. Look, they know you don't have a wife and kids, so it makes you more portable for the coming weeks."

Unclenching his jaw, Nick glared at his administrator. "Fine. I'll do it. But not past the end of January. Figure something else out beyond that. I want the position at Emory waiting for me to step into when I return, just like we discussed before this came up." The coveted Emory job was what Nick had been working toward for the past couple of years, the position he'd been working his way toward at Grady Hospital while he'd been up to his elbows in gunshot, car accidents, and stab wounds every day. This had been part of the "paying his dues" portion of his training—and an integral step in learning to be the best trauma surgeon around.

Dan nodded and stuck out his hand to shake Nick's. "I'll speak with the powers-that-be. The job's had your name on it since Doctor Jacobs announced his intent to retire last year. I'll see about getting the paperwork drawn up."

Nick felt the warm wave of negotiative success wash over him. Then, the cold splash of reality. He was headed to Ministry Alabama for the next month or so. Good, God. He could hear the banjos twanging already.

Chapter Two

RACHEL'S EYES WERE nearly crossed from the photo editing she'd done the last few days trying to get things finished up before Thanksgiving. Closing her computer, she headed to her bathroom to take a shower. It had a magnificent claw foot tub that Rachel assumed to be original to the home. The apartment she'd rented was on the top floor of a very old house owned by an equally elderly lady named Mrs. Wiggins. Clearly Mrs. Wiggins was baking again, based on the delicious smells wafting up through the wooden floorboards of the house, into Rachel's nose, and into her stomach, causing audible growling.

Living alone was nothing new to Rachel. Neither was forgetting to eat. She wasn't the cook her sister or mother were, and she found no joy in shopping for food and preparing meals for one. She was lucky that both her mother and sister lived nearby and fed her regularly or she might *become* a skeleton in Mrs. Wiggins's attic.

As she turned on the ancient shower, she couldn't help

but appreciate this apartment find in the heart of the historic district of Ministry. The house was enormous, and the upstairs had been divided into two apartments years ago. Her recent next-door neighbor, Jane, had just moved out. Jane had found her Prince Charming in the form of a handsome, single doctor who worked at Ministry General. He'd gotten an unexpected offer at a larger hospital in Birmingham, and he'd asked her to marry him and move there. Rachel hoped to be as lucky with a new next door neighbor with whom she would share walls. Mrs. Wiggins didn't need the money, and would be more likely to leave the place vacant until she found someone suitable than accept just anyone into her home as a renter. So, that was a relief.

The water finally was warm enough for Rachel to step under. The water pressure wasn't the greatest today, so it took longer to rinse out the conditioner from her thick hair than normal. The good news was there was enough hot water to last. She would take the good with the bad these days.

Living here, Rachel couldn't help but think of the similarities to her childhood home in the New Orleans Garden District. She'd grown up in one of those historic old houses the tourists stopped to take pictures of when they came to town. It was large with high ceilings and rich oak floors that smelled of fresh beeswax. This old house had the same feel of history and belonging. And the smell of beeswax. And low water pressure; because there were some things about old house one couldn't change.

Just as she'd stepped onto the bath mat and wrapped a towel around herself, Rachel heard her phone ringing in the bedroom. Dashing out, she nearly tripped over a large calico cat. "Dang it, Spags, I almost squished you." Spags was Mrs. Wiggins, her landlady's cat—her *alive* one, who sometimes dashed inside her apartment when the door was open and she wasn't looking. Mrs. Wiggin also had two formerly-alive kitties she'd had preserved by Junior, the town's taxidermist, for perpetuity.

She grabbed the phone off the bed. "Hello?"

"What time will you be here?" Sabine asked.

"I've been editing all day and I just stepped out of the shower. About an hour, maybe."

"Can you pick up a few things at the store on the way? Ben's out in the barn."

Sabine was quite pregnant, and they had an adorable squishy little toddler named Janie, so Rachel occasionally ran an errand here and there for her to help out. "Sure. Text me a list."

"Great. See you in a bit."

Rachel was headed over to help her mother and sister prepare food for Thanksgiving dinner. They would be eating at Evangeline House with Sabine's inlaws, the Laroux family, but Sabine and Rachel had Louisiana traditions they maintained for Thanksgiving and other holidays as well. So, there was bread pudding, crawfish pasta, and a few other non-traditional favorites to prepare. They would bring the dishes over as their contribution when they went for dinner tomorrow.

Plus, it gave the three of them a chance to spend time cooking and enjoying the holiday together before joining the great, big Laroux family celebration. They'd been through a lot in the past couple years, and this together time was healing. Their struggles, as a family, were a big part of why Rachel had recently made her home here.

Dad was now out of the white-collar prison, having served his time, and made parole. His crimes hadn't been of a violent nature, but he'd caused a lot of damage to many—especially his family—their mother, in particular. He was now living on the coast of Alabama at the beach. Mom and Dad had divorced, and Mom had recently found much-deserved happiness again with a very nice local man, Norman Harrison. But Dad had been the love of her life, so there was still a lot of unresolved anger toward Dad for the pain he'd caused them all.

So, Dad's re-entry into their lives was an ongoing process. Rachel had been slow to forgive his ruining of their family. A ruining that had begun years before she'd had any idea he wasn't anywhere near the man, or the father, she'd believed. And she'd been a daddy's girl. She'd adored her father and trusted him blindly as only his baby girl could.

So, her deep, bitter disappointment at discovering his betrayals was existentially shattering to Rachel. She'd begun to heal now, but it was likely going to take the rest of her life

SUSAN SANDS

to truly forgive her father, and not to doubt the motives of men, in general, after what he'd done to her mother and their family.

⟫⟫⟪⟪

"DR. SULLIVAN, THANKS for coming to town so quickly. We weren't sure what to do when Dr. Dawson announced he was taking the job in Birmingham. Left us in a real pickle—he did." Nick shook the hand of the chief of staff at Ministry General, who was dressed in camouflage from head-to-toe. Did Nick really want to speculate if there was a dead animal slung over the hood of his 4x4 out in the parking lot?

Nick steeled himself against noticeably hesitating to shake the man's hand, in case he'd not scrubbed down after he left the woods. "Deer season?" Nick asked.

"He he. Son, we take our time in the woods when we can get it around here. Just came off my stand at the lease. They said you were coming today, so I didn't want to miss you."

Nick appreciated the effort. "Thanks for coming in."

"Suzette's our department manager; she's around here someplace. She'll show you the ropes. When are you wanting to get started?" the older man asked.

"I'm here, so I might as well start now, if you need me," Nick answered. He was checked into a tiny motel off the highway, and had nothing else to do until he found a larger place to stay.

"Well, son, I like your spirit." Dr. Granger slapped Nick

on the back and said, "Well, I'll leave you to it. Got to go home and shower. I'll be back when your shift ends. Just remember, we move at a slower pace here than in the big city. You'll have to remember to be tolerant with our staff and our patients at first. I've seen it before, folks coming from bigger places. There's a learning curve—not necessarily one that goes upwards, if you know what I mean." The old doc gave Nick a wink and a nod then moved away, and left him staring, eyes glazed. Nick hoped his expression didn't display the abject horror Dr. Granger's words had just instilled within him.

Nick took a breath. And then another. It was only for a month and a half, at most.

"Hey there. I'm Suzette."

Nick turned to see who'd spoken. The rather husky voice did not match the face. She was stunning. "Hello. Nicholas Sullivan." He stuck out his hand to shake.

"Dr. Granger said you were coming in today. Lordy, we've been worried getting a replacement since Dr. Dawson said he was leaving us. Of course, Dr. Smith covers the third shift, but this is a job that takes three of you without making somebody do overtime."

Lordy, was right. Suzette appeared to have stepped right off the pageant stage and into a pair of hospital scrubs minus her crown. She was just under six feet tall with platinum blonde hair.

"It's nice to meet you, Suzette. Could you show me

where my office will be so I can unload a few things?" He had his messenger bag slung over his shoulder.

"Well, sure. It's right this way." He tried not to notice the way she sashayed ahead of him, her shapely hips swaying. Surely, she realized her walk was worthy of a runway in New York or Paris. Suzette led him into a nice-sized office with windows and a large antique desk and a comfy-looking sofa. The hospital was an old, historic building, like everything else in this town, but it had been renovated, and even seemed quite up-to-date from what he'd seen so far.

Nick put down the heavy bag that held his few desk items and laptop on the sofa.

"Here's the key. I've hung a couple lab coats over on the hook in the corner. Your name tags are on them, and I've got your electronic key fobs to gain access to all the secured areas at the nurse's station. You'll have to show identification and sign for those."

"Great. You've managed to get a lot done quickly." He pulled out his wallet and showed her his government issued ID. She then removed the high security items and handed them to him.

His amazement must have been somewhat evident, because Suzette gave him a smile that might have held a tiny bit of scorn, and she said, "Ministry might be way out in the sticks, but we run a fine establishment and a tight ship."

Touché, Suzette. "From what I've seen thus far, I'm pleasantly surprised, I must admit."

She nodded, accepting his compliment as her due.

Nick filled out a mountain of additional paperwork, careful to take his credentials and key fobs with him when Suzette introduced him to the staff working the current shift. He had to admit to again being impressed by the efficiency of the nurses, CNAs, and even by the maintenance engineers who all seemed to be extremely proficient and friendly in dealing with patients, and in their movement and interactions with one another.

He'd interned and worked in multiple hospitals for over ten years now and knew when things were functioning as they should. It was a combination of organization and cooperation by the chief of staff, the charge nurses, and a positive working environment. When people were treated well, trained well, and paid well, it motivated them to perform at a much higher level.

For a small, podunk town, he was pleased by what little he'd seen. Nick relaxed just a bit. At least he could slide into his work here without it being the worst-case scenario. His fears of walking into a Mayberry RFD episode had been replaying like a black and white movie reel in his head, complete with the classic *Before the Shot* Norman Rockwell print on the wall of the treatment rooms. He'd reserve judgment on that until he'd seen them.

"You're going to be the attending on call covering the ER and general surgery. So, pretty much anything that comes in will go through you before we call in a specialist."

"Everything?" So, here was the rub. Small towns meant less compartmentalization. More generalization.

"Well, our nurses and nurse assistants handle the small complaints after you've had a look. You know, constipation and such. But you'll deliver your share of babies and treat folks for trying to impress their kin here." She smiled, nearly blinding him with her dazzling white smile.

Shaking his head, he asked, "Trying to impress their kin?"

"Aw, you know, when somebody says, 'hey y'all, watch this,' and then it doesn't go so well."

Ah. Yes. Nick nodded. "I've seen plenty of that in my day."

Just then, the double doors swooshed open. The tiny brunette triage nurse approached, her rubber clogs squeaking, and handed Nick a chart as she spoke. "Female, twenty-eight weeks pregnant, complaining of upper belly pain. No bleeding. This is her second pregnancy. First one went full-term."

He took the chart. "You want me to handle this one?" he asked, uncertain of his current authority.

"Dr. Griffin left you in charge. Said you wanted to start immediately." She grinned at him then and said, "Oh, and since you're new, the patient is the mayor's wife."

"Well, then, I'll leave y'all to it. I've got paperwork to do," Suzette said. "Let me know if you have any questions, and keep me posted on Sabine's condition," she flung over her shoulder as she sashayed away.

The nurse said to Nick, "Dr. Sullivan, I've put Mrs. La-roux in treatment room one." She pointed down the hallway. "It's marked. Georgie, our nurse on duty is with her now."

"Thanks."

Chapter Three

"I'M OKAY. I didn't need to come here," Sabine said for what seemed about the hundredth time.

"Clearly you're not fine. I saw you double over in pain and you could hardly walk," Rachel said, trying not to shout at her very stubborn sister.

"It was gas. Have you ever been pregnant?"

That shut Rachel up.

But then she couldn't help herself. They were siblings, after all. "No, but if I was, I would go to the doctor if I had that kind of pain."

The door opened and a doctor wearing a white lab coat entered the small treatment room. Rachel was expecting Dr. Griffin. This was *not* him. She'd overheard Ben tell Sabine they'd wrangled a new temporary doc from Atlanta at the last minute, but there hadn't been any discussion of his resemblance, or being a possible body-double to Matthew McConaughey. *Alright, alright, alright.*

"Good afternoon, I'm Dr. Sullivan. I understand you're

having some pain." He nodded to Sabine, and then to Rachel, but didn't make eye contact. His focus was all on Sabine. Very professional.

Sabine flushed. "I'm embarrassed. I think I'm fine, maybe some gas, but my sister, here, and my mother insisted we come in." Sabine gestured toward Rachel.

Dr. Sullivan's polite gaze moved to Rachel and he smiled. His eyes were a nice hazel gray, and his expression polite.

"Well, let's make sure you're right and your sister is wrong, why don't we?" He pulled the stethoscope from around his neck and placed it inside his ears and listened to Sabine's chest, then had her lie down on the padded table. He placed the instrument on her belly and listened intently. "Your baby's heartbeat is strong and steady. Are you feeling a normal amount of movement today?"

Sabine nodded. "Oh, yeah. This little stinker is a kicker."

He nodded. "Have you had a lot of heartburn thus far?"

"Some. When I eat red sauce or pepper."

"Have you had any spicy foods today?" he asked.

Sabine grinned and nodded. "I've had boudin and smoked sausage."

"Don't forget about the gumbo," Rachel reminded her.

"Your bowel sounds are quite audible." Dr. Dreamy grinned. "Sounds like you've upset the balance in your gut. You're far enough along to take an over the counter antacid, let your stomach settle, and see if you feel better by morning.

If not, you should make an appointment to see your obstetrician tomorrow."

"See? I told you." Sabine made a face at Rachel.

"But." He held up a finger. "Let's do a quick urinalysis and blood glucose while you're here." He turned and made a quick note in Sabine's chart and handed it to the nurse assistant, who left the room, presumably to arrange for Sabine's tests.

Rachel turned to the hunky healer and said, "Thank you for making sure, Doctor."

He looked at her then. Really looked. And his mouth went slack—just for an infinitesimal second—before he recovered. Rachel almost missed it. She wasn't sure whether to be flattered or embarrassed. Rachel glanced at Sabine. Sabine hadn't missed it either.

In fact, the gleam in Sabine's eye promised retribution for Rachel's earlier *told you so* attitude. "Doctor Sullivan, did you just arrive in Ministry?"

He smiled at Sabine. "Yes, today, in fact."

What was her sister up to?

"I know this might sound unusual, but would you consider having Thanksgiving dinner with our clan tomorrow? My husband is the mayor, and has a huge family. They hold all their holiday gatherings at their family's event planning business, The Evangeline House. We would love for you to join us."

He looked like a deer in headlights. Rachel understood.

It was unusual for Sabine, who was normally so reserved, to turn on the full Prudhomme charm. But when she did, she was a sight to behold. Her midnight black hair and silver-gray eyes were downright hypnotic. "Uh, I've got to find a place to rent still."

"So, you're free. Wonderful. We'll have a cocktail and hors d'oeuvres at noon, then the meal at one o'clock. There will be lots of kids and babies, and likely some swearing. We dine casual, so come comfortable."

"Sabine, he might not want to subject himself to such chaos as the Laroux family gathering," Rachel suggested and shot her sister a *look*. What happened to her gas?

"Nonsense. It's Thanksgiving. He should be with family—somebody's family."

Rachel looked over at the irrationally handsome healer who was patiently observing their conversation. "I'd be delighted to attend Thanksgiving dinner. I do have family here, of sorts. I just haven't let them know I'm in town yet."

"Oh. Who are you related to here in Ministry?" Sabine asked, clearly interested.

"Judith and Jamie Dozier-Fremont." He squinted his eyes and winced a little as if waiting for a reaction.

Rachel and Sabine looked at one another. "Judith and Jamie are our dear friends," Sabine said, reassuring him he was indeed related to fine folk. Rachel hadn't missed his unsure expression, and understood it perfectly.

"They are?" Dr. Sullivan seemed surprised. The nurse,

Georgie, had returned with a test tube, and made a small snorting sound.

"Well, sure. When was the last time you saw them?" Sabine asked.

"It's been several years. We only saw each other on holidays and in the summer at our grandparents. They were—*characters*—best I remember. I still see some shenanigans on Facebook." He grinned, possibly a little embarrassed at that reveal.

"Well, they're grown women now, and they still have strong personalities, but we consider them friends. But I do suggest you contact them immediately, because if they find out you're in town and they hear it from someone else first, you might have a problem," Sabine warned.

Rachel giggled. "A serious problem." Rachel pictured Judith and Jamie, the doppelgangers for the Doublemint twins on the old Wrigley's gum commercials. They were sassy, Southern, and had big attitude, Junior League pull, and were, by far, the most sought after for sorority recs in the county. If a Dozier-Fremont got behind you, you were *in*. In whatever or wherever you wanted to be.

"I'll take your advice and contact them in a day or so," he said, and put a hand on the doorknob. "I'll leave you in Denise's capable hands for labs."

He quickly glanced at Rachel and the corner of his mouth quirked up. "See you both tomorrow. Can I bring anything?"

"Not a thing," Sabine answered.

"Every ounce of strength and resilience you possess," Rachel said and smiled sweetly.

"Noted," he said and left the room.

>>>×<<<

WHEN THEY WERE back in the car, Rachel let her pregnant sister have it. "If you weren't carrying another adorable squishy niece or nephew in there, I would call you terrible names and maybe punch you in the arm."

"Why? The poor guy just arrived in town and has no plans for Thanksgiving dinner."

"Oh, and he's a dead ringer for Matthew McConaughey. That couldn't have factored into it. That and your need to find me a nice, handsome young man. You and Mom."

"I didn't notice. This guy's nowhere near that old. But his response to you didn't escape my notice, or the lack of a ring on his finger. Doctors always wear wedding rings if they're married to keep women from throwing themselves at them," Sabine said.

"Oh. You know what?" Rachel giggled a bit. "He's headed for deep trouble. Word's gonna get out that he's new in town and single. I almost feel sorry for him." She'd made a few single friends in town, and the disparity between the number of single women and men was exactly what she and Miss Maureen were discussing after the wedding the other night. The local women were on the hunt for fresh man meat—always.

"Why can't you keep an open mind? Maybe you've met a great guy with a good job, and just go from there?" Sabine asked.

"Because things are never as they appear—people aren't as they appear."

"Maybe in this case, the good doctor is just a nice single guy. Ben shared that they had to strong arm him just a little to get him over here from Atlanta." The goings-on in a town this size involved everyone, and almost always, the mayor.

"Why would anyone move from practicing medicine at a big hospital in a city like Atlanta to Ministry? Unless he was trying to get away from something?" Or, maybe, someone? Rachel thought.

"Well, from what I heard, he drew the short straw because his contract was coming due. You know they must have had some leverage there," Sabine said.

"Maybe," Rachel turned in the driveway to Sabine and Ben's incredible stone and wooden-beamed house. Ben had owned the house for several years before he'd met Sabine. His goal in life had been to fall in love, settle down, and have kids. Ben was a happy guy. Because he was crazy about her sister, and they'd been blessed with little Janie and the squishy-to-be. Not to mention the animals Ben had used as his props to propose to Sabine in front of the entire town: Their large-pawed Labrador retriever, Ala, who co-dependently went nowhere without his sidekick Bama, the supposedly low-allergy Siberian breed feline. It was a love-hate relationship.

Mayor Ben was standing on the porch, holding a squirming Janie, with the dog and cat at his feet. Ben was a fine-looking man, Rachel could admit. He'd been the most sought-after bachelor in most of Alabama before he'd met her sister. Ben had taken the attention from women of all ages as his due, having been the baby of four older sisters. He'd been surrounded by females his entire life. But while Ben had dated pretty much the entire population of five counties, he'd not been interested in getting serious with anyone but Sabine.

Ben stepped off the porch and approached the car to assist his wife with his free hand. Rachel hoped she would someday find a man who adored her half as much as Ben did Sabine.

"Is everything alright?" he asked, a worried frown between his brows. Janie grinned and babbled.

"I'm fine. I told you before I left that it was gas, and a little heartburn." Sabine accepted his kiss and smiled. "The new doctor just arrived today. He seems nice." Sabine shot Rachel a wink.

"Your wife invited him to Thanksgiving dinner."

Ben laughed. "The more the merrier. Good thinking, honey. He probably didn't have anywhere else to go."

"That's what I thought," Sabine said.

Rachel wanted to pull her sister's hair.

"Honey, you alright?" Mom called out the door, an apron tied around her waist. She still wore a potholder on one hand.

Sabine waved. "Fine, Mom. Just gas."

They made their way up the porch steps and into the kitchen, where the amazing smells of the dishes they'd been preparing still filled the room. Ala, the dog, who was physically full grown, but not yet out of his puppy phase at just over a year old, suddenly found Bama's swishing fluffy tail irresistible, and gave chase, much to Bama's annoyance. She yowled in displeasure, and her claws found purchase in Rachel's shin and ankle before using them as a springboard to make her getaway.

"Aaah. Your cat is trying to kill me," Rachel yelped in pain, grabbing her ankle.

"Oh, no. Are you alright?" Ben asked, handing Janie over to her grandmother.

"She flayed me," Rachel said, sticking out her leg and pulling up her black leggings. Sure enough, there were three somewhat deep welts about four inches long that were oozing blood.

"Ouch. I'll grab the first aid kit," Ben said.

Sabine came over and had a look and wrinkled her nose in sympathy. "Sorry about that. These animals can be such a menace."

"I'm thinking maybe the cat and dog as siblings weren't the most inspired idea your husband ever had," Rachel said.

Ben returned then with the peroxide and bandages. "Wrong. It's how I got Sabine to agree to marry me." He grinned. "Plus, asking her in front of the whole town didn't hurt."

Sabine laughed. "The cat and the dog are a mixed bag, but I was a cat person and he was a dog person, so I guess it was a selling point. And it would have been hard to say no considering the position you put me in." Sabine elbowed Ben in the ribs.

"Everything went according to plan." He squatted down to where Rachel's injured leg was resting. "This is going to sting a little."

"Ouch!"

He laid a gauze square over the scratches and taped around it with steri-strips. "All better?"

"Yes. Thank you."

"This will make it better." Her mother handed her Janie, and she totally forgot about her very minor injuries.

"Boo-boo?" Janie lightly touched her leg.

She was the cutest thing *ever*. "Yes, Ala and Bama were naughty and gave me a boo-boo."

Janie touched her chubby fingers to her lips and then to the bandage. "Kiss boo-boo. All better."

Rachel might as well just have melted into a puddle on the floor right there. "All better. Thank you, Janie. Auntie Rachel loves you so much." She picked up her squishy little niece and proceeded to play all their giggly games—The

Fanny Wiggle Walk being the all-time favorite.

This town might not have much to offer a young single woman as far as excitement was concerned, but it had her family, and for now that was quite enough.

Chapter Four

N ICK TREATED A compound bow hunting accident gone wrong, where the arrow ended up in the hind quarters of a human wielding the bow instead of his prey. Nick wasn't sure how that had happened. Fortunately, it was more humiliating to the bow-bearer than a serious injury. A teen boy was admitted with side pain that was presenting as appendicitis, the usual kitchen knife injury from holiday food prep, and then, almost as if Suzette had fated it, a case of constipation in an elderly woman.

When his shift ended, Nick filled out charts and paper-work, much like he did in Atlanta. Besides the slow drawls of the staff, he continued to be amazed at the up-to-date facility and efficiency of everyone here. There were more *bless your hearts* and promises to pray for one another by staff and other patients. But that didn't bother Nick. Kindnesses of any kind never had. He'd been raised in a church-going family, though nothing like the small-town churches here, he believed in prayer and blessings. It wasn't uncommon in

Atlanta, a Southern city, to hear some of the same. Many of the patients there were brought in from smaller towns and suburbs outside the city to receive a higher level of care than was available in their more rural areas.

As he drove back to the motel at the edge of town, he remembered the phone number Suzette had handed him on a piece of paper, along with all the others. "Now, you might want to give Mrs. Wiggins a call. She owns a big old house in the middle of town and has an available apartment to rent, last I heard. Dr. Dawson's girlfriend moved out and left with him last week. I haven't heard that anyone else has rented it. If I didn't have a husband to live with, I'd take it. It's a cool place."

Nick guessed she would know, because isn't that how it worked in a town this size? Everybody knew pretty much everything? But he wouldn't pass up the opportunity to grab a prime place to rent, because it wasn't likely such places were easy to come by on short notice.

He hadn't brought much stuff with him, so hopefully the apartment had the basic furnishings. He would know soon enough. But first, he stopped by what appeared to be the local diner that looked as if it had been around for at least a hundred years, judging from the retro architecture of the building and the sign. He hoped the food was edible. The dozen or so cars in the parking lot must be a good sign.

The bell on the front door jingled as he walked in. There were several folks sitting in booths who looked up with interest as his arrival. The faces were a mix of young and old. It was around eight o'clock in the evening, the Wednesday before Thanksgiving.

"Well, hey there, young man, you must be our new doctor."

Nick turned toward the voice. A woman who likely was involved in the ribbon-cutting at the opening of the diner stood, her short hair dyed bright red. She grinned, showing her two or three remaining teeth. "Hi. Yes, how did you know?"

"Aw, sugar, we've been expecting you. Don't get many strangers in town, you know." She laughed—more of a smoker's cackle really. "I'm Thelma, come on over and have a seat, Doc." She led Nick to a booth with upholstered seats in worn red Naugahyde.

He stuck out his hand. "I'm Nick Sullivan."

"Aw, aren't you sweet." She blushed, or at least that's what it resembled. She shook his hand, her face crinkling and reddening.

"Do you have a menu?" he asked.

She laughed again. "Sure, honey." She reached behind the counter and handed him a well-worn laminated menu that looked again to be as old as the diner itself. "Don't get many requests for menus. Most folks have it memorized and just order their favorites. Haven't added anything new in a long time."

He took a moment to look through the local fare.

"I'll get you a drink while you look, if you'd like," Thelma suggested.

"Okay. I'll take a decaf and a glass of water. Thanks."

"Sure thing. Be right back." She shuffled away, her scuffed white orthopedic shoes a throwback to earlier times.

"You might want to stick with the patty melt and hash browns as a newcomer," a male voice from behind said.

Nick turned to see an older man, a dead ringer for one of his favorite actors, Sam Elliott, wearing a plaid shirt sitting across the booth grinning. "Thanks for the recommendation."

The man nodded. "Name's Howard."

"Nick Sullivan," Nick replied.

Thelma set the glasses in front of him with a *thunk*. "Howard, don't you be harassing my customers, you hear?" Thelma challenged.

"Wouldn't dream of it, darlin'." Howard/Sam blew Thelma a kiss.

Thelma narrowed her eyes at Howard. "Howard used to be some kind of spy or something. That's all we know. He married Maureen Laroux, so he's one of us now. But he's a real pain in the butt, you know?" Thelma said this in a conspiratorial tone, but Nick could tell she adored Howard despite her words.

"You know I've got your back, Thelma," Howard said. Even his voice sounded like Same Elliott's.

Nick broke this exchange up by saying, "I'm going to

take Howard's advice, Miss Thelma. I'll have the patty melt and hash browns, please."

"Coming right up." Thelma nodded, and shot Howard the stink-eye.

"Don't pay any mind to Thelma. She has an active imagination. Welcome to Ministry."

"Thanks. Seems like a nice place," Nick said. "Did Thelma say you were married to Maureen Laroux? Is she hosting the big Laroux family Thanksgiving dinner tomorrow?"

Howards bushy gray eyebrows lifted. "Yep. You coming?" Howard, man of few words, asked.

"Yes. I was invited by Sabine Laroux today."

"Well, I guess I'll see you tomorrow. Look forward to it." Howard stood then, and left a twenty-dollar bill on the table, and turned to leave. "Happy Thanksgiving everybody." He raised a hand to the folks in the diner just before heading out the door. The response was returned enthusiastically.

This place was from a storybook. Like every made-for-television movie he'd ever seen. Nick sat and ate his old-fashioned patty melt in this authentic diner—he couldn't even call it retro because it was the real deal—and pondered his current reality.

If he sat and thought about it, he might work himself up into a panic attack. Well, maybe not that, but the reality of where he'd landed sank in. He wasn't in Atlanta anymore. And here he would stay until the new year. Would the job be available at Emory when he returned, or were they just yanking his chain? The patty melt became hard to swallow suddenly.

⟫⟫⟪⟪

RACHEL LOADED HER camera, as she planned to take candid photos today during the family get-together. Funny how she considered herself part of Sabine's husband's family. The Larouxs did that to people. They pulled a person in and made them feel as if they belonged. Sabine hadn't had that sense of belonging within a community since she'd been a little girl living in uptown New Orleans, where private schools, the country club, and tight-knit social circles had created a safe and happy childhood for Rachel and Sabine.

Of course, their father had been the District Attorney of Orleans Parish, and they'd had all the privilege of wealth and status. Rachel was involved in every club and activity available because she'd been constantly seeking something new and challenging. She'd attended an all-girls' school and had been a fierce competitor in academics and sports. She'd been athletic and had lettered in tennis and soccer in high school. She'd also loved art and drama. There'd never been a dull moment.

Sabine, on the other hand, had been the exact opposite. She was excessively bookish. She'd spent most of her time reading with her cats, which had seemed boring to Rachel, who never sat still. The two girls looked nearly identical, though Rachel was a few inches taller, but they'd had such diverse interests, it was hard to understand one another as teens. But they were closer now than they'd ever been. The events of the last few years had done that.

Things began to change for the family when he'd brought their half-brother, James home one day and explained the situation to their mother. Dad had fathered a child with a cocaine-addicted debutante, who'd passed away. Mom never viewed Dad the same, but, saint that she was, took James in and tried her best to raise him as her own. But their father spoiled him, not allowing him to be disciplined, due to his sad birth circumstances. The result was a holy terror in their home who screamed the place down when things didn't go his way, and when he got older, he became meaner.

Sabine and Rachel had had to lock their doors to keep him out of their rooms when he was little. They'd tried absolutely everything to love him and incorporate him into their home and lives. But he refused to be anything but a nightmare.

James only listened to their father now, and only then because Dad held the purse strings to keep James in line. James had graduated from Tulane Law, so he was an intelligent, and very good-looking young man, but he lacked human compassion.

As Rachel dressed, she thought about her family and their Thanksgivings past. They'd had a great big house on St.

Charles Avenue right off the streetcar line in the prettiest part of the city. There was a brick wall surrounding the backyard that served as something right out of *The Secret Garden*. There'd been a pool, a gazebo, and lush semi-tropical gardens year-round. Holidays were always spent together as a family. Meals were massive and prepared mostly by her mother's hands, with the help of the elderly Hattie, her mother's right hand and dear friend, who'd worked for them throughout their childhoods.

Hattie had a hand in raising Sabine and Rachel, and even James, but she had passed away during the worst of the drama between their parents, which had made all of it so much harder to bear.

Dad wasn't here for Thanksgiving this year. The past two years he'd been incarcerated in the criminal detention center a couple hours from here. The white-collar prison had been a slap on the hand compared to the punishment the media suggested he deserved for his crimes. Rachel hated to think about all that. Dad's misdeeds had been criminal, and he'd hurt a lot of people, so it had been hard to be his children through the trial, and after.

And before. Because before the trial, he'd been exposed for having several affairs after James had come to live with them. He'd cheated on their mother publically, then behaved as if Mom should just take it in stride as the wife of a powerful political figure. Mom hadn't taken it in stride. And Dad had made it impossible for her to get a divorce. He'd used his connections and influence to keep her with him. Because, despite everything, he loved her. It was ugly and messy and very confusing for Rachel and Sabine.

It had been emotionally damaging to them all. Then, it all hit the fan when the charges were brought against Dad for all the illegal things: jury tampering, collusion, and numerous other offenses. He'd sworn he was trying to keep the bad guys from getting off on technicalities by ensuring the charges stuck. He'd turn a blind eye to the law and justice system somewhere along the way. It meant all the convictions during his twenty years as assistant district attorney and district attorney were called into question and had to be retried.

Many of the involved parties were now dead, and much of the evidence gone missing or considered tampered with, or inadmissible. It was a continuing disaster for Parish and would be for many years.

So, the entire Prudhomme family bore the cloak and the stain of their father's sins. That's just how it was, especially in a place like New Orleans, where the political stew was rife with corruption already. Of course, Dad saw very little wrong with his brand of justice, save getting caught. Even now, while he hated that he'd hurt his family, his true regret was not having done more to bring more criminals to justice.

Rachel shook her head to clear it, trying to keep from being dragged down by this yet again. These Alabama folks didn't care so much about her past in New Orleans. They knew about it, and every now and then, someone tried to get the lowdown on her ex-con father, probably because it was pretty interesting, so Rachel supposed she couldn't blame them. It *was* a rather fascinating story. Maybe someday she would write the family memoirs. In fifty or so years.

Rachel glanced in the mirror to check her appearance before leaving. Her eyes were a slightly deeper color than Sabine's, more toward blue than that cool silver. She had a slimmer build and pretty much towered over her curvier sister. Rachel felt like Lurch next to Sabine, no matter how much they resembled one another.

Just as Rachel had slung her camera bag and purse over her shoulder, a knock sounded at the door. She frowned, not expecting anyone.

"Hellooo—" she heard Mrs. Wiggins's creaky, high pitched voice on the other side of the door.

Rachel smiled and turned the knob. "Happy Thanksgiving, Mrs. Wiggins!"

"Well, Happy Thanksgiving to you too, dear." Mrs. Wiggins was about four-foot-eleven in her one-inch wedges. She held a small tin of something in her hands.

"That smells wonderful."

"It's shortbread. I make it every Thanksgiving. I wanted to bring you some while it was still warm." The little lady shoved it into Rachel's hands.

"How special. Thank you." Rachel leaned down and hugged her sweet landlord.

"It looks like you're on your way out, so I won't keep you."

Something niggled at Rachel about this. "Do you have plans today?"

"Well, no. My granddaughter was going to come pick me up, but her car isn't working, and she's not going to make it."

"Well, I insist you join me at The Evangeline House. Miss Maureen wouldn't hear of my leaving you here alone on Thanksgiving."

"Well, I wouldn't want to intrude—"

Rachel didn't allow her to finish. "Of course you wouldn't be intruding. Did you want to get a sweater?"

"I've got one right here." The elderly woman whipped out her tiny grandma sweater from a hook on a door in the hallway. Where had that even come from? Rachel was slightly amused, but happy to bring Mrs. Wiggins along as her guest, knowing a hundred percent that it would be expected should any of the Larouxs find out Mrs. Wiggins was alone today.

※》》《《※

WHEN NICK ARRIVED at The Evangeline House, it sounded through the heavy old mahogany door as if a party was in full swing. He rang the bell, but no one answered. He knocked hard. No answer. So, figuring he would be out here all day otherwise, he opened the door slowly. The scene that greeted him was a brand of chaos he'd not expected at such a grand establishment.

Amidst the lush fall décor, there were children running amok—and animals—two big dogs being terrorized by a large furry cat, if his eyes didn't deceive him. And then there were adults, who behaved as if none of this were occurring right under their noses, and feet. He counted at least three, no four gorgeous pregnant women, including Sabine Laroux, and a couple babies in arms. *What a menagerie.*

"Oh, there you are. Happy Thanksgiving." Sabine caught sight of him standing there, likely with his mouth open in shock, and possibly horror. She excused herself from speaking with a young African American woman who was also smiling and very pregnant.

He plastered a smile on his face and returned her hug as a greeting, remembering he was holding a bottle of wine and a large mixed bouquet of flowers. He'd stopped by the market after his shift yesterday and fought the crowd who were snapping up all the last-minute items for today's festivities.

"Happy Thanksgiving. These are for the hostess," he said. The much-spoken-about Maureen Laroux must be around here someplace.

"How sweet. Come with me and I'll introduce you. She and Rosie are in the kitchen." Sabine grabbed his hand and led him out of the main room.

He noticed the interested but welcoming glances darting

his way as they moved toward what he guessed was the kitchen. It was a huge and charming renovated mansion, clearly used for entertaining large groups. The place seemed to go on endlessly. The day was mild, so the back-patio doors were opened wide, allowing the guests to spill out onto a gorgeous outdoor area.

Were all these people family? He hadn't seen Rachel, Sabine's sister, in the crowd yet. Not that she was why he came, but it would be nice to see another familiar face. And hers wasn't hard to look at, he had to admit.

They entered the kitchen through a swinging door. An older woman wearing potholders on her arms was just turning around from pulling a large foil-covered pan from the giant oven. A milar-aged black woman was slicing a loaf of bread. Both looked up as they entered.

"Maureen and Rosie, I'd like to introduce you to our new doctor, Nick Sullivan. He's come bearing gifts." Sabine took the wine and flowers from him and placed them on the counter.

The older women turned and smiled warmly at him. "I'm Maureen, and this is my oldest and dearest friend, Rose. It's lovely to meet you, Dr. Sullivan. We are simply thrilled you could join us today." She pulled off the potholders, moved toward him and took his hands in hers as a dear friend might.

He nodded to Rose and Maureen. He was instantly charmed. "Call me Nick, please. Thank you for opening your amazing home to me. It's wonderful to meet you, Rose. It seems I don't have enough flowers."

Rose laughed. "Nonsense, honey. Maureen's the flower-lover around here. This boy's a charmer, Mo. We'd better keep him a secret in this town or those gals will be all over him."

"Well, it's certainly an honor to be here."

"Nonsense. You're likely going to want to go running, screaming down the street right back where you came after you see what you've gotten yourself into around here."

Maureen circled her hand in the air to demonstrate her point.

He laughed.

"Thank you for the wine and flowers, my boy. Now, you go on and make yourself a cocktail to calm your nerves before they find out you're here. You're gonna need it." She winked.

"Before who finds out I'm here?" he asked, but Maureen and Rose had already moved away.

Sabine laughed. "She's talking about her family. They're not shy, and they have various ailments. And you're new to the area, so, you'll be asked questions. *Lots* of questions."

"I'll get that drink now. Excuse me." He couldn't help but smile. These people were absolutely fascinating. Nick had thought he would be bored, and maybe he would be very soon. But not yet. He wasn't bored yet.

BY THE TIME Rachel had buckled Mrs. Wiggins into the car, gathered several tins of freshly baked goods Mrs. W insisted they carry with them (because showing up to Thanksgiving empty-handed would just be *rude*), and made the drive over to The Evangeline House, it was closing in on dinnertime.

Rachel hated to display any impatience where her guest was concerned, seeing how the lovely woman had offered her a place to live in the heart of town with such reasonable rent, but molasses moved faster in the dead of a Northern winter, Rachel was certain.

"Let's get you up the steps and I'll come back for the goodies, okay?" Rachel suggested as she helped Mrs. Wiggins from the car.

"Looks like a real humdinger of a party."

There were numerous cars parked in front of the house, in the side parking area, and down the street. Rachel couldn't help but smile at the woman's obvious enthusiasm for the social gathering. "Yes, well, they're going to be happy to see you."

Rachel didn't bother knocking, knowing she'd not be heard over the noise.

"Hey, Rach. Oh, hi, Mrs. Wiggins. Happy Thanksgiving! So glad you could join us," Ben said, and then helped the woman inside toward a comfortable chair in the heart of the action. Everyone in town knew Mrs. W. She'd been here since pretty much the birth of them all. "I'll let Mom know you're here."

Once Mrs. Wiggins was settled, Rachel said to Ben, "Thanks for the help. I need to get my camera and some other things from the car."

Ben nodded, and then tapped his sixteen-year-old nephew, Dirk, on the shoulder, and said, "Hey, buddy, can you help Rachel carry some stuff?"

"Sure, Uncle Ben." The young man, just having morphed from his awkward years turned to Rachel. "Oh, hey, Rachel. You need some help?"

"Thanks, Dirk. Mrs. W baked some desserts and they're outside." Dirk followed her, and together they managed everything in one trip.

"This stuff smells awesome." Dirk inhaled as he came through the kitchen door with the tins.

"I know. Nobody bakes like Mrs. Wiggins," Rachel agreed. "Thanks for your help."

"Is there anything I can help you carry?" a deep, and somewhat familiar voice asked once they were back inside.

Rachel turned to see Nick Sullivan, a drink in hand, standing at the corner of the kitchen island. "Oh, hi. No, that was everything. I brought my landlady to dinner at the last minute since her granddaughter's car wasn't working and she would have been alone today," Rachel over-explained.

"Seems everyone in your family can't stand for anyone to be alone on Thanksgiving," he said and smiled.

Rachel nearly dropped her camera bag. His face entirely transformed when his smile reached his eyes. A very warm and druggish sensation quite literally made her knees want to buckle. How foolish was that? Like a romance novel description or movie with accompanying music in the background for production value.

"Whoa, you okay?" He came over and took the bag from her.

"Huh? I'm fine. Just a little hungry, I guess. I've been rushing around trying to get us both here before dinner was served. I guess I forgot to eat breakfast."

"As a doctor, I can tell you that's not a good idea," he admonished, but smiled again, causing a similar response, though this time she was more prepared for it.

"Oh, hi, Rachel. I'm so glad you brought Mrs. Wiggins with you to celebrate Thanksgiving with us. So sad about her last-minute change in family plans." Miss Maureen had entered the kitchen. Clearly Rachel hadn't noticed.

"Can I help you do anything in here?" Rachel asked.

"I'm just about ready to start bringing food to the table. I'm going to round up my children and have them help. And Rose is here too. She refuses to behave like a guest."

Rachel smiled and nodded. "I saw Anna and Derek out there in the fray. I figured Rosie must be around here someplace. Let me know how I can help," Rachel said. Rachel had been introduced to Rosie and her family soon after she'd moved to Ministry. Anna, Rosie's youngest daughter, had recently met and married her husband, Derek. They were expecting their first child soon.

"Oh, Rachel, did you notice if Ivy and Mason Monroe had arrived?"

"No. I spoke with Ivy yesterday, and she said they may not make it because of some problem with work at the inn." Ivy was a friend of Rachel's who lived with her father. They were renovating the Ministry Inn, the historic inn on Main Street that had been in their family for generations.

"Oh. I had so hoped they could come and meet everyone. Mason and I grew up together." Then she smiled at Rachel. "Why don't you go around and introduce Nick to everyone while we bring in the food?" she suggested.

"O-okay. Sure." Rachel didn't think that would be her answer. Now they would all assume he was her date.

"Thank you. It might be awkward to show up as a stranger at the dinner table," Nick said.

"Nonsense. Everyone at my table is used to it," Maureen said, a twinkle in her eye.

"Well, no time like the present." Rachel led Nick out of the kitchen into the main family living area where most of the guests were gathered.

She said hello to her mom and her boyfriend, Norman, and introduced them to Nick. "Well, hello there, Nick. It's lovely to meet you. Thank you for quieting any fears we had yesterday regarding Sabine's intestinal distress. You can't be too careful, as you know." She patted Nick's hand.

"No, ma'am, and you're so welcome. It was a pleasure meeting both your daughters."

He smiled at Mom, and her mother cut her the *look.* The look that said, *Oh, he seems nice, Rachel; better grab this one.*

Yep, exactly why she hadn't wanted to do this introduction thing. And, so it went as she brought him around to meet the others. Ben's sisters were the worst about matchmaking, because they were all happy in their marriages, and wanted everyone else to find that same contentment. Helping things along, for them, was acceptable and expected behavior. And they believed themselves experts.

As the introductions continued, the gleam in their collective eyes meant trouble, Rachel knew.

As the food was carried into the dining room and placed on sideboards, and on the table, Rachel's stomach growled audibly. She hadn't eaten breakfast, and perhaps her response to Dr. Nick was simply a low blood sugar issue, which explained a lot, and was a relief.

The last thing she needed was a childish crush on a cute doctor whose past she knew nothing about and had no plans of staying beyond New Years. And she could admit that her choices in men thus far hadn't been stellar.

Chapter Five

N ICK REALIZE AT some point during Thanksgiving dinner with the Laroux family that this was how families were supposed to be. These people weren't perfect. They laughed with and at one another. They were loud. They were fun. They interrupted. And yet, the setting was pretty-darn picture-perfect, something his mother had always strived for, but in a different way. Her idea of perfection was everyone speaking quietly, eating with perfect manners, and no chaos of any sort.

His mother was miffed that he was currently missing their family's Thanksgiving feast. Missing holiday dinners the last several years wasn't unusual for Nick, as he'd been at the mercy of a rotating hospital schedule. Only administrators and the most senior staffers had first pick to take off on holidays. It had been hit or miss for quite a while now.

"So, Dr. Nick, did they have to twist your arm to get you to come up here to our little town?" Howard, Miss Maureen's husband, whom he'd met at the diner last night asked.

If they only knew. "Well, it seems I drew the short straw," Nick said honestly, and everyone at their table laughed. "I was at the end of my contract, so there was some bargaining. But so far, I'm impressed with the facilities and staff. And, of course, with the hospitality."

"Well, if you need anything while you're here, don't hesitate to call on us," Miss Maureen said.

"I can't thank you all enough for welcoming me to your lovely home today. I might have been eating a leftover sandwich from the diner in my motel room if you hadn't."

"Nonsense. We don't believe in anyone being alone during the holidays," a tall blonde, who looked to be about nine months pregnant, said from a ways down the table. "I'm Emma, by the way." She waved and looked down at her belly. "Twins. And there's no way you can remember us all."

"Congratulations. And I definitely need a reminder—or for everyone to wear name tags," Nick said.

"Name tags wouldn't be enough. We'd have to wear a family tree attached," another youngish woman said from the other side of the table, obviously a sister to the pregnant blonde. This one looked a few years older, but was still very attractive, with shorter, darker hair. "Name's Maeve." She pointed to the next table. "My daughter Lucy is over there." Lucy, who looked to be around twelve, heard her name and waved.

"Clearly, I'm not worth mentioning, but we met earlier

in the living room. I'm Junior, and I'm married to Maeve, father to Lucy." Junior waved. "I can handle all your taxidermy needs."

Nick tried to hide his smile. "I guess you're pretty busy this time of year."

Junior rolled his eyes. "You wouldn't believe what people want to preserve for perpetuity. I've got pictures."

"Not over Thanksgiving dinner, please, Junior," the one named Cammie, who Nick recognized as the Southern celebrity television chef said to her brother-in-law.

"Party-pooper." Junior made a face at her.

"Junior did a fine job on my kitties," Mrs. Wiggins piped up. "They are still so life-like, you'd never know they passed three and four years ago. I still carry them into my bedroom at night so it feels like I've got everyone with me when I fall asleep." The old woman's smile showed no comprehension of anything amiss in her words.

"Well, lovely lady, I'm thrilled I could make your loved ones continue to bring such happiness," Junior said.

Nick's mother would have fallen face-first into her gumbo by now from the shocking conversation. And by the lack of tradition in the food. Nick tried not to laugh at the absurdity of what he'd just heard. The faces all around the table were a mixed bag of amusement and slight distaste, but no one seemed particularly shocked or horrified at the idea of stuffing a domesticated animal to prolong an old woman's joy.

"Now, y'all need to behave. We have guests who may not quite understand our peculiarities discussed at the dinner table," Miss Maureen said, but she grinned as she said it.

"Not on my account," Mrs. Wiggins, the other lonely soul said. "Y'all are more fun than a barrel of monkeys." She giggled. "And Dr. Nick, did I hear you're staying at the motel? Do you have more permanent plans for a place to stay while you're here?"

"I have a phone number to call someone about an apartment to rent." Wait. He pulled out the crumpled paper from his pocket, having intended to make the call this morning. "Are you Dolly Wiggins?"

≫≫⧽⧽⧽⧽

RACHEL *MIGHT* HAVE groaned out loud. Mrs. Wiggins was going to ask Nick Sullivan to move in next door. To be her neighbor and share a wall and a hallway. A house.

"Well, yes, as a matter of fact, I am. And I do have an apartment to rent. How long will you be staying here in Ministry?"

"Not long. Just over a month, until New Year's, most likely," Nick said. But he paused, perhaps at the idea of dead cat's eyes, staring at him.

"Well, the place is fully furnished, and I guess I don't have a problem with a short-term lease, so long as you have references," Mrs. Wiggins turned to Rachel and beamed. "Rachel, here, rents the apartment next door. If you decided to move in, you'll already know your neighbor."

Rachel forced her mouth to make a smile shape. This was not something she wanted—this gorgeous single doctor moving in next door. Sleeping next door. She wondered if he slept naked.

Her face was likely bright red, because it felt super hot, and she now noticed that everyone at the table was staring at her. She should say something pleasant. "It's a really nice place. And Mrs. Wiggins is a fantastic landlady."

"Sounds perfect," Nick said. He was giving her a funny look. Almost like he could tell what she was thinking. Well, there was no way he could know she'd been thinking *that*. Or, it could still pertain to the stuffed cats. *Who knew?*

"Why don't you gather your things after dinner and come on over this evening? I've just had the place cleaned, and it's ready to go," Mrs. Wiggins suggested. "You can sign a month-to-month rental agreement. Electricity, cable and water are included in the rent."

"You're a lifesaver," he said to the woman. Rachel couldn't say she blamed him. She wouldn't want to stay at a cramped motel more than a night or two if it wasn't necessary.

"Well, that worked out splendidly. My two guests making a wonderful connection—what providence." Miss Maureen raised her glass, and others followed suit.

A strong sense of foreboding swept through Rachel then. A tingle, sort of. A flush, maybe. As she lowered her glass and took a sip, she glanced over at Nick. He was staring directly at her, an odd gleam in his eyes.

She would bet money he slept naked.

>>>><<<<

RELIEF SPREAD THROUGH Nick like a wave. Part of his not wanting to come here had been the suddenness of it, and not having a plan, especially for a place to live. He'd left Atlanta so abruptly, there'd not been time to do anything. He wasn't exactly a fly-by-night kind of person. He'd been taught from a young age to make a solid plan and keep to it.

"Nick, you like football? We're big SEC fans around here, but we're split in half about our teams for both college and the NFL," Ben said.

Beau, JoJo's husband chimed in. "Football game's already started, but we're recording. The Iron Bowl is Saturday, and we *always* get together and watch that. About half here went to Alabama, and the other half Auburn. Cammie makes snacks." He grinned at Cammie, who smiled back.

"Roll Tide!" somebody yelled, and then several *whoops!*

In reply were a couple, "War Damn Eagle!" Glasses clinked all around at all three tables. The babies squealed and children chattered.

Nick laughed then. "I'm a Dawgs and Dirty Bird fan. Big time."

"*Boo!*" The jeer came from Rachel's mother, who then

smiled at him to soften the insult. "We're all hardcore Saints fans, Rachel especially. My former husband had season tickets for twenty years. You know the Falcons and the Saints play each other on December eighth in Atlanta, which is two weeks from today, right?"

Nick nodded. "I've got tickets to the game. I've had them since before I knew I was coming here."

"Are you still going to the game?" Mrs. Prudhomme asked.

Nick shrugged. "I haven't even thought about it. I'll have to check the schedule at work."

"Be a shame to miss it," she said.

"Yes, ma'am. I was looking forward to it," Nick said. And he was. One more reason to be annoyed at the powers that be for manipulating him into this move.

⟫⟫⟪⟪

RACHEL HAD EXCUSED herself from the table before the football conversation and just now returned with her camera. She was snapping candid photos of everyone. They were all smiling and relaxed. There'd always been tension at his house. Either Dad had had a cocktail more than Mom approved, or someone had shown up ten minutes late—the important stuff.

Nick doubted anyone would notice if someone showed up late around here.

"Dears, as much as we'd all like to talk football stats, we

should give some thought to this year's Christmas celebration," Miss Maureen called out.

"Who's in charge of the parade this year?" someone asked.

A list was produced. "That would be Ben and Sabine," one of the sisters answered. He wasn't sure which one.

"Of course, he's in charge of the parade. He gets to ride on the back of the convertible as the mayor and wave at everyone," Emma said and rolled her eyes.

"Has anyone rented the snow-blowers yet?" Junior asked.

Snow-blowers? Didn't they realize they were in Alabama? Nick wondered.

"Yep. We'll have snow again this year one way or another," the blonde Emma answered.

"When is the tree being delivered?" Miss Maureen asked Junior.

"It's coming from North Carolina next week," Junior said.

Sabine explained to Nick, "Tomorrow it all begins. Many of the residents will come and help take down the fall decorations and store them. The Christmas decorating will begin in full force the day after that. It's a long-standing tradition."

"Since our family hosts so many of the big events in Ministry here at Evangeline House, we coordinate the holiday events. The Christmas festival, being the largest. There's a giant tree put up in the square. The whole town takes part in decorating it," Miss Maureen added to Sabine's explanation. "Every child makes an ornament."

Miss Maureen went down the list. "We've got a tour of homes, the 5k Jingle Jog, the Christmas pageant, the cookie bake-off and swap, photos with Santa, live television all week on Cammie's show, the parade, the tree lighting and decorating, caroling, and fireworks."

"Wow, sounds like a very festive time," Nick said.

"Oh, it's *way* over-the-top, but what can you say? We love Christmas around here. People come from miles around to celebrate the season with us. But we *refuse* to decorate for one holiday until the one before it is over," the sister, JoJo, spoke up.

"And Matthew, here, films Cammie's cooking show live in the square for a whole week. Cammie, isn't Jessica Greene coming this year as your guest?" Maeve asked. Matt was Emma's husband. It was all very confusing, but Nick was getting an immersion crash course in the Laroux family tree.

Cammie made a face. "If she shows up. Live television is unpredictable." She nodded toward Matthew. "Cammie used to be Jessica Green's assistant on *her* cooking show until Cammie was unfairly blamed for setting the woman's hair on fire during an unfortunate crêpe Suzette flambé incident, and Jessica fired her. The woman went on every talk show in North America and made a stink," Emma said.

"I think I remember that," Nick said. Even in Atlanta, he'd heard bits and pieces about this vendetta. Southerners loved a feud. It made great headlines on the news.

"Well, the whole thing turned when the truth came out, and now Cammie has her own show, and Jessica is out on her—" Junior began.

"We get it, Junior," Maeve said. "Anyway, Jessica is now begging Cammie for any airtime she can get."

Nick nodded. "Sounds like that might draw quite a crowd."

"People love a dramatic saga," Cammie said.

"Or a catfight," Junior said and snickered.

"I'll lend you a few of my recipes if you need them," Mrs. Wiggins offered.

"I might hit you up for your shortbread recipe, if you don't mind, Mrs. Wiggins. It's widely known around here. In fact, isn't it time for dessert, y'all?" Cammie asked.

"You bet," Miss Maureen said. "Let's clear this food and make room." Like a well-trained army, the Laroux children, along with Anna, Rose's pregnant daughter, magically cleared away dinner plates, casserole dishes, and soup tureens, and made the switch to clean dessert plates, silverware, and far more desserts than an army could eat in one sitting.

"Wow, this is amazing," Nick said, marveling at such efficiency.

"We've had plenty of practice serving at events over the years. Pressed into service at a young age, you know," Ben said, as he placed a large, steaming dish of bread pudding in front of Nick.

Nick sighed in appreciation, turned to his right and caught Rachel's eye. She appeared a little flustered—face flushed—and just as soon as their gazes met, she raised the camera up to her eye.

⟫⟫⟫⟪⟪⟪

BY THE TIME Rachel pulled into the drive and unloaded Mrs. Wiggins and her various tins, she was exhausted. The laughter, the over-eating, and the crowd made her want to seek refuge and solace in her tiny, quiet apartment. In her pajamas, and without a bra. But she was acutely aware that within the next hour or so, her blessed bubble of peace and tranquility would likely be shattered by a man moving in next door.

Rachel was a special kind of introvert; she loved spending time with people, but needed to retreat to her own corner to refuel with alone time and quiet afterward. That's why photography made perfect sense as a career. She shot weddings, parties, and other events, interacted with clients, and then hurried back to her solitary space to edit her work.

She figured the good doctor would be at the hospital most of the time, so hopefully, his becoming her next-door neighbor wouldn't cramp her style much. It's not like they were dating or anything. Heck, they weren't even friends, and only barely acquainted. But something about his entering her territory and invading her space rankled. Rachel had just gotten her bearings around here. She was booked with shoots through the first of the year, so she had job security for the foreseeable future. She was content for the first time in a long time, and was finally beginning to relax a tiny bit in her surroundings. Change wasn't something she welcomed right now. This new neighbor meant she would have to put on a bra, dang it.

But she still changed into her comfy, loose, cotton pajamas, which were decidedly decent by any standards. She pulled her hair up into a messy bun with a clip and flipped on the TV for background noise, and football. Rachel curled up on her sofa, connected the cord from her camera to the laptop, and transferred the many photos from today's gathering. This was the kind of editing she most enjoyed—photos of people she loved all together. She'd caught them unguarded and relaxed. They were laughing and talking. Their love for each other was evident in every shot.

She grinned at a picture of her tiny niece, having just stuffed chocolate cake in her mouth, giving Ben an open-mouthed kiss. Ben's expression of surprise having been given two-gifts-in-one cracked her up. This was a Christmas gift no-brainer.

A knock on the door startled her from her screen. "Coming," she called. She exhaled. *That* was why she dreaded a new neighbor.

"HI, NEIGHBOR," NICK said, and noticed Rachel had changed to night wear. "Long day?" It was barely seven-thirty at night, and though it was chilly outside, and dark, it seemed early for bed.

"I changed the moment I got home. Pajamas are my mainstay."

He held his hands up in a defensive gesture. "I wouldn't want you to change on my account. Just passing through."

"Can I help you?" She raised a very well-shaped eyebrow.

"Do you have a hammer? I'm low on essentials since I left home with pretty much nothing to come here."

She looked like she might shut the door in his face. "I have a hammer. Is there anything else you need?" *So you don't bother me again.* Nick got the implied message.

"Just a hammer—for now."

She stepped back, opening the door for him to enter. As he followed her inside, Nick was enveloped by the warm, cozy atmosphere of her place. He couldn't put a finger on exactly what made it seem so welcoming. The décor, maybe; her sense of style was eclectic, a mix of items both old and new in muted colors with tons of framed photos scattered around. The place smelled of roses, a delicate version of roses. The same scent surrounded Rachel. He'd first noticed it the night they'd met at the hospital. It was fleeting, and light.

"Here's my tool kit. Just in case you end up in need of, say, a screwdriver or an extra nail or two." She was holding a metal tackle box-sized tool kit by its handle.

"Great. I might need a screwdriver," he said and looked around. "I like what you've done with the place."

"Thanks. I spend a lot of time here, being self-employed. I need to like my surroundings."

"Well, the house is fantastic. I feel fortunate to have found this place. I hope you don't mind my barging into your sanctuary," he said, and couldn't help but get stuck when a long pass was thrown on the screen. He held his breath to see if it was caught for a touchdown.

She noticed. "Are you a fan?"

"Not a Cowboy's fan, but a football fan. We talked about it at dinner when you left to get your camera in the kitchen. I hear you're an Aints fan." Saints fans had been heckled for years with this dropping of the S.

"Watch it buster, or you can forget about borrowing my hammer." Her eyes sparkled dangerously. "So, I'm guessing you're one of those pathetic squawking dirty bird fans."

"Guilty. We rise up." He used the Atlanta Falcons slogan from the year before when they made it to the Super Bowl, but lost at the very end in a real heart-breaker.

She shook her head as if that was the saddest thing she'd ever heard.

"So, I was saying that I hope my moving here won't be an issue for you. I know it's sudden."

She gave him a somewhat pained smile. "Of course your moving in won't be a problem for me. But I'm pretty private and a bit of a homebody, truth be told."

Message received. "Well, I'll do my best not to get on your nerves, except on game day. My coming here was a pretty big blip on my radar and I'm still trying to get used to the idea that I'm taking a break from my life to do this."

"I get it. I moved to be near family after living my entire life in New Orleans. It was—an adjustment."

"I thought I detected a little bit of an accent between you, your sister and mom."

"We up-towners aren't so blessed with the strong accents as those in some other parts of the city." She seemed a tiny bit defensive.

"No offense intended. I like it." He grinned. "Thanks for the tools. I'll bring them back tomorrow." He stepped outside, feeling like the ambience had just been sucked away.

"You can leave them outside the door when you're finished. No rush." She shut the door behind him.

As he opened the door to his own apartment, he caught himself smiling. Rachel Prudhomme was a prickly woman. It amused him that she fought her irritation with his intrusion into her solace. Clearly she'd been taught to be a lady and use good manners, despite wanting to call through the door for him to go away. And despite his being a Falcon's fan.

And he was getting a kick out of annoying her for some reason. That wasn't usually his thing, so it made him pause. He'd avoided conflict with women like the plague for awhile now, since he and Monica split a few months ago, and while that made him sad, he'd been enjoying his own blessed peace and silence. So, he should appreciate and empathize with his new neighbor instead of feeling the inexplicable need to pester her.

He was still smiling though. Maybe the next month or two wouldn't be so bad. He'd consider it a break from the hassle of his normal life. If yesterday's patient load was any indication of how things were to be here, his stress level would be significantly lower at work, and being away from his mother would be its own vacation. Speaking of his mother, he'd been avoiding listening to the voicemail he'd received earlier. It was Thanksgiving, after all, and he would call her after he got things squared away in his new place.

He'd brought a set of sheets, pillows, and his grooming items, and of course, clothing. The things he would normally take with him on an extended stay. Not that he'd been anywhere away from work for more than a weekend in a very long time. Nick figured he would get whatever else he needed once he got here.

The television was tiny, but Mrs. Wiggins mentioned the cable was connected. He hoped it was, because being single and alone in a new place seemed awfully quiet right now, plus, he wanted to catch the game that was on. He liked football, and Rachel had a large, lovely flat screen next door, and right now he was feeling a fair amount of screen envy. He envisioned his fifty-two-inch ultra HD at his townhome back in Atlanta and sighed. Just a couple months.

The apartment was old, but it was charming. The living room windows were large and ran the length of the room. They overlooked Ministry's historic Main Street. The heavy shades were pulled up, and could be let down at night. Long, heavy patterned curtain panels hung at each end of the windows were held back by heavy iron hooks. The sofa and large club chair were slipcovered in a textured beige cotton with large colorful striped and floral throw pillows. There was even a sisal throw rug that pulled everything together.

Everything blended without the feeling of matchi-ness. It was quaint for a furnished apartment. In Nick's experience, an already furnished place meant a hodgepodge of stained leftovers from former tenants. Not that he'd ever lived in a nasty place, but he'd had lots of friends during college and medical school who hadn't been as fortunate. He hoped the bed wasn't as old as the television. Sleep was an important commodity and worth a decent mattress, even for a month or two.

Nick's phone rang then, and he saw it was his mother's number. The urge to ignore the call was strong, but it was Thanksgiving, and he *was* thankful, after all.

"Hey Mom. Happy Thanksgiving."

"Happy Thanksgiving, dear. I'm assuming you've worked another holiday because I haven't heard from you."

Was this a rhetorical statement? Or, did she require an answer?

Before he had a chance to reply, she asked, "Well, did

you work, or have you avoided your mother?"

Shit. "I was invited to Thanksgiving dinner by a family here in Ministry, so no, I was off today. I did start work yesterday though."

"It wasn't those tacky cousins on your father's side, was it? I mean, they have plenty of money, but no class at all. Small-towners."

Nick closed his eyes. He could imagine his mother's mouth tighten in disapproval of *his father's people.* Mom grew up in the city, and Dad had more of an acceptable rural gentry upbringing. How the two of them were still living together, Nick couldn't imagine. He hoped to never marry unless he found someone who accepted him for who he was, and not what he could financially contribute to a marriage.

"No, it was the Laroux family. They own the event-planning business in town. I saw one of them yesterday in the emergency room for something minor, and they invited me for dinner." He smiled at the memory. It had been so *nice* of Sabine.

"They invited a random stranger to their family dinner? How *odd.* Rednecks are so hokey. I guess you had a fine time whooping it up with people who weren't your own blood."

He recognized her attempt at humor by using Southern colloquial phrasing, and affecting a country hick accent as well. But he caught the whiff of jealousy that he'd spent time on Thanksgiving with someone other than her. It hit Nick as very offensive, since he considered the Laroux family quite respectable and not at all "a bunch of rednecks." They were small-town Southerners to be sure, but to assume everyone here was toothless and spit tobacco in the streets was haughty, even for his mother.

"Mom, you know there are plenty of people that even you would find acceptable company here, the Larouxs being among them." He tried not to lecture, but she kind of deserved it.

"Well, excuse me. The last I heard, you were grumbling about going down to a, how did you put it, backwoods, podunk, town in Alabama?"

She had him there. That was exactly how he'd anticipated this place would be. "You're right. I was expecting the worst. Fortunately, I've met some nice people and it's not so bad. At least, it's not bad so far. I shouldn't have judged the town or its people, either way. I was pissed that this move was out of my control."

"Language, Nicholas." He could feel her disapproval across the miles.

"Well, I *was*." He hated when she corrected his word choice like he was still ten years old.

"Your brother was here earlier with Stacey. She's very pretty, but I don't know if she's quite the kind of person we want in our family. I wish he'd stayed with Debbie. Now, *she* was quality. Have you heard from Monica?"

He ignored that last question.

"People aren't graded on a scale like apples, Mom. And if

Chuck didn't love Debbie, why would you want him to stay with her?"

"Sometimes love isn't the best reason to get married. The most solid marriages are based on mutual interests and common goals. Love fades, passion dies. Be smart and go for something that lasts."

He couldn't help himself. "Like you and Dad?"

"Exactly. Now, I need to make sure your father isn't sneaking another scotch, so I'll let you go. I expect to hear from you regularly while you're—away."

"Goodbye, Mom."

Nick flipped on the ancient television that sat inside an antique armoire, and he was relieved to see there was basic cable connected to a rather aged box sitting beside the TV as well. The picture wasn't what he was used to, but for now, it kept the silence at bay. Well, not exactly silence. He could hear the muffled sounds of Rachel's television through their shared wall. It was mildly comforting to know there was someone on the other side.

He'd not experienced this unpleasant sensation in a long time. It was hard to put a name to it—was it loneliness? In a world filled with people, he was sitting in a new place, surrounded by things that weren't his, alone, on Thanksgiving. He guessed he might be just a little lonely. It was rather humbling.

Chapter Six

"RACHEL, ARE YOU sure this is a sexy pose?" Judith Jameson asked as she hiked her leg up on a stump. She and her sister, Jamie, had called last minute to book a sitting to surprise their husbands. They'd come up with the idea of a slightly sexy/naughty series of photos on a lark.

"Um, maybe lower your leg just a bit, I'm a little worried about your balancing on that log in those heels, Judith." It was all Rachel could do to keep a straight face. They were both dressed in bright red velvet Mrs. Claus outfits that the lady herself likely wouldn't have approved of.

"Good Lord, Judith, you don't need another broken leg," Jamie called to her sister.

That had Judith lowering her leg immediately. "Fine. How's this?" She struck a less risky but still sultry pose.

"That looks fantastic. Your husband will love it," Rachel promised. Both women were lovely and blonde, and very fit. They were sisters married to brothers, which was a bit baffling, but Rachel figured sometimes it happened when there weren't that many to choose from. Supposedly it was a safe bet, genetically.

"So, Jamie I just heard from Suzette that Nick Sullivan is here in Ministry working at the hospital while they find another doctor," Judith said to her sister as she struck another pose.

"You mean Daddy's brother's son, Cousin Nicky? Lordy, we haven't seen him in a coon's age. Why hasn't he called us if he's here in town?" Jamie asked.

"I don't know, but I mean to find out. Pretty rude if you ask me." She stuck out a hip and pouted for the camera. "Hey Rachel, do you think I can get poison ivy at the end of November out here?"

Rachel laughed. "I don't think so. Besides the pine trees, everything looks pretty dead on the ground." But Rachel's ears had perked up when she'd heard the two women discussing her new neighbor.

"I heard he and his girlfriend split up. Monica, was it?" Judith asked her sister.

Jamie nodded. "Yep. She was that super-model looking one, wasn't she? His cranky momma was proud of her. She made the Christmas card the last two years. Must've been serious, or she'd never have been allowed on *the card*." Jamie said those two words with such affect, it made Judith laugh.

Judith said to Rachel, "Our cousin Nicky is a surgeon from Atlanta, and his mother is a real uppity bitch. She's never approved of his daddy's people—us. So, over the years, we've done our best to irritate her whenever we've gotten the chance."

Rachel smiled. "We met at Thanksgiving, and Mrs. Wiggins offered him the apartment next door. So, now he's my new neighbor."

The women shared a look, then grinned. "He's single, as we're sure you just heard," Judith said, her tone sly.

Rachel let her camera hang from the strap around her neck and held up both hands in a defensive gesture. "Nope. Don't even think about it. I'm not in the market, especially for a temporary fling."

They looked disappointed. "Well, we can vouch for him. He is a nice guy. Not sure why he and his super-model girl broke up, but I guess it happens," Judith said.

"She wasn't a super-model. She was a doctor. Just looked like a super-model," Jamie clarified.

"Okay, good to know," Rachel said.

"I just thought about something," Jamie said.

"Well, spit it out," Judith said to Jamie, her tone impatient.

"He's going to be fresh meat here in Ministry for the women. Especially now that Ben Laroux's off the market. Oh, Lord, Sister. Can you imagine?" Jamie laughed.

"I can. He'd better suit up. As soon as they catch his scent, he'll need to install a second set of deadbolts on the front door over at Mrs. Wiggins's house." Both women laughed like it was the funniest thing they'd ever heard.

The same thought had occurred to Rachel the first day she'd met him, but she didn't want Jamie and Judith to think she liked Nick. "It can't be that bad," Rachel said.

"You've seen Nicky, right?" Judith asked.

"Sure," Rachel said.

"Gonna be a bloodbath," Judith assured her.

Rachel had to smile then. The single gals in town were a mostly man-hungry bunch, she had to admit. She'd met and made friends with several of them since moving to Ministry, and Nick Sullivan *was* attractive, no, she could be honest—he was hot. Yes, they would be all over him, given the chance.

"Move, Judith, quit hogging all the film, or battery life, or data. You've had your chance. It's my turn." Jamie all but shoved her sister out of the way and took her place in front of the camera.

"I've got some great shots, Judith," Rachel assured the woman, who, judging by the murderous look in her eyes, appeared ready to get into a rolling, scratching, and kicking catfight with her twin. "There's a Thermos with hot chocolate by my bag, if you'd like some."

Jamie smiled sweetly at Judith.

Judith narrowed her eyes, then said, "I'd better let my sister get started. This might take all day. She's not exactly a professional." Judith sashayed over to the Thermos and poured a cup of the steaming cocoa and perched on a folding chair and covered up with one of the light stadium blankets

Rachel had packed for the shoot. The temperature was hovering around fifty today, but considering the scant clothing the women were sporting, Rachel anticipated they might get a little chilly.

"Whoop. Let's do this," Jamie giggled. Jamie had a seemingly less intense nature than Judith. She worked at appearing carefree, but Rachel could see the sharpness and intellect in Jamie's eyes though her viewfinder. Jamie had far more on the ball than she let on.

It was likely a sore spot between the sisters, since Judith liked to take the lead in most situations.

"Yes, well, we're going to need to get to the bottom of Nicky's situation," Judith said.

"What's there to find out?" Jamie asked. "He's gorgeous, single, and living here in Ministry for awhile."

Judith narrowed her eyes. "There's always more to it."

Rachel turned back around to focus on Jamie, who was waiting for Rachel's direction. She was ready to change the subject from her new neighbor now. "Jamie, give me a big smile. Perfect."

A high-pitched scream rent the air from behind.

⋙⋘

"I TOLD YOU those heels were a stupid idea," Jamie said as she held a small ice pack on her sister's ankle.

"Do you think it's broken? I don't think it's broken," Judith said.

"It would serve you right to have to pull that scooter back out of the attic," Jamie fussed at her sister.

They were on the way to Cypress General and Rachel was driving. How had this even happened?

Rachel pulled the car into the patient drop-off at the emergency entrance to the hospital, put the car in park, and walked inside to get help, leaving the women in the backseat.

Rachel approached the counter. A young woman, who was smacking gum, greeted her. "Hey there, I'm Candy, how can we help you?"

"Hi Candy. My friend fell and twisted her ankle. She needs help from the car."

Candy picked up the phone, pressed a button, and spoke into the receiver, "Hey, I need some help out here, y'all. Yep, a wheelchair. Thanks."

Candy hung up and addressed Rachel. "Somebody's comin'."

Sure enough, an orderly came out immediately pushing a wheelchair. The young black man appeared to be in his early twenties. Rachel thanked him for coming so quickly, and led him to where the sisters were still squabbling in the backseat of her car.

"Let's get y'all out of there so we can see about your injury," the orderly, Jacob, according to his name tag, said.

"My sister, here, is a klutz," Jamie said as she climbed out of the car, making way for Judith's exit.

Judith was rolled inside, and Candy got to work on her

insurance info and triage.

"Is Dr. Nick Sullivan the doctor on duty?" Judith asked.

"Yes ma'am, he is," Candy answered.

"Tell him it's his cousin Judith."

"I'll tell him, but you still have to fill out your paper-work," Candy replied.

Judith waved her hand toward the clipboard then toward Jamie. "Handle that, Jamie. I'm in too much pain." Then, she made a dramatic face for effect.

Jamie narrowed her eyes at her sister and grabbed the clipboard and pen. "Something makes me question the extent of this injury."

Rachel hadn't even considered that Judith might be fak-ing her injury. Why would she do such a thing? Then it occurred to Rachel that Judith might be setting Nick up. Forcing a face-to-face since he'd not done the cousins the courtesy of contacting them since he'd been in town. Hadn't Sabine warned him there would be consequences?

Judith was called back into the treatment area a few minutes later. Fortunately, there appeared to be only a few family members waiting for patients sitting in the waiting area, so if Judith was faking, at least she wasn't taking a legitimately sick or hurt person's place in line.

"C'mon, Rachel." Judith waved her hand for Rachel to accompany them.

Rachel frowned. She couldn't think of a way to say no without being rude, so she went.

They were shown into the same treatment room where she'd been with Sabine only a few days before. Déjà vu, seriously.

"Hey there, Mrs. Dozier-Fremont. This doesn't look nearly as bad as the last time they brought you in," the nurse said with a smile.

"Lord, no, honey. Last time I thought I was gonna *die.*"

She'd gently removed the ice pack they'd pulled from the small first aid kit in Rachel's car. Heading out onto the backroads for a shoot with these two required preparation. Snacks and drinks, blankets, and a first aid kit.

Rachel looked over at the ankle in question. Okay, it was a little swollen, and maybe slightly bruised. That relieved her mind somewhat that this wasn't a total setup, though she didn't wish an injury on her friend.

The door opened and Nick Sullivan filled the doorway. He wasn't an overly large guy, but he was finely built and wore a lab coat as if it had been expertly tailored to fit his broad, muscular shoulders. *Sigh.* Rachel squirmed just a little in her chair, hoping her fluster didn't show.

He grinned at the small group of women. "Well, hi there, cousins." Clearly he'd read the chart before stepping into the fray.

"Well, mercy, aren't you a sight for sore eyes, Cousin Nicky?" Judith said from her spot on the treatment table.

Jamie hopped up and hugged Nick. "We heard you were here in town."

"Looks like you've found me. Sorry it had to be under these circumstances. Judith, let's have a look at that ankle." He moved around where he could examine her, but not before he acknowledged Rachel.

"Hey there, neighbor." He gave her a little side-eye smile. Was that a wink?

"Seems like we were just here," she said. OMG, did her face just turn beet red? It did; she could feel it. It was on fire.

"We were." He nodded.

"Rachel, here was taking our pictures. We don't normally go around wearing such get-ups." They'd each pulled on a sweatshirt and a sweater over the top of their matching bosom-revealing dresses, but the red velvet skirts were short, short enough to raise an eyebrow or two around town. "This is a little embarrassing, but we were taking *special* pictures as a gift to our husbands for Christmas," Judith said.

Rachel noticed the slight pause in Nick's manipulation of Judith's ankle as he digested this information. "Well, I'm sure they'll both be appreciative of the gesture."

What else was the poor guy supposed to say? These women were in their early thirties, and they were his first cousins. How awkward. Rachel had no comment to make on the subject.

"Rachel is an excellent photographer. Folks in town book her for everything: weddings, graduate photos, baptisms—you name it, Rachel's your girl," Jamie chimed in, not to be ignored.

"I'll keep that in mind in case I need any photos taken," Nick said.

Rachel had no way of shutting these women up. "Or, I could just give him a business card. He knows where to find me most days, y'all. We live right next door to each other."

"Oh, that's *right*. Y'all don't need our help, do you?" Jamie laughed, as if she'd just figured something out.

"How's your momma and daddy?" Judith changed the subject, thankfully.

"They're probably exactly how you remember them from last time you saw them," Nick said. He rotated her ankle and Judith winced. "Let's get an x-ray of the ankle, just in case." He nodded to the nurse.

"I broke the *hell* out of my other leg almost two years ago falling off a runway practicing for a pageant. This doesn't feel like that." She showed him her scar from the surgery.

Rachel remembered hearing about that. It had happened at Emma Laroux's studio, and had sounded like a pretty big deal.

"I saw the photos on Facebook," Nick said. "And you're right, this isn't like that. But you could have a hairline fracture. I want to be certain you don't before I let you out of here.

"She puts *everything* on Facebook," Jamie said, and made a face.

The nurse helped her into the wheelchair. "Jamie come with me to get my x-ray."

Jamie hesitated, and Judith gave her a hard look that brooked no argument. "Well, fine."

That left Rachel in the treatment room with Nick. "So, you spent the day with those two, huh? And you ended up here with them? God bless you," he said, and there was laughter in his voice.

Rachel smiled. "They're mostly harmless once you get to know them. Judith really did seem like she was in pain. And Jamie didn't want to drive with Judith 'kicking up a fuss,' as she put it."

"Well, as their closest relative at the moment, I thank you."

"You're welcome."

"And thanks for the use of the toolbox. I'll drop it by tonight."

"Oh, you can just leave it in front of the door anytime. I'm not planning to fix the sink or hang a picture anytime soon."

Rachel's awareness of Nick's very fit body in such a close space was wreaking havoc on her heart rate. She might require a little mouth-to-mouth if he didn't back off soon.

When she looked up, he was staring at her mouth. Rachel had been stared at by men her entire life—even before those stares were appropriate. She understood desire when she saw it in a man's eyes.

This man was dangerous to her peace of mind. He was too good-looking, and thus-far hadn't shown her any faults or weaknesses, which would have been a good thing, had she been a normal woman. But his biggest check in the negative column was that he was here in Ministry temporarily, and she couldn't allow herself to like him, or to get the least bit attached.

"Well, thanks again for loaning me the tools. I know you weren't exactly thrilled by the intrusion."

Now, he made her sound like a bitch, which she'd not meant to be. "I'm sorry if I seemed unfriendly," Rachel said, slightly shamed.

"It's okay. It was a long day."

"No, I'm truly sorry. I sometimes come across like that, but I don't mean to."

"So, make it up to me. We can be friends, can't we?" Nick asked.

"Uh, sure." *Crap.* Now she'd gone and done it; by trying to undo her unfriendliness, she'd opened the door to their getting friendly.

"Friends hang out together sometimes, as do neighbors. And I'm all alone here and don't know a soul, besides those two." He pointed toward the door where Jamie and Judith had recently exited.

"Um, I guess." *Dammit, dammit, dammit.*

"I've got a couple of casseroles in my refrigerator that need to be eaten."

"Casseroles? Where did you get casseroles?" Rachel was curious.

"They've been arriving here at the hospital with welcoming wishes from some, uh, residents in town."

It dawned on Rachel then. "The single women," she said and nearly snorted her laughter. "They've found you."

He had the grace to look embarrassed. "I guess. There are phone numbers included." He grinned then.

"Sounds like you don't need me to share your casseroles."

"But, I would prefer your company to meeting random women over casseroles. It's never been my preferred way of dating."

"You could always get that right-swipe, left-swipe thing on your cell phone," Rachel suggested.

The horrified expression on his face indicated he was highly opposed. "Dear God, do *you* use that to find dates?"

She laughed. "Not yet, but I've had friends who do. I can't say any of them have reported finding their life mates that way, but I'll keep you posted."

"Oh, come on. It's just casserole between neighbors. What do you say? I'll return your tools," he said.

Rachel suddenly had an urge to climb on his lap and see what doctors wore under their scrubs. "I'll make you a deal. You bring the casseroles over to my place so we can watch football on my TV. Yours is unacceptable."

He stood and stuck out his hand to shake hers. "My screen envy has been getting the better of me since I moved in. I get off at six. I'll see you at six-thirty."

"Deal." They shook on it, but Rachel couldn't help but feel as if she was sealing some kind of fateful bargain with consequences far beyond tonight's dinner. Then she realized it was Saturday. "You mean you don't have anything better to do on a Saturday night?"

"Nope. Not a thing. Looks like you don't either."

He was right. But only because she chose not to. That's her story and she was sticking to it.

The door opened then and the nurse, Georgie, re-entered holding the x-ray, which she then handed to Nick. "The x-ray tech says to tell you he e-mailed the digital film to Dr. James's office. He'll check it and give you a call if he sees anything."

"Thanks. Oh, and could grab a set of crutches to get Judith home?" She nodded, and Nick stuck the film on the lighted holder and took a moment to study it.

"I don't see any evidence of a break, but if I hear differently from Dr. James, the radiologist, I'll give you a call."

"Well, that's a relief," Judith said.

"I'll give you a prescription for 400 mg of ibuprofen for the inflammation, and I want you to keep weight off the foot for three or four days. It's most likely a mild sprain, but those can be quite painful. Apply ice for twenty minutes with half hour breaks during the next forty-eight hours."

"Should she get the scooter out?" Jamie snickered.

"It wouldn't hurt, if you have one handy. That way, you won't be tempted to bear weight on it while moving around to the bathroom and such," Nick said, his manner all doctor.

"Well, shit," Judith swore. "I'm glad it's not broken, but I'm busy decorating my house for Christmas right now. I don't have time for this."

Rachel employed great self-control in not rolling her eyes then. "It's just a few days. Maybe your husband can help you out with that."

Judith did the eye-rolling then. "Ha. He already can't find his backside with two hands, and it's attached."

"Don't worry, Sister. It won't kill you if my house gets done first." Jamie smiled sweetly at Judith, whose face turned an angry red.

"Over my dead, rotting corpse will that *ever* happen. I'll amputate first," Judith ground out between her teeth.

Rachel, Nick, and Nurse Georgie all exchanged a look of horror. No one knew what went on between these siblings. Seemed best to step back and stay out of the death race to complete the Dozier-Fremont twins' Christmas décor.

Jamie giggled, clearly tasting victory.

The nurse, Georgie, came back inside holding a pair of crutches. "Dr. Sullivan, someone dropped off a pie for you. I didn't want you to forget it when your shift was over." She tried to suppress her grin.

"Now we have dessert," Nick said to Rachel with a laugh, leaving Jamie and Judith staring back and forth between the two as if watching a tennis match.

"RACHEL, WE CAN'T thank you enough for dragging us all over town and country today. I know you have better things to do with your Saturday," Judith said once they were back in the car headed home. Fortunately, they'd all ridden together on the outset of this adventure when Rachel had picked the two women up at Judith's house around noon.

"It's part of the job. Sometimes things go as planned, and well, sometimes they don't."

"So, Nicky said y'all were having dessert 'cause somebody brought him a pie. Does this mean you're having dinner together?" Jamie asked.

Rachel knew this was coming. Best to downplay the situation. "Seems you were right about the gifts of food welcoming him to town."

"You mean the women in town?" Judith asked.

"Nick did mention there were phone numbers attached to the dishes," Rachel said.

Judith and Jamie both laughed. "Yep. It was only a matter of time. I'm surprised nobody's taken an ad out in the Ministry Gazette," Jamie said.

Judith took up the thought. "It would read, 'Fresh meat in town, y'all. Send your casseroles and desserts to the hot, single doctor—and best of luck to you.'" Judith cackled at her own cleverness.

"Well, he has all this food and prefers not to let it go to waste, that's all."

"Uh, huh. Sounds like he chooses to not make a few

phone calls and share it with you. That seems a little selfish if you ask me, don't you think, Sister? I mean, them going to all that trouble to make their most effective man-gettin' family recipes, and he doesn't even call to thank them or ask them to share—" Judith indicated her sister should weigh in.

"Very selfish. Gonna be some seriously pissed off gals around town, especially if he doesn't return that fancy casserole crockery. You know, returning the dish is a big part of the man-meeting process around here."

"I'll mention that to Nick while we're enjoying our dinner. Perhaps he should write proper thank yous and send texts."

"Oh, girl. He'd better show some manners or they'll want him even more," Judith said. "Nothing some women crave more than a challenge. Might only make things worse if he ignores them."

She had a point. It might even be worth mentioning to Nick. "I'll tell him you said so."

Chapter Seven

NICK'S CURRENT CHALLENGE was convincing Sally Jo Jordan that indeed she did not have skin cancer.

"But I looked on that medical website online and it showed a mole that looked *just like this one.*" She unbuttoned her blouse to expose ample cleavage in a very sexy black lace push-up bra. And yes, there was a mole. "Momma says it's my beauty mark, but I'm worried about skin cancer, you know?"

"I know the Internet can be a scary place when it comes to researching medical conditions. This mole is what we call a benign neoplasm, which means it shows no signs of being cancerous. It's perfectly round and symmetrical, with regular borders. It's not terribly dark in color, and shows no signs of flaking, oozing, or bleeding."

Sally Jo blinked at him, showing no real sign of comprehension. "So, I don't have cancer? Are you sure you don't want to have a closer look?" She shoved her chest closer. He wore a pair of lighted, magnified glasses, or loupes, to get a good look at the not-at-all suspicious brown mole, which basically put his face in her bosom. Nick now pushed the loupes from his eyes down, and around his neck.

"You can button your blouse now. If you still have concerns, I can give you a referral to see a dermatologist," he said. Just then, his eyes met Nurse Georgie's and she was clearly holding in her hysterical laughter with every ounce of control she possessed—just barely.

"Have you eaten the casserole I sent?" Sally Jo asked, completely changing the subject.

"Um, I'm having it for dinner this evening. Thanks for the welcome." He didn't mention that he was sharing it with Rachel.

"I've been waiting to hear from you." She wore a pout on her full lips, her blouse still open.

He turned away and made a point of noting something in her chart instead of continuing to peer at the woman's near-naked chest.

"It's been pretty busy since I started here, but I do appreciate your kindness. It helps not having to cook."

"You'll let me know how you like it, won't you? It's my granny's recipe," Sally Jo said.

"Um, sure. I'll return your dish as soon as I finish with it."

"My number's on the bottom of the dish. Don't break it. Granny's had that dish since she got it with Green Stamps when her and Granddaddy got married. So, it's special, you know."

He did now. "I'll be careful. Thanks again. Here's the referral if you want to follow up with the skin specialist."

She left the top button undone. "Call me."

Georgie followed Sally Jo from the room, but not before she turned and shot him an epic smirk.

Once Georgie had seen Sally Jo out, she quickly returned to the treatment room as Nick completed the chart. What a waste of healthcare dollars.

"You're going to get a lot more of that if you don't call these gals," Georgie warned.

"But I didn't ask them to send me food," he said and ran a hand through his hair.

"They're coming after you whether you want it or now. Best to go ahead and call to prevent this nonsense."

"Don't you have something to do?" he asked her.

She just grinned. "Don't say I didn't warn you."

Nick stopped on the way home and picked up a nice bottle of wine and flowers. He realized this wasn't a date, but his mother had taught him to show class no matter the situation. Not that he always followed her high-brow advice, but he knew how. In this instance, it seemed like a good idea.

Rachel Prudhomme was a down-to-earth kind of sexy he hadn't been experienced with in a long time, which wasn't to say his ex, Monica, wasn't attractive, because she was. But there was something about Rachel that appealed to him from the moment they'd met. Maybe it was her lack of affectation and drama. Toward the end, Monica became all drama all the time.

Rachel thought the casserole brigade was hilarious. Monica would have likely blamed Nick for leading the women to believe he was interested in their gooey offerings. Not that he and Rachel were in a committed relationship, but the contrast between the two women's responses was so obvious to Nick.

He climbed the stairs with flowers, and apple pie, a carton of vanilla ice cream, and a bottle of wine. And a goofy smile on his face. He hadn't experienced this kind of nervous anxiety about seeing a woman in a long, long time.

⫸⫷

"HEY. I MADE chicken and dumplings. Do you want some?" Sabine asked Rachel through the phone.

"Um. No. I'm good for tonight."

"You going out?"

"No. I'm staying in."

"Did Mom bring you something?"

"You know I'm perfectly capable of fending for myself, don't you?"

"Hmm. I know you eat cereal way too much, and if we don't feed you, your nutrition suffers."

"Well, I've got good food coming my way tonight, so don't you worry."

"Really? From what source?" Sabine asked, clearly suspicious.

Why had she said that? In Rachel's haste to reassure Sabine that she wouldn't starve and die without their help, she'd argued herself into a corner. "Uh. My neighbor is sharing a casserole with me."

"Handsome Dr. Nick? Do tell." Sabine wasn't letting her off the hook, despite the chaos in the background at her house. Rachel could picture her little squishy squealing in her high chair throwing Cheerios to the dog, who nearly trampled the cat to get them.

Shit. "Well, it seems he's been the recipient of the town welcome wagon. He didn't want to waste the food, so we're eating together."

"How did this invitation come to pass?" Sabine was engaged now.

"I brought Judith to the hospital for a sprained ankle."

"Judith hurt her ankle again?" Sabine sounded concerned. She'd known Judith awhile now and they'd become friends, and it was well-known that Judith was a patient of Sabine's.

"It was the other one—long story. Anway, we had a minute alone while Judith was having her foot x-rayed, and he suggested we eat casserole together that someone dropped off at the hospital." Cliffs Notes version.

Rachel heard another shriek and more barking in the background at Sabine's. "Hmm. Someone? That sounds interesting. You know casseroles are for funerals and man-getting around here."

"Yes. I've been reminded of this several times today."

"Better be careful eating another girl's casserole." Sabine snickered into the phone.

"Shut up and kiss Janie for me."

"Call me tomorrow. Oh, and we'll need help with the decorating, you know. Takes the whole village—or town—to get the job done."

"When does all that start?" This was Rachel's first year living in Ministry for the annual Christmas festival. She wasn't sure how all the prep went down.

"It's already started, but we're going to head out for a couple hours to the town square after the kids go to bed to prep for the tree if you're free after dinner. If not, we'll catch you tomorrow."

"Okay. I'll see you later. But only if you keep your questions to a minimum."

"Fine."

>>><<<

RACHEL STOPPED AT the store after dropping the twins off and picked up a bouquet of yellow roses, a couple bottles of wine, and a fresh baguette. Who knew what kinds of gastric masterpieces they would be consuming and what the pairing might require? So, to be certain she had the right wine to go with the food, she thought she'd better be safe than sorry.

Coming from New Orleans, where food and wine were such a deeply ingrained part of everyday culture, Rachel found it second nature to consider such things. Maybe it had been her upbringing as well. Food was comfort and always part of the conversation.

Rachel wondered if she should turn on the game or music while they ate. It wasn't as if they were dating. Music created ambiance, and she wanted to avoid that, so she flipped on the TV. Her alma mater, LSU was playing A&M at seven, but the Iron Bowl was still on, and Alabama was making a show of spanking Auburn at the moment.

The red wine was breathing, and the white was chilled, and the bread was in the oven. She took out a couple dinner plates, dessert plates, and some silverware. Her stomach growled. Now, Rachel was ready for the food to arrive. She refused to admit her anticipation for the appearance of the one bearing the gifts, though she could envision him quite clearly in her mind's eye. Every hunky inch of him.

He bothered her. As in, attracted her. And she didn't need that right now. But she couldn't come up with a good reason to tell him to keep his distance either. He seemed to be a decent guy, he smelled nice, and he was drop-dead sexy. *And* he came with life-long cousin references. Who could argue with those? She'd done worse in her life.

Rachel jumped when she heard the knock at the door. Her stomach was in knots.

She opened the door to see the reason for her knotty

stomach wearing potholders and juggling hot dishes. "Here, let me help you." She grabbed a bottle of wine from under the crook of one arm and a nosegay of flowers from the other. "Bring that over here." She pointed for him to place the large crockery on the stovetop.

"Thanks. Things started slipping by the time I made it over here. I've got more in my apartment." He smelled good again.

"I'll help."

"Thanks." She followed him next door inside his place and he handed her a pie.

He used the pot holders to pick up another hot rounded dish. "Wow. How many of these do you have?" she asked, laughing.

"There are two more in the fridge, but I figured I would save them for later."

She shook her head and rolled her eyes. "You'd better send thank-you notes or there's gonna be hell to pay." They walked back to her apartment, and she grabbed the bread out of the oven as soon as she put down the pie.

"My mother is big on thank-you notes. I'd rather just make a phone call or thank someone in person," he said, placing the other hot dish on her stove.

"We're Southerners; where *are* your manners?" She affected a strong deep, low-country Georgia accent and drawled out every syllable in her best Scarlett O'Hara impersonation.

He laughed and rolled his eyes.

"Looks like we've got plenty of wine," she said.

"Everything here has cheese in it. I think any kind of wine goes well with cheese."

Rachel pulled the foil sheet off the first dish. "I can't tell what's under the cheese."

"I didn't have the courage to look."

"Well, here goes." She dug into it with a large serving spoon, scooping out a good-sized helping onto a plate.

"I see chicken, maybe mushrooms, and that could be water chestnuts and broccoli. Looks edible," Nick said, thinking about his last patient of the day.

Rachel nodded. "Let's check the other one." She scooped into the next one and a strong fishy odor hit them. "Ooh, this one looks like tuna noodle surprise."

Nick grimaced. "None for me, thanks. I don't do tuna."

Rachel laughed. "The smell is enough to put me off. It's funny; before I broke the cheese seal, I couldn't smell it."

"Cover it back up."

"I'll just put it down the garbage disposal." Because it was still hot, Nick held the dish with potholders, while Rachel spooned out the tuna noodle surprise into the running disposal until it was gone. But the smell remained.

They were shoulder-to-shoulder and hip to hip, and Rachel was very physically aware of him, despite the smell of tuna.

"I'll light a candle," Rachel said, moving away and grabbing her favorite half-burned kitchen candle and lighting it.

"Do these windows open?" Nick asked, obviously working to get some fresh air inside.

They were both laughing, trying to quickly rid the tiny apartment of the noxious odor.

"Yes. There's a crank on the right side at the end. They're very old, so be careful," she said.

He gently cranked the old window open and a cool breeze blew in, lessening the stink almost immediately. "Whew. That was bad. Do you think whoever brought that dish over did it as a prank?"

Rachel giggled. "I don't know. Whose name is on it?" She turned over the dish to see if there was a name on the bottom.

"That one didn't have a card with it."

"Well, the dish has the name, *Davis,* on back written in Sharpie marker."

He wrinkled his brow. "That name is somewhat familiar."

"Did you see a patient by that name?"

"No, but I know who provided the one we're actually eating today."

"The cheesy chicken?"

"Yes. But I saw her as a patient today, so I can't give any particulars."

"A patient? Did she really have an ailment?" Rachel appeared interested.

He flattened his hand and tilted it side to side as if to show maybe/maybe not. "It's questionable, but suffice it to say, I think she was *impatient* that I hadn't yet called to thank her. I told her I would be having the dish as tonight's dinner. I didn't mention you were sharing it with me."

"Well, now you'll have to report back to her and let her know how you liked it."

"At least she didn't supply the stinky tuna noodle surprise. I don't think I could keep a straight face and lie about that one."

"Keep in mind, people often send food as a thank you around here. So, not all *this* is necessarily from women who want to find out what's under your scrubs." She blushed then.

His eyes widened at her suggestion regarding his scrubs. "Do *you* want to know what's under my scrubs?"

"We're not talking about me. *I* didn't bring you a casserole," Rachel assured him.

He nodded. "Gotcha. Well, now that the smell is gone, I'm still hungry. You?"

"Starved."

They sat down, each tore off a piece of the bread, and decided red would pair best with gooey, cheesy, chicken broccoli casserole, and shared dinner, while keeping one eye on the game in the background.

"Pie?" Nick suggested once they'd consumed seconds of the surprisingly tasty dish.

"Not yet. I'm so full I can't take a deep breath, but I promised my sister I'd go out this evening and help get things ready in the square for the big Christmas tree. It's supposed to be delivered in a day or two."

"It's a nice night. I'll come with you," he said.

The two of them showing up together couldn't be a good thing. The gossip would fly, but she couldn't very well tell him to take a hike after he'd fed her so well.

"Okay. Let me make sure the TV is set to record the game. Maybe we can have pie later."

"Sounds like a plan. Too bad Auburn couldn't pull it out. Alabama is such a powerhouse every year. It would be nice to see somebody trounce them once in a while."

"I want to see LSU do it one of these days. We hate Alabama with a passion in our family."

"Geaux Tigers, huh? Well, you'd better not let anybody around here hear you say that. You'll never work again."

SEC football was a very serious matter five months out of the year, and then it was talked about the other seven. "I can keep my mouth shut, except on game day."

She turned off the set and stood, slipping her shoes on. "Is it all set to record?" he asked.

The look she gave him questioned his intellect.

"Right. I'll take that as a yes," he said, then picked up the glass container from the countertop. "I'll stick what's left of this food in your fridge, if that's okay."

"Sure."

>>>×<<<

COULD A WOMAN be any more perfect? She was stunningly gorgeous, she actually ate real food with cheese, and bread, without worrying about gluten and fat, and she truly loved football enough to set her DVR to record the game.

Now they were headed to help her family and others get things ready for Christmas. If someone had told Nick his life would change so drastically within a week, and he would actually be enjoying it, he'd have never believed them. But right now, his stress level was as low as it had been in years.

"You have a funny look on your face, like you're surprised about something," Rachel said.

"You're reading my thoughts, apparently."

"So, tell me. What are you thinking?"

"I'm headed out to help with Christmas decorations in Ministry, Alabama on a Saturday night and I'm fine with it. There's actually nothing and nowhere that sounds more appealing to me at the moment."

She laughed out loud then. He hadn't heard her do that since they'd met. "You poor, poor man. I'm so sorry."

"Well, you seem okay with it too. Here you are doing the same thing on your Saturday night. Does that mean you should be pitied as well?" he asked.

Rachel shook her head. "No. I'm here because I choose to be. I decided after my dad got out of prison that my place was here, with my family. It wasn't chasing the next paycheck and freelancing all over the place. I put down roots here. So, while it may not be very exciting, it's where I now belong."

He nodded. "I don't know what happened with your father, but it sounds like it was hard on your family."

Rachel's expression clouded. "He wasn't the man I thought he was my entire life."

He sensed her discomfort with the subject. "I wonder if we ever know anyone," Nick said, thinking of his own parents and Monica too. She'd seemed to be one person and then she'd changed so drastically to someone he didn't recognize.

"Sounds like you've got your own load of baggage," Rachel said.

"I guess." He wasn't one to discuss his family woes either, and certainly not his love life.

"Well, I hope you find peace with yours, because I'm still working on it," Rachel said, her voice sad.

"I'm sorry you've had to go through that," he said, as they stopped just short of the square, where at least a dozen people were stringing Christmas lights on the bushes, laughing, while Christmas carols played in the background through speakers.

Rachel turned to him then. "It just goes to show that you can't trust anybody." Then, she waved toward her sister, who called them over.

That left Nick staring at her back. She was one tough nut.

Chapter Eight

"HEY, YOU TWO. Thanks for coming out," Sabine said.

"Should you be here doing all this?" Rachel asked.

"I feel fine. Plus, we've got a doctor nearby if I get gas again." Sabine rolled her eyes at Rachel and grinned at Nick. "C'mon, we've got lots to do. I do get tired earlier than I used to, so get cracking."

Rachel laughed and they followed her sister toward the truck beds filled with lights and garland.

"Hey, Nick, could I get your help over here?" Ben called.

"Sure." Nick glanced at Rachel, and she waved him away.

"So, how was dinner?" Sabine asked when Nick was out of earshot.

"Dinner was fine. Some kind of chicken with cheese."

"You know that's not what I meant and you know it," Sabine said.

"It was fine. He suggested coming with me to help decorate. I'm not sure why anyone would offer to do that." Rachel looked around at the lights going up on the main street and had to admit it was very pretty.

"Maybe he wasn't ready for *dinner* to be over," Sabine's eye's twinkled.

"Well, we *will* be going home together, since we live in the same house right next door to each other." Rachel pointed to the upstairs of Mrs. Wiggins storybook house a half a block away.

"Funny, but as much as you refuse to admit it, he likes you, and I see the way you look at him." Sabine gave her a speculative look. Rachel hated it when her sister did that.

"Well, he is hot, and he smells nice; and so far, the only thing I have against him is he's a man and I hardly know him."

"Well, that's progress, and I'll take it."

"So, what's going on here?" Rachel gestured to the work in progress in the town square.

"Right now, we're hanging the lighted garland all around to get this area ready for the giant tree's arrival Monday or Tuesday. We have a lot to accomplish before the scheduled events begin next weekend. Emma's been working overtime with her students preparing them for the Christmas pageant," Sabine said. Emma was a former Miss Alabama and was now the town's pageant coach.

"Yep. I'm taking photos during the event," Rachel said.

"As you know, it's on the seventeenth, so we still have a

few weeks, but that takes a lot of prep."

"I don't envy Emma that job." Pageants had never been something either of them had been involved in. Maybe it was more of a small-town Southern thing. Pageant coaching kept Emma Laroux in a full-time job, year-round, so clearly, they were very popular here.

"She has her pageant committee, so that's helpful. They've been doing this for many years, so they're very efficient."

"Is it the same group that does the Pecan Pie Pageant?" Rachel asked. Because that was a well-run deal. She'd been hired to photograph the event, and as far as little and big girls competing in fancy dresses with costume changes and a talent event, Rachel was amazed at how little drama and confusion there seemed to be.

"Yes, it's pretty much the same organizing body, with a few different faces. It's a similar setup, but no talent competition, and only one gown per girl, which makes the evening go faster."

Rachel nearly laughed that her clinical psychologist counselor sister was talking small-town beauty pageants. Not that organizing this kind of thing was completely foreign to her, because she'd been a state senator's wife in Louisiana in her previous life, which seemed like a hundred years ago to them all.

Having been a politician's wife, Sabine had done a lot of community organizing, mostly charity events and benefits.

Sadly, Sabine had been married to someone who'd been a corruptible fool. Her former husband was now in prison for solicitation of underage prostitutes, and for kidnapping and drugging Sabine to prevent her from divorcing him.

It was why Rachel was so protective of her mother and sister. Both the men in their lives had proved to be total shits after they'd sworn to love and protect them. Those same men had been supposed to be reliable for Rachel too. She'd trusted them.

"Mrs. Wiggins told me she would like to be involved with the cookie bake-off and swap," Rachel said. "Who should I speak with about that?"

"Hmm. I think one of Ben's sisters oversees that. I'll ask and let you know."

"Hey, Rachel, could you come over and hold this ladder?" Ben called.

"Sure." Her brother-in-law wisely didn't ask his pregnant wife to do it, and Rachel was grateful.

Rachel stood at the bottom of a ten-foot ladder while Ben threaded lit garland at the top of a pergola in the square. There were four such structures on every side of a center green area, where the giant tree would be placed by a crane when it arrived by truck.

She'd been hearing about the particulars for weeks about how this would all go down. "How are they going to secure the tree, Ben?" She didn't know that detail.

He glanced down. "They'll attach steel cables on all sides

to loops set in the concrete from previous years. The tree sits down into a heavy vice that stabilizes it before the cables are attached. So far, it's worked well. It's not going anywhere. We had a structural engineer come out from Auburn and draw up the plan."

"Sounds like y'all have this down to a science around here—this Christmas thing," Nick said from where he was threading lights into the garland.

"Yeah, you'd think *we* would hire a company to do the decorating, wouldn't you?" Ben said. "But I'm told that would take away the *specialness* of what we do here in our little town."

"You not feeling so special right now, brother-in-law?" Rachel teased.

"Stop complaining, Husband. I was up on a ladder beside you last year," Sabine reminded him. "You set a good example for the residents."

They heard a male laugh. "Yeah, Brother, shows 'em you're not too big for your britches," Junior said from behind them. He'd arrived with more lights.

"Junior, get your ass up here on this ladder," Ben sniped at his brother-in-law.

It was nearing eight-o-clock and more people had trickled in and were stringing lights and garland. "Looks like the Saturday night crew has arrived."

"Seems late to get started," Nick said.

"Not for a Saturday night. Plus, the football game just

ended. Gave everybody a chance to eat and get the kids to bed. Lots of sitters are employed this time of year," Sabine said.

"Bring 'em on, I say," Ben said.

Maeve, JoJo, and Anna walked up carrying containers of hot chocolate and cups. "Anybody thirsty?" There was a folding table set up, so they placed the drinks there.

Pretty soon, there was a large team of volunteers decorating the square. They'd brought more ladders and were now hanging large wreaths with big, red bows at intervals, in addition to the lights and garland.

"Once all the lights and greenery are in place, we'll put up the fun stuff," Sabine said.

"The fun stuff?" Nick asked.

Rachel could tell by his expression that the overkill on all this was surprising to him.

Heck, it was surprising to her as well. She'd been a part of it the last couple years, but hadn't gotten involved in the planning and execution.

"What do you consider fun stuff? This looks pretty *fun* to me," Rachel said, gesturing toward the festive-looking lights and such.

"This year, we're placing oversized candy canes, snowflakes, and snowmen on all the storefronts downtown. Plus, we have all our events: the cookie bake-off and swap, the Christmas pageant, the big tree decorating, the fireworks, the 5k, the Christmas concert, the caroling, the tour of homes, and photos with Santa. If we had some actual snow, it would be perfect."

Sabine listed all the upcoming events as if she were reading from a list. "But you'll have snow blowers, right?" he asked with a grin, clearly referencing the conversation from Thanksgiving Day dinner. This idea of snow blowers seemed to amuse him.

"Yes, but only for the main celebration events. And that only works if the temperatures are low. Otherwise, things just get wet and smushy. I guess you take the good with the bad."

Rachel could see how blowing precipitation on a sixty-degree day in the South might make mud in a quick minute.

She glanced over at Nick and had a feeling he was thinking the same thing.

$$\gg\!\!\!\ggg\!\!\!\lll\!\!\!\ll$$

THE CLIMATE AND temps here weren't so different from those in Atlanta most of the year. Winter was unpredictable year-to-year. Nick remembered several holidays bundling up and sledding down the big hill on the side of their house on ice and snow, and some where they'd played flag football out in the front yard in shorts and T-shirts in seventy-degree weather. But mostly, it was just dreary and somewhere in the middle around Christmas.

Last year, his mother strongly hinted he should propose to Monica. Monica had made her expectation clear that she expected a proposal. This had made the entire holiday season very uncomfortable for everyone. He wasn't ready for marriage. Maybe he just hadn't been certain of his feelings for Monica at the time. His *not* proposing had made her insecurities worse, but it was an impossible subject to broach without actually telling her he was having doubts about the depth of his commitment to their future. A true conundrum. He'd taken the coward's way out instead and bought her a ridiculously expensive necklace.

Being surrounded by all this Christmas activity was bringing back some of those feelings of inadequacy he'd felt about being the cause of all that frustration and unhappiness.

"You okay?" Rachel asked.

"Sure. I'm fine. Just remembering last Christmas." That was true enough, but he wasn't sure about sharing his innermost thoughts with someone he barely knew, or with a woman who'd made it pretty clear she wasn't interested in him.

The multitude of twinkling clear lights all around them shone in her eyes and gave, at least, the impression of real interest. It felt genuine.

"You seemed pretty deep in thought. Did something bad happen last Christmas?" she asked.

He shook his head. "Not really bad. I just didn't live up to expectations is all. I was in a relationship and everyone thought it was time for a proposal. I didn't."

"Oh. I guess *everyone* was disappointed."

"You could say that. My mother was at the top of that list. My girlfriend too."

"Now I'm dying to know what happened."

"I obviously didn't propose, and we broke up recently. I didn't feel what I believe a person should feel for someone they plan to spend a lifetime with." Nick regretted that. The not feeling for Monica. Maybe he had the problem, but he hoped not.

Rachel's expression became very sad and serious. "That's a shame. I have my doubts about finding that kind of lifetime commitment and happiness. I mean, I believe and hope Sabine's found that with Ben, but it didn't happen for my mom and dad, or for Sabine the first time."

"So, you're a cynic about finding true love," he said. They'd walked away from the fray just enough where they could survey the scene without anyone hearing them and had enough privacy to speak freely.

Rachel shrugged. "I'm not sure what you would call it. Daddy issues, for sure after what happened. It affects how I view relationships now, and how hopeful I feel about my future in finding a classic happy ending. I've become a skeptic."

He nodded. "My parents' marriage is one of the worst shams I've ever experienced. My mother is a miserable human being, but swears marriage isn't about finding the person you love, or who completes you. No, she says it's all about making a smart match, and that all the flowery stuff fades away."

"What do you think?" Rachel asked.

"I don't know. I hate to think I'll end up like either my mother or my father. I'd rather be alone than make another human being that miserable."

Rachel shrugged. "*My* mom's happy now, but only because she finally left my dad. He cheated and lied for years. But he swore he loved her."

"Did he?" Nick asked. "Love her, even though he cheated and lied. Is that possible?"

"He loved her. But he had such an ego, and thought himself so important and powerful, and above mere morals, that my mother should accept it. She didn't. When his powerful, important ass went to prison, she was finally able to divorce him without having to fight all the legal battles."

"Do they still talk?" Nick asked.

"No. Not really. She hasn't forgiven him, but she has moved on. Mom's very happy with Norman, and we are thrilled they're together. If anyone deserved another chance to find love, it's Mom," Rachel said.

"Sounds like it. Do you think it takes learning from those kinds of God-awful mistakes and getting hurt that badly to get to the heart of real love?"

"Kill me now. I'd rather avoid the whole thing," Rachel said with certainty.

"Me too," Nick agreed.

They both laughed. "I guess watching other people screw

it up royally makes us just as screwed up."

"I never thought about it quite like that, but I guess it does make a person want more and better when it comes to their own futures. I just know I won't ever settle for what my parents have. That's why I broke it off with Monica."

"How long were you together?"

"Almost three years."

"That's a lot of history to be with someone you weren't sure about," Rachel said.

He nodded. "I know. She made it—hard to break it off."

They'd kind of slipped away from the crowd without saying good night, but nobody but Sabine would notice, so Rachel kept walking toward home.

"My mom says it's never good to be the one who loves the most. Sounds like Monica loved the most in your case."

Nick winced. "I guess she did. That sounds pretty awful."

"I've never been in love, so I've never had my heart broken by a man, besides by my dad. And that was enough."

"Sounds like he did a number on the whole family," Nick said.

"In so many ways," Rachel agreed.

They climbed the stairs to their respective apartments. Once they arrived at her front door, Rachel stopped, put her key in lock and smiled at him. "I had a nice evening, Nick. Thanks for insisting we share your casseroles."

"I'm just sorry casserole number two stank up your

apartment so badly."

They shared a laugh at that. But then, it became awkward, because he wanted—no—needed to kiss her then. It was a shared attraction, he was certain, but he didn't want to blow the moment with more words, so he took a chance and stepped forward, gently putting his fingers gently through her hair at the base of her neck.

He lightly leaned forward and tentatively kissed her, tasting her lips for a brief instant. She didn't resist. In fact, she surprised him by reaching out, and pulling his face toward her a second time. The pressure of their lips wasn't so light then, and out of nowhere, as if a magnet had switched on, their bodies were instantly touching: legs, hips, chest, and lips.

Rachel sighed and pressed against him, and then she kissed him again. "This is such a bad idea."

"It doesn't feel like a bad idea," he murmured against her lips.

"I thought I heard you kids coming up the stairs. Oh—my." Mrs. Wiggins's eyes widened behind her glasses like an owl's might. "Well, I guess you two are getting to know one another."

They sprang apart like busted teenagers.

Rachel's cheeks were bright red. "Hi, Mrs. Wiggins. We were helping outside with the decorations. I told Sabine you wanted to help with the cookie swap and bake-off. She's going to find out who's in charge."

Mrs. Wiggins wore a half-smiling, but still speculative, expression on her wrinkled face. "Thanks for checking on that, dear," she said to Rachel.

"Well, I'll say good night," Nick said.

"Don't let me stop you," Mrs. W said, grinning fully now.

He moved toward his door.

"Did you want the rest of the casserole?" Rachel asked.

"Uh, I'll get it later, if that's okay." He unlocked his door. "Well, good night."

"Good night," Rachel said. He could hear the laughter in her voice.

Then, just before he closed the door, he heard Mrs. Wiggins's exaggerated whisper. "I think he's embarrassed."

⟫⟩⟫⟩⟫⟨⟨⟨⟨

RACHEL SAID, "I have to admit that I'm pretty embarrassed getting caught kissing my next-door neighbor in the hallway."

"Oh, nonsense. At least he had the decency to kiss you outside your door like a gentleman."

Rachel hadn't thought about that. "I guess so."

"He's a nice boy, that doctor. We don't have fraternizing rules here, so no need to worry. I know what goes on between healthy young people."

"Mrs. Wiggins!" Rachel couldn't hide her shock at the older woman's openly discussing *fraternizing*.

"Don't act so shocked. How do you think we all got here, sweetie? S-E-X, that's how." She whispered the word loudly.

"Well, we're not fraternizing, besides dinner and that one kiss, so don't worry. I'm not looking to get serious or have S-E-X with anyone right now."

"I'm just saying that if you do, you won't be in the doghouse with me. He's a catch, that one. And if *you* don't catch him, somebody else might. And I hate to see him go to somebody I don't approve of."

»»»«««

"WELL, RIGHT NOW I don't think he's with anyone else, so you shouldn't have to worry too much about it. And he's a full-grown adult, so if it happens, I guess neither one of us can say much about it."

Mrs. Wiggins patted Rachel's hand. "Be smart, dear. Just be smart, and if you think the two of you have a shot together, don't dilly-dally."

"I'll keep that in mind. Thanks for the talk."

The woman nodded sagely and headed back down the stairs in her careful, slow manner.

"Good night, Mrs. Wiggins."

"'Night, dear."

Rachel turned to go inside her apartment, her face still flushed from horror and shame. Then, she noticed the pie sitting on the table. He'd forgotten about the pie. And there was still football to be watched. Maybe tomorrow.

The window was still opened where they'd aired the place out from the tuna noodle surprise. No hint of the horrible smell remained, and it had gotten chilly inside, so Rachel cranked the window closed, but not before she glanced outside and noticed the transformation tonight's efforts by the townspeople made. The clear lights shone brightly up and down the main street of Ministry. Rachel leaned to the right and could see the square, where they'd been earlier, all lit up.

If only her life could transform so beautifully and quickly. If only someone like Nick had come here to stay, and Rachel could find the kind of peace and happiness Sabine had with Ben. If it happened for other people, why not her?

Christmas made Rachel believe—believe in magic and miracles. And holding out that kind of hope was dangerous. Because it made those nebulous happily-ever-afters begin to feel real and tangible for people like her—for just a little while, amidst the lights, carols, and stories of Christmas babies and wise men.

As Rachel placed the few dishes in the dishwasher, she wondered what Nick was thinking on the other side of their shared wall. They'd both exposed some sensitive information about themselves to each other tonight. She'd gotten the feeling he wasn't the type to go around discussing his personal life with just anyone.

She certainly wasn't the type. In fact, the few times she'd dated the same guy more than a few times, her discomfort with sharing personal details had most certainly been a deterrent in moving forward with relationships. She was slow to trust anyone. Because of her father, and because of Richard, Sabine's ex-husband.

Making herself vulnerable to someone seemed unwise. Tonight, however, she'd come very close to doing that with a guy she barely knew. But he'd shared too, so it hadn't felt quite so scary in the moment.

Then, he'd kissed her. *Wowza.* What a kiss. As far as kisses went, it shouldn't have affected her that way. His hands hadn't been touching her anywhere but on the back of her neck and lightly on her face. But her entire body had awakened with only that slight touch. And of course, the touch of his lips on hers.

Her formerly intact lady parts were on high-alert now and screaming at her. Rachel wasn't happy about that. He'd introduced a physical restlessness, and a desire she'd not experienced in a long time—maybe never.

Then, Mrs. Wiggins had shown up, and as far as Rachel was concerned, saved the day. Rachel wasn't certain what might have happened next if she hadn't appeared on the scene. Based on the state of her body's response to just Nick's kiss, things *might* have gotten out of hand. What if he'd actually gotten to second base?

The possibility existed that Rachel would have thrown her legs around his waist and begged him to take her on the floor in the hallway. How humiliating that she couldn't rule it out.

For all her big talk about it to Sabine, Rachel hadn't been with a lot of guys, sexually. Rachel hadn't wanted her sister to worry about her not being well-adjusted or lonely. Making jokes about meeting guys here and there seemed like the thing to do at the time.

Truth was, Rachel understood men thought she was attractive, to the point of being intimidated by her. She'd played on that enough to scare most of them away. Those who were courageous enough to approach her, she typically brushed off with some excuse or other.

She'd had a couple boyfriends in college, but nothing too serious. It just hadn't worked out.

Chapter Nine

NICK HAD JUST finished treating a beastly case of gout in treatment room two. Mr. Davis had allowed the situation to get so far out of control that Nick considered admitting the poor man because he was in so much pain and couldn't bear any weight on his ankle.

But the farmer promised to take his meds, use the wheelchair for the next week, and stay off the foot. Nick understood how important pushing through pain was when one's livelihood was at stake, but some of these folks were going to kill themselves in the process. It concerned him how many older folks he'd seen in the last week who just refused to adjust their activity to allow for their age and condition.

Nick was still considering ways to communicate the importance of self-preservation when his reckoning finally came.

She was loud, and she wasn't taking no for an answer. "I want to speak to Doctor Sullivan. He has something that belongs to my momma."

"Angie, you're not allowed back here unless you're a patient. I'll give him a message."

Nick heard Candy, the receptionist, try to dissuade someone named Angie.

"You gonna call the cops on me?" the woman sneered. "Thought not."

The reckoning manifested itself in the form of a tall brunette, with very large hair, in skin-tight jeans, red cowboy boots, and an impressive, uh, chest that was encased in a tight reindeer sweater whose eyes were exactly in the nipple positions, for lack of a better explanation.

She spotted him as soon as she burst through the double doors, with Candy nearly hanging off the woman's arm, still trying to dissuade her. "So, you're the snotty piece of shit who can't be bothered to pick up the phone and return a casserole dish when somebody spends time cooking you a welcome dinner?"

"Excuse me?" Nick was taken aback at the woman's manner, and, he had to admit, the sweater with the strategically placed reindeer *eyeballs*. Was she even wearing a bra underneath? It was like a horrible train wreck where one couldn't look away.

With great effort, Nick dragged his eyes from the shocking scene on the woman's chest. "I'm sorry. I apologize if I've offended you. I don't think we've me. I'm Nick Sullivan." Nick stuck out his hand.

"I'm Angie Davis." She narrowed her eyes, but shook his

hand anyway. "I'm not used to being ignored, and I don't appreciate it. Didn't anybody tell you who I was when I dropped off the tuna noodle casserole?"

He shook his head, but suppressed a shudder at the memory of the smell when they'd broken the cheese seal. "I have your dish ready to return. I figured you'd stop by to pick it up. I'm not used to this custom. It's not something people do where I'm from. Sorry." He shrugged.

"Well, anybody with any home training or good sense should realize that when someone leaves a phone number, you should make a call." Her well-groomed eyebrows shot up, making her point that he had neither.

He walked over to where a variety of casserole dishes were stacked on the counter. He'd been avoiding those phone calls, hoping the containers would magically find their way back home.

"Ah, here it is. Tuna noodle surprise." Then, he cringed that he said it aloud.

"Why did you call it that? It's Momma's special recipe. Are you saying you didn't like it?" the screamer called Angie demanded.

"I didn't say that." He handed over the oval glass dish. "Here you go. Thanks for your kindness. But you can't be back here if you're not a patient." His patience with Angie of the obscene sweater was at an end.

"How *dare* you? Do you know who I am?"

He tried hard not to roll his eyes.

"Excuse me Dr. Sullivan. You have a patient in treatment room three," his nurse said.

He took the chart for his next patient as if it had just saved his life. And he nearly kissed Georgie on the mouth.

"Sorry, Angie, was it? We're in a hospital, and I have a patient. Thanks again for the casserole." He turned away, and nearly sprinted toward treatment room three.

Not looking back, he was surprised when he opened the door of the exam room and there wasn't a patient.

"Sorry, Doctor. I thought you needed rescuing. I grabbed a patient's chart you'd seen earlier. Angie is the sheriff's daughter. She's a bully when she doesn't get her way. Two years ago, she had her cap set for Ben Laroux, like most of the other women in town, and was extremely pissed when he wouldn't date her."

"So, do I need to worry about retribution?" he asked, and laughed a little, but wasn't entirely sure it was a joke.

"Well, I don't know how much influence she has with her daddy these days, but I hope she doesn't go home and tell them you insulted her momma's tuna casserole," she said. Her expression was filled with empathy, and maybe just a little pity for his situation.

"Oh, shit. All I need is the local sheriff pissed that I insulted his sweet wife's cooking. You know, a heads-up when the dish came in would have been nice."

Georgie laughed then. "Then we wouldn't have had this much entertainment in watching how you handled it. Take it from me, you might want to give the others a call and tell them thanks for the casseroles."

"What are the expectations that go along with this phone call?"

She shrugged. "This is their shot at an introduction so you'll notice them. They surely hope it will lead to more. The single women in this town wait for someone like you to show up. When you do, they do what they can to work things in their favor. You really can't blame them."

"I'm not here to stay. I'll be gone by New Year's."

"Yes, well, that gives them less than six weeks to change your mind, doesn't it?" She laughed and stepped out the door, leaving him to ponder her words.

⟫⟩⟨⟨

As RACHEL WORKED through editing the remaining shots from Thanksgiving, she stopped short when she came across a full head-shot of Nick, smiling at someone or something. It was unguarded and natural. And undeniably gorgeous. The impression that he was the real deal through her lens lent a credibility to her gut instinct. She trusted her camera lens. It rarely told the lies people did.

His teeth were white and straight, his hazel eyes were clear and devoid of shadows and secrets, though maybe a little regret or sadness lurking in the depths? His face had enough character to lend credibility, his nose was just off-center, as if he'd had it broken as a kid, but not so much that it detracted from his good looks. Rachel stared at the honest photo and secretly hoped he lived up to the ideal she'd captured.

The shot was admittedly such a good professional candid that he might like to have it to frame as a gift for his mother—or someone. Rachel understood how much people appreciated photos of loved ones in this world where objects were so easily purchased and discarded. Good photos were still unique and not easily replaceable.

She loaded high-quality glossy paper in her photo printer, and when she'd completed her software magic, printed out the photo in both color and black-and-white.

He was model-perfect, and the photo was excellent, she had to admit. This was quality enough to grace any magazine spread. Nick might consider a second career in print work if the whole medical thing didn't work out.

A knock on the door interrupted her train of thought.

"Coming," she called.

When she opened the door, the same face that was currently on her printer greeted her. "Hi there."

"Hey. I stopped by to see if we were grounded."

She laughed. "Actually, quite the opposite. Mrs. Wiggins let me know that she had no rules against *fraternization*. And she understands what goes on between young people."

His eyebrows went up. "What goes on?"

"S-E-X." Rachel whispered it loud like Mrs. Wiggins had.

Nick laughed at that and stepped toward her, wiggling his fingers. "It does? Wow, that's great."

She slapped his hands, giggling. "I didn't say *we* were having S-E-X."

He shrugged his shoulders. "Aw, well. I have to say, that kiss was pretty major last night. We could do that again."

"You're in a mood this evening, aren't you?" His playfulness had lightened her own attitude.

"It's you and all your S-E-X talk. Actually, I just got off work, and stopped by to pick up the dish. It's come to my attention I'll have to return it."

"Oh. Okay. Come in. I need to wash it. There's still half a cheesy-chicken casserole inside. I was going to heat it up. And there's pie. Have you eaten yet?" No more kissy talk.

"Uh. No. I guess I could eat it again, if you don't mind my barging in a second night in a row?"

"You provided the food, so fair is fair." Rachel was getting all tingly just having him inside her apartment.

He shut the door.

She walked into the kitchen area to take out the food from the fridge, leaving him standing in the other room. "Why do you have a picture of me on your printer?"

Shit. "It was one I took at Thanksgiving. I thought it came out so good you might want to frame it for your mother as a Christmas gift or something."

He grinned. "Thanks. It's a nice photo. She'll like that."

"Why did you think I had a picture of you sitting on my

printer?"

He gave her a sly look. "If I told you, it would sound extremely conceited."

"Uh-huh. If you'll notice, I also have one of my brother-in-law with cake on his face and one of my niece, so you're in good company."

"Should I go next door and get a bottle of wine?" He changed the subject.

"I've got some here. You can get a couple glasses for us."

He moved into the kitchen and pulled down the glasses from the holder. She pointed to the bottle of corked wine and he brought them to the table.

"So, I have an interesting story to tell you about a lady in a reindeer sweater."

They sat at the table once the food was hot and ready to serve. "Sounds like a good one. Do tell."

He regaled a story about Angie Davis, the sheriff's daughter, sender of the stinky tuna noodle surprise casserole, barging into the hospital with much dramatic flair, sending Rachel into peals of laughter.

"Oh, she did *not*."

He pointed to where the reindeer's big eyeballs were positioned, describing in detail the sweater, and Rachel nearly fell out of her chair. "Stop it! It's too much!"

"And I *might* have called it *tuna noodle surprise*, not realizing my mistake, which led her to believe I wasn't particularly fond of the dish."

"You did NOT." Tears were now rolling down her cheeks.

He nodded, tears of laughter leaking from his own eyes.

Once they'd stopped laughing, Rachel took a sip of her wine. "You've done it now, buster."

"Done what?"

"Started the gossip train. Now, they're just going to try harder."

"Harder than the casserole competition and the fake illness visits to the emergency room?"

"Wow. Now they're coming in to see you at the hospital? Faking illness? That's bold, even for Ministry's single contingent. They must feel pressed for time."

"I'll only be here through New Year's. Maybe that's why I'm getting the full-court press." He told Rachel what his nurse, Georgie, had said about that being an extra incentive.

"Sounds like you're in a pickle," she snickered.

"It might solve my immediate problem if Mrs. Wiggins told everyone that you and I were dating since she caught us kissing."

"Who said she won't spread that around? She is quite the information source."

"She's a gossip?" He sounded shocked.

Rachel nodded. "One of the biggest. Though she doesn't mean any harm, she's just lonely, and it's her way of being relevant."

"Sounds like a perfect non-solution to me. If people

think we're dating, I won't have to deal with the onslaught."

"How is it a good idea for me? Maybe I don't want people thinking I'm dating someone. Might hurt my single reputation."

"How was single life treating you? I mean, you were eating cheesy chicken with me and watching football last night."

And having a fantastic time. "Fine. I could take a break from all the guys breaking down my door, I guess."

"I would be shocked if you didn't have every guy between here and Birmingham chasing after you."

She shook her head. "I'm living in Ministry, Alabama, remember? They barely have Internet here. Well, that's not quite true, but it's small and well off the beaten path, besides its well-known Christmas festival and Cammie's cooking show."

"Anyway, I'll owe you, big time. And I can call the women who left their phone numbers and cookery, and regretfully break the news that I'm no longer on the market."

"You dodged a bullet with Angie Davis. She'd have eaten you alive. I'll have to think about payment." In the form of sexual favors, perhaps.

"Did you watch the Saints game?"

"Of course I did, and my Who Dats kicked butt. The Falcons don't start until eight-thirty, so I'm about to turn on the game I recorded last night. You're welcome to watch if you'd like. I'll be editing photos on my laptop, but I like having a game on in the background."

"That would be great. I'm either going to buy a bigger TV while I'm here, or make a quick trip to Atlanta and bring mine back for the next six weeks. We're in the middle of the season. I can't watch it on that tiny screen next door."

"I get it. I like my big screen—no explanation needed." Now that Rachel had extended the invitation, she would have to wear a bra while doing her editing. But having her sexy new fake boyfriend watching football with her would be better than sitting here alone and braless, she supposed.

"We could practice our fake-couple kissing," he suggested, and then grinned at her.

She shot him an eye-roll. "Nope."

"Okay, but it was a really hot kiss, you have to admit."

"Nope; not admitting to anything." She shook her head, and refused to make eye contact with him as she searched the menu on the screen for the recorded game.

"I'm going next door to get a beer. Want one?" he asked.

"Yes, please."

Rachel found the recording and pressed "play." She wasn't entirely sure why she'd agreed to be Nick's fictitious girlfriend. It sounded like a hokey idea, this playing pretend, but the fission of excitement that went through her at his suggestion was undeniable. Maybe she was playing with fire; maybe they both were. But it was only for a few weeks. What harm could come of it? They were both full-grown adults.

NICK'S PHONE BUZZED in his pocket the minute he'd closed the door of his apartment. It was his mother. *Great.* He didn't really have anything new to report, but if he avoided her, she would get her feelings hurt.

"Hey, Mom."

"How's it going in Alabama?" she asked.

"I'm fine. How's Dad?"

"Oh, your father's right as rain, like always. It's me you should be concerned with," she said, cryptically.

"Are you having a problem, Mom?"

"Not right now, but I could be, so you should always inquire."

He rolled his eyes, though there was no one to see. Typical Mom. "Glad to know you're well."

"I called to ask if you were still planning to come to the Falcons/Saints game Thursday?"

Nick grimaced. He'd nearly forgotten about it, even though he'd been looking forward to it when he'd bought the tickets initially. "I doubt it, Mom. I haven't spoken to anyone about covering my shift at the hospital."

"Well, I was really looking forward to seeing you, and so was your father." She did sound legitimately disappointed.

"I know. I'm sorry. If there's any way I can still make it, I will. I'll let you know as soon as I find out." He grabbed a couple longneck Buds from the fridge.

"Monica's been asking about you."

That stopped him cold. "How's Monica?"

"She's as lovely as ever, of course. But she misses you, Son. You should give her a call. You owe her that much, don't you think?"

"I don't think my relationship with Monica is your concern. I don't want to hurt your feelings, Mom, but Monica and I are no longer in a relationship."

"I know you were upset with her for some of the things she did, but now that you've taken some time away, I hope you'll come to your senses and realize how perfect she is for you."

Nick sighed. "Mom, this is not something you should get in the middle of, though obviously, that's what you're doing. Did you tell her I was supposed to come home for the game?"

"Well, I might have mentioned it."

"I want you to tell her I'm doing well. But I'm not making plans to see her if I come home for the game, so you should probably let her know to keep her distance either way. It's only going to be harder for you both if you hold out hope that she and I plan to get back together, because we're not."

"What an awful thing to say, Nicholas. The two of you were together for a long time. It couldn't have been time wasted."

"I don't consider it wasted time. The relationship just didn't work out in the end. People decide to go their separate ways for lots of reasons."

"A relationship is an investment of time and emotion, Nick. You shouldn't have wasted so many of her child-bearing years if you didn't plan to put a ring on it. That was poorly done of you."

"So, I should have just stuck with her because we spent a few years together even though I didn't love her the way people who build lives together should?"

"Yes. You've got your head in the clouds if you think that kind of love can sustain anyone for a lifetime."

He nearly laughed out loud, but settled for a choking sound, because he was unable to stop it from bursting forth.

"What was that about? That sound? I guess this is about your father and me?"

"I don't know Mom. Clearly you've got thoughts on the matter."

"I love your father. Not like I did when we met; it never panned out to be the great hearts and flowers kind of thing I see on the movies, but we got pregnant right away with you, so we did what was proper. And we built a life and family together. That's what people did back then. These days, young people say they *just aren't feeling it* and split up no matter how it affects their children or their reputations."

"And so you stayed together and were miserable all these years to save face, and taught us that it's better being miserable and together so long as you put up a good façade for the neighbors?" The beers in his hand were dripping onto the floor.

His mother sighed into the phone. "Divorce is rarely a good solution, especially for women, you know. Or, maybe you don't."

"Well, I would never do Monica the indignity of marrying her knowing I didn't love her enough."

"I think you have an over-inflated idea of what love is. Your expectations are going to let you down. Best to find someone you can live peacefully with, and who can give you beautiful children."

"Surely you wish more for Chuck and me." Nick was shocked at his own mother's lack of hope for a better life for her children and their future happiness. "I mean, we don't have to end up like you and Dad. In fact, I really hope we don't."

"What's wrong with us?" She seemed shocked that he would suggest there was a problem there.

"Are you kidding? You just admitted you settled, big time, because you were pregnant and didn't want to embarrass your family or upend your status. That sounds like the biggest case of throwing in the towel I've ever heard."

"No, it's staying strong. But he does drink too much and goes out of his way to do everything on the earth to annoy me."

"Could be that he is trying to get your attention."

"Ha. He's been trying to get me to leave him all these years. But I wouldn't give him the satisfaction."

The reasoning behind her alternating statements baffled

Nick. Who was she trying to argue with? Herself or him?

"Well, Mom, I'm going next door to watch the football game with my pretty neighbor. Here's hoping I have a nice evening, despite our conversation."

"You're doing *what*? You just broke up with Monica. She believes the two of you are going to reconcile." Mom was getting shrill again.

"No, she doesn't. I haven't spoken with her in months, and I made it clear we're over." He paused a moment and lightened his tone to a less harsh one. "So, I'll let you know about the game as soon as I know. Love you, Mom." He hung up then.

Nick took a couple cleansing breaths. Why did he continue engage with his mother like that? She could get to him like no one else. His parents were a hot mess, and had been as long as he could remember.

Nick replaced the sweating, less-cold beers with new ones and headed out the door. He'd taken so long trying to pacify his mother and her neuroses, he hoped Rachel hadn't locked the door.

Nick opened her door and noticed the game was on, so he stepped inside, but didn't see Rachel at first. He took another couple steps and peered over the back of the sofa. She was slumped on her side, her laptop having slid onto the cushion beside her, the screen in sleep mode.

She appeared uncomfortable, but who was he to wake her while she slept? He placed her beer in the refrigerator. He should have left then—he should. But it wasn't late, and the game was on. It was likely she would wake up soon and wonder where he was, right?

So, he slipped off his shoes and eased his feet onto the battered coffee table. It was a repurposed wood rebuild—cool to be sure, and indestructible. He appreciated that her tastes ran toward such décor. His mother preferred the priceless items that were so tastefully and artfully placed, that a quick turn in any direction in her home might mean the destruction of something so valuable it would send her into a tizzy of epic proportions.

Mom's tizzies were something Nick gratefully left behind when he departed for college years ago, except for the occasional ones when he got caught in the snare of her drama before he realized what was happening. They were unforeseen, and sprang suddenly from Mom's normal whiny remarks into a full-blown shit-storm of passive-aggressive commotion, like tonight.

A cold beer and a football game in the presence of a nice, pretty girl did a lot to soothe his nerves. Even if she was a sleeping beauty. Just watching her sleep gave Nick peace. He had an in-sync sensation when Rachel was nearby. So, like a weirdo, he sat in her apartment and watched the football game, and occasionally, watched her sleep.

RACHEL WOKE WITH a start. Nick was there, and he was

staring at her. "What the—?"

"You fell asleep."

She swiped the drool from her mouth. Aw, dang. "You've been watching me sleep? That's pretty creepy." Her eyelids felt like the 40-grit sandpaper she used to refinish her nightstand were grinding on them when she blinked.

"You're beautiful. You know that, don't you?" Nick grinned at her.

There was warmth in his hazel eyes that made her feel things in places throughout her body that hadn't had attention in a long time. Places that tended to tingle lately only in his presence. "What?" She blinked another scratchy blink. "I just wiped drool off my face."

"Rachel, I'm proud to call you my girlfriend, you know." He sounded like a fifteen-year-old boy.

She sat up, setting her laptop on the sofa beside her. He was on the cushion in the center where the sectional made the turn.

"*Fake* girlfriend, you mean." She laughed awkwardly, because well, this was not exactly a comfortable conversation.

"Semantics." He waved that minor detail away with his hand as if it were a trivial thing. "We can go out and enjoy our time together. It will be fun to play pretend with you."

"You know this really is an odd thing we're doing, right?" She just wanted to make certain he understood.

He nodded. "Yep. Very strange. But I'm still looking forward to it. You know this isn't the kind of thing I normally do either. I'm not usually so impulsive. I'm a pretty serious guy in general."

"Um, okay." She looked over at the TV as the Falcons scored a touchdown, and the sideline judge called a penalty, which then caused Nick's attention to immediately shift to the game.

"No way! He totally crossed the plane before his knee was down."

They both watch the replay that clearly showed the player stretch his arm, football in hand to cross the plane of the goal line before the player's knee hit the turf, which meant the touchdown was legit. Nick whooped loudly and stuck his hand up toward Rachel for a high-five validation of his excitement to share the joy. She reluctantly complied.

"Fine. It was a touchdown. Barely," she conceded. The Falcons were her least favorite team in the league.

"That was big of you," he said and laughed.

"Not a fan, as you know."

"Aw, c'mon. You can find some joy to share with me. Plus, you're closer to Atlanta here in Ministry than New Orleans. You should adapt, right?"

"We're right in the middle, I'd say. And, I don't see the adaptation happening anytime soon. Sorry."

"How would you feel about going to the Saints/Falcons game Thursday? I've got sweet tickets on the fifty-yard line. Of course, I'll have to get somebody to cover for me at the hospital, but if we time it just right, we could make it a quick trip."

"Seriously? That sounds awesome!" She hadn't meant to react so quickly at the prospect of seeing her Saints play in person, but dang it, it had been a long time since she'd been to a game. The only drawback is they wouldn't be at the Superdome in NOLA.

"I'm not sure if I'm going to be able to swing it, so I'll get back to you tomorrow and let you know if it's doable."

"Okay. I'll double-check my schedule. I've got some Christmas photos with Santa scheduled, but I can add some additional times to make up for the ones I miss." She grinned. "Thanks for inviting me. This really does sound like fun. I promise not to rub it in when my boys wring your dirty birds' necks." She smiled sweetly.

"On second thought, maybe I should leave you home."

Chapter Ten

T HE GIANT NORWAY spruce was being delivered to the town square today. Rachel had been asked by the editor of the local newspaper to photograph the delivery and setup process. She'd somehow ended up covering events that made news in the area. She'd soon need to hire an assistant full time if demand for her services continued at this pace. She often hired a weekend helper for big events, but only when she needed an extra pair of hands to manage. Between the weddings, pageants, school photos, senior portraits, and every other event in Ministry, Rachel's business was booming.

She'd been working on a website, but hadn't completed the process yet. Right now, Rachel was working on booking her shoots through The Evangeline House and taking jobs word-of-mouth, and keeping up with everything on her smartphone, which linked directly to her iPad and computer's calendar. If there was a breakdown in that process, it would be disastrous to her business.

Her dream was to have a studio of her own on Main Street where she could house a real photography business. She would have expensive lighting and equipment so her work would reflect her vision. Right now, she had the bare essentials in equipment. Just enough small, portable lights and filters that she shoved in the back of her small SUV and dragged with her wherever she went. Rachel could only imagine how much the quality of her work would improve if she were able to invest in a home for her business.

She'd imposed a few times for special projects on Sabine's sister-in-law, Emma's husband, Matthew, who was a cinematographer, by trade. He was now a director/producer, but had begun his career in high-end photography and video work. He had a studio in their home that made Rachel want to cry in homage. Matthew had been kind enough to allow Rachel to use his space for a few shoots. But she hated to ask unless the situation was dire.

So, as she worked and saved, Rachel made plans for her dream studio. Before long, she would have enough money for the down payment on a storefront with an apartment above. She had her eye on the space if she could persuade the owner to sell.

"Hey Rachel, how tall you think the tree is this year?" Junior asked and rubbed his beard as if it would help him figure out the puzzle. He wore a coon-skin hat, its tail hanging down the back of his head like a mullet. Likely one of his creations in the taxidermy shop.

He and Rachel were standing on the green about thirty feet from where the guys in hardhats were placing the truly giant specimen. It was magnificent. "Hmm, maybe about sixty feet tall? It's hard to say since it's not completely upright yet." She zoomed in on the group of men carefully guiding the trunk into the deep recess, amidst all the branches that obscured their progress. They'd had to use a chainsaw to cut dozens away thus far.

"Seems bigger this year. Maybe a sixty-fiver. Last years was about fifty-eight. This bastard's huge." He turned and cupped his hands over is mouth and called out to someone. "Hey, girls, come check out the tree."

A couple young girls in their early teens ambled toward them. Rachel recognized them as Samantha Harrison, Cammie and Grey Harrison's daughter, and Junior and Maeve's daughter, Lucy. They both had their phones out and were staring at the screens and looking ahead alternately, so as not to actually bump into anything or one another along the way.

"Wow, Dad, it's *huge*," Lucy said, marveling at the enormous sight. Lucy had an open and friendly personality that wordlessly included everyone in her conversation without even trying. Everybody knew where they stood with Lucy. In short, she was Junior's daughter all the way.

"Yeah, epic," Samantha agreed, almost in a whisper. Now here was a girl Rachel could identify with. She was dark-haired with incredible green eyes that matched her dad's. She was a sweet child, but not quite as open and bubbly as Lucy. Sam had some sad and scary skeletons rattling in her closet, even at such a young age. Not anything the young girl was responsible for, but like Rachel, Sam had some terrible junk done to her by a parent she'd trusted.

Cammie arrived, pint-size Stephie in-tow. Cammie was pregnant with another little nugget as well. The water here might just have sperm swimming in it. It seemed just that easy to get pregnant around here. Either that, or those Larouxs were just that prolific.

Lucy scooped up Stephie and pointed to the grand tree, now being hoisted to its full height. "Look, Stephie. It's soooo big."

Stephie squealed and clapped her chubby hands together, dimples deepening with delight. "Twee, twee; it's soooo big." Stephie had just turned two and enjoyed teaching her cousin, Janie all the words.

Sam was Stephie's older sister and stood next to Lucy and Stephie. Samantha had lost her mother in a single-car drunk driving accident when she was ten.

Grey's and Cammie's second-chance was a love story that could melt the hardest non-believing heart. It was the kind of tale that gave Rachel hope.

Sam loved Cammie. They were as bonded now as any healthy mother and daughter. "Wow, this one is even bigger than last year," Cammie said.

"I guess it is. Last year was kind of a blur for me," Rachel said.

Cammie smiled. "Yeah. Imagine it was. Do you think your dad will want to come for Christmas?"

Rachel frowned. "I hadn't thought about that. Mom and Sabine haven't mentioned it, but he wasn't here for Thanksgiving. Maybe we should invite him to drive up from Orange Beach for the day." She hadn't thought about including her dad, even though she should have.

"I don't mean to stick my nose where it doesn't belong. I just wondered what his status was since he's gotten out," Cammie said. Rachel knew she meant well. The Larouxs were notorious for wanting everyone's family to be as happy and intact as their own.

"I really should be in closer contact with him. As much of a disappointment as he's been to all of us, it's Christmas, and we're all he has," Rachel said.

Cammie smiled, then they heard Sam call, "Mom, can you grab Stephie?" Fast as lightning, Cammie turned to give chase to her slippery, speedy little toddler, whose chunky legs were carrying her as fast and as far away from them as possible with every second.

"A little help here, girls, please," Cammie called to Samantha and Lucy when Stephie managed to slip past Cammie, who was likely pregnant enough to realize thirteen-year-olds had a better shot at catching the tiny bolt of greased lightning who was headed across the grass at a dead run.

If Rachel hadn't had the camera with her very large, expensive lens strapped around her neck, she'd have given chase as well. But the two girls were every bit as fast as the toddler, and had her well in hand in under a minute.

"Wow, she's so fast. I had no idea," Rachel said to Cammie, who was slightly winded, watching the little girl giggle, as she'd now turned her little run-away into a game of dashing back and forth between the two girls.

Cammie laughed. "She does that every chance she gets. I can't let her down in parking lots or at the grocery store. She takes it as a sign to run fast and free, and let's face it, I'm not as fast as I used to be."

"I don't know how you maintain a daily taping schedule and raise an active toddler, a tween—and a baby on the way. I can barely remember to feed myself," Rachel said.

"I've found that we can handle more than we realize. We're women, after all. But, I'll admit to wondering how life will change when this little one makes his appearance. We're a manageable group right now; I'm afraid my scales are soon going to tip."

Rachel smiled. "Oh, I'll bet you'll handle it just fine."

"One thing at a time here. If we can get through this holiday taping week without my feet blowing up, I'll call it a step in the right direction," Cammie said.

"Do you think Jessica Greene will make it to do the show?"

Cammie shrugged. "Who knows? Her publicist reached

out and practically begged for the opportunity on her behalf. She's hoping it will spark a comeback of sorts if it goes well with viewers."

"You're awfully kind to say yes. I mean, she did fire you from her show not so long ago," Rachel said.

"Well, the woman has had a couple awful years since then. Now that I've pretty much taken over her role with viewers, I can afford to show her some grace."

"Careful she doesn't throw the grace back in your face," Rachel said, remembering some of the awful things the woman had said.

"We'll be live, so no matter how it plays out, the truth will be there for all to see. It's a risk, I guess, but I've definitely got the home advantage in this situation," Cammie said.

"I guess." Rachel hoped so. Jessica Greene wasn't known for her cooperative and drama-free nature.

"What's up?" Matthew Pope, Cammie's producer had approached without either of them realizing it.

"We were discussing Jessica Greene's upcoming appearance on the live show. Rachel has some concerns about her causing a ruckus," Cammie told Matthew.

"Just let her try her shenanigans on my watch. She's lucky I wasn't there the first time." Matthew was Emma's husband, but he was fiercely protective of his sisters-in-law as well.

Matthew focused on Rachel and asked, "How's the photography business?"

Rachel understood he was asking as one professional to another, which she appreciated. "I'm super busy. I'm saving for my own studio space in town."

"That's fantastic. I know how hard it is to drag equipment around for studio shots. You do know that you've got a standing offer to use my studio whenever you need it, right?" he asked.

"That's so generous, but I hate to impose, or to use your fancy equipment."

"Are you kidding? You're family, Rachel. Emma would have my head if she thought for a minute you were struggling and I didn't help in every way possible. But that's not why I'm offering. Artists should always give a hand up to one another. What we do is hard to make a living at. Many don't understand our vision. When you find success within your creative outlet beyond a hobby, you're in a lucky minority."

Rachel nodded. "I tried my whole life to find the right sport or activity I wanted to pursue, but nothing fit until I picked up a camera, and my life changed the second I looked through the viewfinder that first time."

Matthew laughed and nodded. "I had a similar experience, but I was a movie and television addict, and would memorize dialogue from my favorite shows. I knew from the time I was a young kid that I wanted to make that kind of magic."

"Too bad you got stuck here doing a cooking show,"

Cammie said and jabbed him in the ribs.

"The *best* rated cooking show on the air for two years running, with the most awards, hands down—including best director."

"Poor Matthew pissed his boss off at the network and got sent here to do my show when we started. He wasn't happy to be here at first, but then he met Emma."

"Let's just say it wasn't where I saw myself long-term." Matthew's expression was near-comical.

"Oh, hey there, Doctor Nick," Cammie said.

Rachel turned to see Nick approach. He was a *really* sexy guy. Had she noticed how tall he was before? Or how well his jeans fit his muscled thighs? "Hi there. I thought you would be at the hospital right now."

"Dr. Granger stopped by and told me to go to lunch. Said he had a meeting and would cover anything that came in while he was finishing some phone calls and paperwork. One of our patients said they were putting up the tree today. I figured you'd be out here taking pictures, so I hoped you might be free for lunch." He grinned at her like he was her real boyfriend.

"Sounds great." She grinned back, remembering their deal. On impulse, she leaned toward him and kissed him quickly on the mouth. She didn't expect the thrill that went through her, or the sudden desire from such brief contact. "Let me take a couple shots of the tree now that it's in place and then we can go. I'm starved."

He covered his surprise at her kiss pretty well, considering. But his eyes darkened with desire for an instant. Then he asked the group, "Anybody else hungry?"

They noticed that the others gathered around them were staring with varying degrees of surprise. Cammie recovered first. "I'm always hungry, but I don't want to interrupt y'all's lunch date."

"Nonsense. Let's all head to the pizza joint and put some tables together," Rachel suggested.

"Sounds like a plan," Matthew agreed. "I'll call Emma and see if she wants to join us."

Really, their dating shouldn't have been such a surprise considering he'd sat next to her at Thanksgiving dinner, and been with her the other night in the square when most of them had been there decorating. But it hadn't occurred to Rachel that coming out officially as a couple might raise some eyebrows.

She wasn't planning to tell anyone, not even her family, that this was a ruse. Rachel had her own reasons for having a sexy fake boyfriend, besides doing Nick a favor. One of them was getting her family off her back about finding *a nice young man*.

She only wished she didn't want to jump his bones so much.

NICK HAD ARRIVED just as Matthew made a profound

statement. *"Let's just say it wasn't where I saw myself long-term."* It sounded like Matthew had landed here from getting his arm twisted by the powers-that-be by his employer as well. Matthew's words had pretty much stopped Nick in his tracks, because, while Nick had experienced that same frustration at being forced to take the job here, he too had found himself warming to this town and its people and way of life.

At first, he'd felt manipulated by others, and he'd been powerless to make his own choice about this abrupt change to his life. He'd not been able to see anything positive about the move or the job change, however temporary. But it hadn't taken Nick long to feel as if he'd been whisked away on some kind of permanent vacation from stress to a new way of life he hadn't ever been exposed to. It was eye-opening and important.

Lately, all he could think about was re-adjusting his prior goals and vision for his life and fitting it into a new and very different one here. He'd spent much of his time since he'd been in Ministry thinking how right this place felt, but wondering if he'd snap out of it the minute he got back to Atlanta.

As Nick approached the gigantic tree, he shouldered some of Rachel's equipment. In that moment, he thought that there wasn't anywhere he'd rather be. She was stunning. Her long black hair streaming down her back as she crouched down to capture just the right angle of the magnificent tree. She was completely unaware of his thoughts or how she affected him. His suggestion of her pretending to be his girlfriend *might* not have been such a phony or foolish idea.

They fit. He'd never been so at ease with another human being. Since they'd met, and in the short amount of time they'd spent together, he'd shared more of his past, and his thoughts about family and hopes for the future with her than he ever had with Monica. It was as if he'd been offered the opportunity to know Rachel, and now he must re-evaluate everything he thought he wanted for his life if he wanted a shot with her.

That sounded ridiculous after barely two weeks. And he had no idea how she felt about him. He figured she liked him well-enough, based on their interactions thus far, but if he wanted a chance with this woman, Nick decided he'd better start working out a strategy right now. He had about six weeks give or take.

As the group of friends and family made their way a couple blocks to the local pizza joint on Main Street, they passed the giant tree, which was now totally upright and being anchored in place by the workmen. Other than Rockefeller Center, Nick had never seen one quite this impressive.

Once they arrived at *The Pizza Pie*, Junior sought out the owner, and arranged for their group to be seated together. Pizza Joe, they called him, came out to welcome his guests, and had several of the wait staff pull tables together to accommodate the party. Several other customers were filing in for the lunch hour as well, and the place clearly did a brisk business, but was well-prepared for the crowd. The hospital was about two miles from here, so hopefully, Nick would have plenty of time to eat and get back within the hour.

Once they were seated, Nick asked, "So I was wondering how do you put lights on and decorate a tree that size?"

They all kind of smiled and laughed, like there was a story behind that. Junior answered, "Well, Nick, a few years back, we decided on full-blown building scaffolding. We tried fire ladders and buckets, and that worked okay, but it was slow-going. So, we looked into how they handled it with that great, big tree they put up every year in New York City. Those Yankees do it right, and since our tree isn't so much smaller than theirs, we decided to give their way a try.

"You mean you build scaffolding all around it to put on lights and decorations?" Nick was amazed at the time, money, and effort the town put into this tree.

"Yup. That's what's going up next. Have to use a crane to place the star on top," Junior said.

Junior nodded toward Cammie. "We're lucky enough to have Grey Harrison's company available to provide the scaffolding. They do major structural renovations of historic buildings. He's an architect and a master carpenter."

Cammie chimed in then. "The town schedules the use of his scaffolding a couple weeks this time of year to get the tree done."

"Who actually spends days threading the lights into the tree?" Nick wondered aloud.

"That's the one job we hire out to professionals. It's just too big of an undertaking for anyone here. A team of about twenty comes in from a company who specializes in commercial work. They use the hundreds of decorations our citizens have made over the years that are special to us, and ones we've all collected and donated to add to the tree. This year, we voted to use colored LED lights instead of white lights only. The company uses solar panels as a power source, in addition to electricity, since it takes so much power to keep it lit."

"That's smart. I can't wait to see it all finished," Nick said.

"It's beautiful beyond words," Rachel said then, her eyes shining. "The kids in town spend their time running and playing on the green, around the tree, after school and during their break for weeks. They wait to take it town until New Year's Day to get the most enjoyment from it."

Rachel was sitting next to him, and he put an arm casually around her shoulders. It felt so natural to want to reach out and touch her—to physically connect with her. Even out in public, though she might think it was for show, it wasn't.

As soon as he did this, Rachel glanced over and smiled at him, leaning in just enough to let him know she was okay with his touch. Nick relaxed and completely forgot about the *pretend* part of their agreement.

SUSAN SANDS

One of the reasons he came here this afternoon was to let her know he'd arranged to take the time off so they could attend the Falcons/Saints game together. He hoped she would still be as excited about the prospect as when he'd mentioned it the other night at her apartment.

So far, he hadn't had a minute alone to discuss it with her. The discussion here was lively, with the current participants laughing and debating how many ornaments and days it would take to complete the decorating of the tree. "Last year, the star wouldn't sit straight, so we had to keep calling the crane operator to come back and fix it," Junior said.

Junior spoke directly to Nick. "In case you were wondering, one of my Christmas festival jobs is making sure the tree is delivered, set up, and decorated on time."

Nick nodded. "I figured you were in charge here. You appeared to have a personal stake in how things go."

"Heaven forbid things don't go well if you're the man in charge around here. The snow-blower broke down one year on my watch and you'd have thought I'd killed puppies."

"Junior!" Cammie shushed him.

"Oh, stop. You know what I mean. People around here always blame everything on the guy in charge, even if it's not his fault. I wonder how they'll react if the snow-blower breaks down if it's Emma's gig?" Junior asked.

"Probably not the same as you, but the sin is often in the delivery. 'Show's over, folks. Machine's broken,' probably wasn't the best way to break the news," Cammie said.

"Can't tiptoe around every dang thing," Junior grumped at Cammie's comment.

Nick quietly handed his platinum card to the waiter while they were distracted, and motioned that both tables' pizza should be added to his check.

When the girl came back for him to sign the bill, Junior's face reddened just a bit once he realized what Nick had done. "When did you do that, Doc?"

"It's my thanks to everyone for such a kind welcome. You've all gone out of your way to include me around here. It' s been—nice." Nick had wanted to do something to thank these people who'd made him feel like part of the town without trying.

"Nonsense. It's how people ought to act. It's common decency," Junior said. "Don't do that again, you hear? I've got the next one."

"Got it." Nick nodded.

There was a sparkle in Rachel's eye. Clearly she'd approved of his actions. He leaned down and whispered into her ear, "We're on for the game Thursday if you still want to go with me."

He pulled back to get her response. Her eyes went from a sparkle to excited. "I'm in," she said. "I'll finish my edits by tomorrow, so I won't get behind. I can reschedule a few things."

"Great. I'll let you know the details by tomorrow."

"See you tonight."

Their exchange didn't go unnoticed, if the interested eyes on them were any indication.

Nick grinned. Good. They sold it. Nobody would doubt the validity of their relationship.

Chapter Eleven

R ACHEL COULD SMELL the baked goods the moment she entered the house. Mrs. Wiggins's shortbread made her mouth water. The pizza she'd eaten earlier for lunch was delicious, but Rachel's sweet tooth begged for shortbread. After lunch, she'd done some errands, then gone and taken photos with Santa at one of the gift shops in town. The crowd of toddlers was growing with every shoot. The closer they got to Christmas, Rachel knew, the busier it would become.

She tiptoed downstairs and tapped on the door that separated the upstairs apartments from Mrs. Wiggins's personal living area.

"Well hello, dear. Did you smell my goodies in the oven?"

"You bet I did," Rachel said, looking around the room, her eyes suddenly clashing with the woman's two formerly-alive cats, as they stared, eyes, not blinking. Rachel tried not to shudder. She noted the doily-covered surroundings, topped with every kind of glass statuette imaginable. Rachel wondered if there were any real treasures buried in this hoarder's paradise.

"Well, of course, I made you a plate, and one for your young man. You can bring it upstairs to him when you go."

"But, we're not—" Rachel tried to deny her relationship with Nick.

"Oh, please, dear. *Everybody* in town is talking. I told you, it's okay with me."

Which was code for, *I've told everyone I saw about the two of you*. Rachel remembered the ruse then. "Thanks, Mrs. W." Even though she had her reasons for staying silent, Rachel hated the dishonesty. This was going to be harder to pull off for her than she thought.

"Did you come for shortbread or did you have something else to tell me?"

"I wanted to let you know that both Nick and I would be out of town in Atlanta for a football game Thursday and Thursday night. I'm not exactly certain what the plans are yet, but he's invited me to the Falcons/Saints game. It's a huge rivalry game between both our favorite teams, but it should be fun."

Mrs. Wiggins clapped her tiny hands together in glee. "Oh, the two of you will have such fun on a road trip together. Thank you for letting me know. I would worry, you know, if you'd been gone and hadn't told me."

"I know. I wouldn't have left town without telling you."

Mrs. Wiggins had become part of her life, and didn't only consider the woman a landlady. She was more like family.

"Could you please deliver this to your young man for me?" Mrs. Wiggins asked, handing Rachel a heavy paper plate laden with shortbread, and covered with aluminum foil.

"Of course. I know Nick will be thrilled to have this. He's a typical guy. Always hungry."

Rachel kissed the older woman's cheek as she accepted her plate of goodies as well, and then made her way back upstairs.

If she was planning to eat those, Rachel decided a run before dinner might be a good idea, *and* seeing how she intended to run the Snow-Shoe 5K next week, it might behoove her to work a little harder than she had been the last couple weeks on her cardiovascular conditioning. Normally, she ran almost daily in the evening. But since her new neighbor had moved in, somehow, she'd gotten out of the habit.

As she laced up her shoes, she heard the door shut next door. A tiny thrill shot through her. That should *not* have happened. The anticipation of seeing Nick made her feel like a high schooler with a bad crush. If she came rushing over there now, it would seem eager of her.

But she did make a promise to Mrs. Wiggins to give him the shortbread, didn't she? So, Rachel couldn't very well break it by not showing up at his door bearing goodies.

So, after she tied the second shoe, Rachel picked up the plate from the table and locked her door, keeping only her cell phone and single key with her.

She hesitated a second, but it was opened before she could knock. "Hey, there. Were you coming to see me?"

"No. Someone else. Sorry, wrong apartment." *What did he expect from that question?*

"Ha. I deserved that. What do you have there?" he asked, looking more interested in what she was carrying than the carrier.

"Mrs. Wiggins baked today, and I promised to drop this by," she said, but still held it away from his grasp. He reached for it again, which brought him in closer contact to her body. He stopped then, and the plate lost his attention as his eyes met hers. The smolder in his gaze made her wonder if she'd made an error in judgment in that silly move.

He grabbed her wrist gently and pulled her inside from the hallway and shut the door, taking the plate from her hand, and placing it on his tiny dining table. "I've been waiting all day to see you." He then leaned down and kissed her as if he meant that statement.

When he lifted his head, she smiled almost drunkenly. "You saw me already today."

"Then I've been waiting since the last time I saw you to do that."

"Oh. Okay. That was nice."

"Again." He kissed her again.

This fake kissing thing was quite a perk to their pretend dating status. It certainly made it easier to pass off as acceptable if it wasn't the real deal or going to continue beyond January. But the desire she experienced in the process was making this far more difficult. Her thin, short, running shorts weren't doing much as far as a barrier between her and his erection, so Rachel knew he was having similar feels.

She pressed herself into his body and felt his response, and heard him groan. "Ah, you're killing me."

"Good. Because I want this," she whispered in his ear.

"Are you sure?" he seemed surprised.

"I *need* this." She slipped her hands under his T-shirt.

He cupped her rear with his hand and pressed her closer. "You feel so amazing. But I don't want to do anything you'll regret."

She moaned. "No regrets. We're full grown adults." She pulled at his shirt.

"Yes, we are, thank God." He lifted his shirt over his head at her bidding.

"I've been dying to see what was under the scrubs," Rachel whispered.

"There's more." He took her hand and led her to his bedroom. "So much more."

Rachel had never anticipated anything so much. "Show me more."

His bedroom was neat and clean, bed made, with a high thread-count duvet and shams. He pulled out a condom from the bedside table with a wolfish grin and tossed it on the bed as if he'd been expecting her.

Rachel wasn't sure how she felt about that. "How convenient."

"Would you rather I didn't have one and we put this off until another day?" His deep laugh made her shiver with desire.

"No, thank you. So glad you're a man with a plan." She would cry if he told her no now.

"So, where were we?" He pulled her into his arms like the best scene from *Gone with the Wind*.

The man had skills, she'd give him that. Not that she was super experienced, but surely those were expert moves, and Rachel was thankful the man knew his way around a woman's body.

Who knew she was such a screamer? She tried to stifle the sounds as she climaxed, but holy cow, nothing had prepared her for such pleasure. The lack of control scared Rachel.

"What did you do to my body?" she asked, amazed, slicked in sweat, and totally satiated.

He laughed out loud at her question. "I'm not quite sure. I've never had that loud a response before."

"I'm a little embarrassed. I've never yelled like that."

He appeared pleased.

"I mean, I haven't been with a lot of guys, but it's never been like that."

"I don't have a double standard when it comes to women enjoying sex, Rachel. I haven't been with a lot of women either, but if you had been with your share of men, it wouldn't make you less attractive to me."

"Wow, that's very progressive of you. And unusual, especially in the South."

He shrugged. "I always thought it was unfair that guys thought it was okay to sleep around with everyone they could and call girls names if they had a boyfriend or two, or more."

"I don't subscribe to sleeping with a bunch of random men, but it's not my business if somebody has more sex than me. I just never felt like it was something I needed to do with people I didn't care about."

"What are we doing here?" he asked, serious now. "This thing between us?"

"Besides the obvious, I don't know. It felt right, but I don't know what to call us." Rachel really didn't know what they were doing. But she was going to give it some serious thought.

"Do you still want to go to Atlanta with me?"

"Are you uninviting me?" She hoped she hadn't blown it with him by pretty much having her naughty way with him.

"Of course not. It's going to be a blast. No expectations, just so you know."

"I still want to go. And let's just play all this one day at a time, okay? I'm not experiencing instant regret, here, so that's good. You?"

"Oh, hell no. No regrets."

They both laughed. "I was headed out for a run."

"Yeah. I noticed the shorts. Nice legs, by the way."

She pulled out a long, bare leg and held it up for his inspection.

And they began again. Nobody went for a run.

⋙⋘

NICK HAD NEVER had his mind blown by sex before. He'd had amazing sex, for sure, but this was different with Rachel. It was unexpected, to begin with. She was honest and open about her pleasure, for one thing. She laughed and yelled when it felt good. There wasn't any embarrassment or manipulation with Rachel. And his body's response to that was beyond any physical sensation he'd ever experienced.

Now that he'd had it, Nick never wanted it any other way. Did it exist with anyone else? Anywhere else? Or only with Rachel Prudhomme in Ministry, Alabama? It was a quandary.

They were leaving at noon for Atlanta. The game was at eight-o'clock tonight, and he'd made plans to stop by the hospital where he'd worked, before moving to Ministry, on his way into the city to pick up some personal mail and say hi to a few friends and co-workers.

It was interesting how little communication he'd had with his familiars since leaving Atlanta. As many years as he'd spent there, and having grown up in the area, it was as if he'd dropped off the face of the earth and everyone had forgotten his existence. Out of sight, out of mind, he supposed.

It might have bothered Nick more if he was pining to return home. But so far, his stay in Ministry had been one grand adventure, with no real downside. He kept waiting for the other shoe to drop and the desperate desire to go running, screaming back to the city to hit like a ton of bricks. His distraction with his lovely next-door neighbor was the obvious reason, but somewhere, deep down, he knew there was more to it than that. The one question he kept asking himself was, *could it last?*

Rachel was waiting when Nick knocked on her door. She had one tote bag and her camera. "Ready?" he asked.

"Ready. Thanks again for this. I've got my Who Dat shirt packed and ready."

He shook his head. "I'll try and protect you since we're sitting in the middle of the Falcon's section in Atlanta."

"Did you think I would sell out?"

He laughed. "No. I didn't, quite honestly. You would never sell out. That's one thing I like about you."

"Well, thank you. I'll take that as a compliment."

"It was meant as one."

They listened to the radio and realized they both had extremely eclectic tastes in music. Maybe not the same music, but varied enough for an open mind.

"How do you feel about meeting my mother?" he asked

when they were about thirty miles outside of Atlanta.

"I'm not sure. Is she going to hate me on sight because I'm not your ex?" Rachel asked, her tone wary.

"I don't know. That's just it; she still has a relationship with Monica, but I can't very well come to town without stopping by and saying hello. I don't want to catch her wrong and expose you to her inappropriate behavior if she's in a stew about something."

"You should definitely see your mom while you're here. Maybe you can stop by and say hi while I sit in the car if you're not planning to stay too long."

"I'll give her a call and feel her out. If she's in a snit, we'll skip it."

Rachel nodded. "I get it. I've been through the difficult parent thing. Your mom has to come to terms with losing Monica as a family member. She might be on a different time frame for acceptance. Probably still holding out hope that you'll work it out."

"I've tried everything I can to convince her that it's over. Last time we spoke, I got pretty frustrated with her. Checking in might be a good thing."

He dialed his mother's number, but she didn't answer, so he left a voicemail. "Hey, Mom, it's me. I'm just outside of Atlanta heading to the game. I thought I would swing by and say hi to you and Dad. I've got my friend, Rachel, with me so we'll be there in about forty-five minutes to an hour, depending on traffic. Call me back and let me know your status."

"Well, I guess our reception will be a crap shoot. Are you okay with an uncertain welcome? The good news is, Mom's reaction can be tempered, and she will feel bad and apologize later. Her mind can be changed. She is moody, and first impressions shouldn't be taken to heart."

"Sounds like my dad to some degree. He often has to be convinced he's wrong about something or someone. It's not easy to do, but he can be made to see reason."

"Exactly. So, you've dealt with this personality before. That's good. It terrifies some people."

"When you've dealt with someone who is edgy and moody, you learn not to take things too personally, and how to navigate them. I'll understand if she doesn't respond well to my being here."

"If they're even home. I'm assuming they will be. They don't get out much these days, especially after about two o'clock in the afternoon. Dad likes a little nap after lunch, and Mom always cooks his dinner."

"They sound very traditional. My parents were outwardly that way until we found out my dad had an illegitimate bastard and brought him to live with us at three years old when his mother died. Then, things got more complicated."

"Wow. I guess so. So, your mom agreed to raised him?" That was admirable.

"She did, but then my dad wouldn't let anyone discipline James. He was wild, and nearly brought the household to its knees. He was a holy terror."

"That does sound complicated—and very unfair to everyone, including James," Nick said.

"And it goes from there. So, your mother sounds like a piece of cake to me," Rachel joked.

"I'll encourage you to withhold your grace toward my mother until you meet her."

"You said you have a brother?" Nick asked.

"Yes. Chuck. He's a few years younger than me. He's in graduate school at UGA in Athens, which is just under an hour from Atlanta in the other direction."

"What's he studying?" Rachel asked.

"He's got a business management degree and now he's getting his MBA. We're close, but completely different, personality-wise. He's a totally laid-back type on the surface, and lets Mom's insults and passive-aggression roll right off him. Drives her crazy that she can't get to him."

"And you take her to task on her bad behavior and she can't get enough."

He nodded. "I can't seem to let her get away with the back-handed insults."

"I've learned from my sister, Sabine, the counselor, that people who act that way are mostly starved for attention."

"Yep. That's the sad part. I know this, and I bite every time. It just drives me crazy the way she behaves."

"Well, I guess we'll see how it goes in a few minutes, won't we?" Rachel asked.

"I'm glad I've prepared you to some degree. At least you know what to expect within a range."

They drove the last half hour in heavy traffic, as they hit the city. It didn't have to be rush hour in Atlanta for there to be traffic. They took the perimeter highway 285 to I-75 to the Vinings exit. Driving through the affluent neighborhoods, Nick worried just a little that his privileged upbringing might change her opinion of him. He understood that she'd had an equally affluent one, but he couldn't help but be a little embarrassed by the show of wealth in his childhood neighborhood.

They arrived at his parents' house a few minutes later. It was a beautiful large, two-story stucco house with a circular drive in front.

"Wow. It's lovely. Did you grow up here?" Rachel asked.

"Yes. My whole life. I attended Pace Academy right down the street."

"Does it look like your parents are home?"

"Yep, they're home." He looked off to the side and saw a low-slung silver convertible. "Uh-oh. Maybe we should go."

"What is it?"

"Looks like Mom's got company. That's Monica's car." He made to leave when a woman came rushing out of the house waving her arms.

"Well, shit." He put the car in park and looked at Rachel for a second. "I can't apologize enough for this."

NICK APPEARED SO upset, Rachel felt the need to comfort and support him in this nasty situation. "It's okay. This isn't your fault. It's a setup. I'll stay here. You go handle this."

His look of relief was profound. "Thank you."

He unbuckled his seat belt and walked toward the slim middle-aged blonde woman dressed in head-to-toe Lily Pulitzer. She could have passed for a woman fifteen years younger than Rachel knew she must be. That kind of upkeep took full-time work. Rachel recognized it from years of living in the Garden District of New Orleans.

Nick approached his mother and she turned her cheek to him for his kiss. The woman then focused on Nick's car, where Rachel sat in the passenger's seat. She wasn't smiling.

Nick was speaking to his mother, who then pointed toward the house. His mom then spared Rachel one more glare before preceding Nick onto the front porch and into the house.

Rachel's natural curiosity made her wish she'd been a fly on the wall with a camera in that house right now.

After about ten minutes, a tall, slim, dark-haired woman came out of the house, clearly sobbing. Monica. All Rachel could think was, *she looks like me, but prettier.*

It was a bizarre sensation. Rachel felt an urge to comfort this distraught woman who appeared uncertain whether to get into her car and leave or go back inside the house. Rachel was a voyeur to Monica's pain. Then, suddenly, Monica focused directly on Rachel, and made a beeline toward the car. Once Rachel was in her sights, the woman's expression turned furious. Rachel suddenly wanted to lock the doors and roll up the windows, which had been left partway down, as the weather was comfortable outside.

"*You*. You're the reason Nicholas won't talk to me." Monica was pointing at her through the window.

Rachel wanted to deny her words, but part of her had a burning urge to not be a victim of this attack by a woman she'd never met. *Where was Nick?*

"Monica, right? You should calm down. I'm sure Nick would be happy to speak with you." Rachel did her best to find words that worked here.

"We were supposed to be together when he got back. He just needed a little space. I can't *believe* he brought you here."

Rachel was becoming annoyed. "But he *did* bring *me* here. Look, I don't know anything about your relationship with Nick, but you can't go around screaming at people who didn't do anything to you."

Nick finally reached the car and tried to gently pull Monica away from the window. "Monica, leave Rachel out of this. She isn't to blame for anything."

"Nick, how can you do this to me? How could you insult me like this? By having *her* here?"

"When I last spoke to Mom, I told her I would call if I was coming in town for the game. I didn't call, so I guess she hoped I would and asked you over just in case. She didn't have any idea I was bringing Rachel, and that was my fault. I left her a message less than an hour ago to tell her we were dropping by. I guess she didn't get it."

"I guess she didn't, did she? Because she never would have set me up like this. Like you did."

"Monica, I never meant to hurt you. I hope you know that."

"You're only saying that because *she* can hear us. I really believed you would change your mind once you got back. I certainly never thought you would find someone else in the meantime. And I can't believe you would come home and not call."

Monica's destroyed expression, Rachel truly felt sorry for the woman. "Monica, we haven't spoken since we broke up. I'm not sure why you thought I would call when I returned. I didn't leave any room for you to question my intentions. I'm sorry things didn't work out between us, but I didn't lead you on."

Nick walked Monica to her car, and she drove away.

He returned to where Rachel was waiting, his posture defeated. Rachel had hoped he was over his ex, and now she saw that he still cared. He cared, but he didn't seem to be in love with her.

He opened the door and sat down in the driver's seat. "I'm sorry you had to see that."

"Yeah. Me too."

"I think maybe today wouldn't be the best day to meet

my parents."

"Do you think your mom set you up, or that she really didn't get your message?"

He ran a hand through his hair. "I honestly don't know. On the one hand, I don't think she would put Monica in that situation. But she may have thought if I saw Monica again I would change my mind and come rushing back to her."

"But, she's you mom and thought she was doing you a favor."

"Are you kidding? She was manipulating me either way. Depending on which scenario is how it went down, one is just a whole lot worse than the other."

"I didn't want to speak ill of your mother."

"That's kind of you, but I know the score. Mom was trying to help Monica's cause because she wants us back together. Period. She's inside sulking now because I let her have it for being so cruel to Monica and to you."

"So, do you still want to go to the game?" Rachel asked.

"What? Of course. I hate that Monica was upset, and that you were as well, but I don't want you to think I was upset because I still have feelings for her. I felt sorry that she was hurt, but not because I want to be with her. I hope you believe me."

"She looks an awful lot like me. Don't you think that means something?" Rachel asked.

"Are you kidding?" He appeared bamboozled by her

question.

"You clearly have a type. I thought you might have singled me out because you missed her."

He shook his head, still denying her words. "I see you so completely different, Rachel. You don't resemble her at all in my mind. Any physical similarities are a coincidence. I guess we all have a type, but that doesn't relate to *who* you are. I mean, I think you are gorgeous and sexy, but you are you. I don't see her in any way when I look at you. End of that story."

She would take him at his word, if she could. But that wasn't her stong suit. She'd mistrusted so much over the past several years since her father's sins and secrets had been revealed by the dozens. Rachel needed to shove her doubt aside, at least for the rest of their trip. She would have all the time in the world to be her suspicious self when they got back home.

It wasn't that she believed he was still hung up on Monica, it was something about their strong physical resemblance that bothered her. Maybe he went for their dark coloring to avoid anyone who resembled his own mother. Now, *that* was something to discuss with her therapist sister when she got home.

"I was planning to stop by the hospital where I worked before we had dinner, but I don't feel up to it. So, we can head down to Ponce City Market if you want until our reservations."

He said, *worked*, in past tense. "Oh, are you moving to a new job when you get back?"

"Not right away, though I've negotiated for a job at Emory once the head of their trauma department retires next year."

"Negotiated, as in agreed to come to Ministry if they give you the big job you want."

He smiled tightly. "Something like that."

"Do you hate it so much? Our little town? Because you don't seem to." She tried to keep her hurt feelings from bleeding into her voice.

He glanced over at her. There was emotion in his eyes. "No. I don't hate being in Ministry. In fact, I feel more relaxed and at peace there than I have anywhere in a very long time. All the years in medical school, internship, and during my residency were stressful and competitive. Even working in a big level I trauma hospital is a non-stop adrenaline dump. So, spending time in Ministry, treating patients for gout and appendicitis has been a welcome break."

"Oh. Well, that's nice to hear." But how long would he be content with that kind of lifestyle?

"And spending time with you. That's been the best part."

A warm, happy feeling spread through her and she tried not to slide into a puddle on the floor of his car. "Me too."

He reached over and put his big, strong healing hand over hers.

"Are you sure you don't want to stop by the hospital?"

she asked. "I don't want to be the reason you don't do something."

"Nah. I thought I wanted to go, but I really can't think of a single person there I miss enough to go to the trouble." He smiled. "I'd rather walk on the greenspace and go to the market. I think you'll like it. The restaurant is nearby."

"Okay. Sounds nice."

As THEY ARRIVED, he played the role of tour guide. "This is the beltline. It used to be the old rail line that connected commerce, and now city planners have turned it into a greenspace, and they've begun a huge renovation of the old, abandoned warehouses and buildings along the rail system and turned them into a residential district."

He suggested she bring her camera when they parked. She soon understood why. They walked on a greenway trail beside huge, beautiful murals painted on the sides of buildings. Like graffiti, but obviously allowed by the city. "This is amazing," she said as she snapped photos as bikes whizzed by, and people walked at a quick pace for exercise, or just ambled hand-in-hand. There were all ages and races represented here: from babes in strollers to the eldest of citizens, using walkers and canes for aid.

The Ponce City Market, she discovered, was housed in the historic Sears and Roebuck building in downtown Atlanta. It was a mixed-use development with shops, restaurants, offices, and loft apartments. "Wow, how cool." It was also an artist's dream—from its open-air food market to Skyline Park on the roof, complete family fun with games and a carnival that offered a spectacular view of the city.

She was suddenly quite glad they hadn't taken the time to stop by his hospital and done this instead.

After dinner, they were heading to the new Falcon's stadium, which had just been completed last year. It was supposed to be a state-of-the-art facility.

It was almost dark by the time they walked toward the restaurant, which was two blocks down from the market, and Rachel got a strange sensation upon entering. Maybe it was the odd stare from the hostess because she was wearing her Saints jersey. It wouldn't be the first one of the day.

"Right this way, Dr. Sullivan." The wispy girl motioned for them to follow.

They were seated at an impossibly tiny table for two beside a window with a fantastic view of the city. "Are we under dressed?" Rachel asked Nick.

"No. I don't think so. I checked when I made the reservation if they had a dress code." They looked around at the other diners. Some were dressed far nicer, but there were several who appeared to be doing the same as Nick and Rachel, based on their red and black Falcons attire.

Rachel tried to make heads or tails of the food choices on the menu in front of her, she really did.

"What is this place? It was tops on Atlanta Magazine's

fifty best restaurants in the city. I can't even figure out what chanterelles are to save my life."

Rachel laughed, relieved she wasn't the only one. "What's vadouvan and sorrel?"

"Beats me."

"I see they have duck, but I'm sorry to say that I don't eat duck."

"I don't eat food I can't pronounce or have to ask what it is. I consider myself a pretty educated person who's been to more than a few nice restaurants, and I don't know what most of these dishes are. I made this reservation months ago when I got these tickets to the game because I wanted to try the place, and I've heard they are nearly impossible to get, but I don't want to eat here in the least."

He stood and reached for her hand. "How do you feel about a game dog?"

She exhaled her relief and took his hand. "Thank you."

"I don't eat food I can't pronounce or have to ask what it is. I consider myself a pretty educated person who's been to more than a few nice restaurants, and I don't know what most of these dishes are. I made this reservation months ago when I got these tickets to the game because I wanted to try the place, and I've heard they are nearly impossible to get, but I don't want to eat here in the least."

The somewhat snooty hostess looked at them in horror as they approached. "Is there a problem, Dr. Sullivan?" She hadn't even addressed Rachel besides the snide glance at her jersey when they'd arrived.

"I realize you don't make the menus, but there are too few selections, and we don't recognize half of what's listed. If you would pass that on, I would appreciate it."

The woman's expression changed to total comprehension. "You know, you're not the first person to tell me that. I've tried to tell the owner and the chef, but since that *Atlanta Magazine* food critic came through and ranked us at the top of their restaurant list, enough people fight to get in just to say they ate here that nobody is listening. I'm sorry you weren't pleased. I will pass it along—again."

"I guarantee it won't last long if they don't make the menu for the mainstream and customer-friendly with so many other great restaurants opening up in the area. Good luck."

The hostess nodded.

They headed out, and Rachel was relieved to be on their way to a big, fat game dog and fries.

"I hope you didn't think I was nasty to the poor girl," Nick said once they were back in the car.

"Nope. She was in total agreement with you. Obviously, we aren't the first or the last who've gone in thinking we were getting a great meal and left before ordering. The food might be fantastic, but for those prices, I wouldn't take a chance on ordering something I don't even know if I like."

He smiled at her then. "We really do think alike, don't we?"

"We seem to agree on a lot of things. Definitely about game dogs being a better choice tonight. Chili-cheese with onions and mustard for me."

"Relish, mustard, and onions for me. Hold the chili."

She made a face at him. "Party-pooper."

Chapter Twelve

N ICK AND RACHEL arrived at the brand-spanking new Mercedes-Benz Stadium at least an hour before kick-off, which gave them plenty of time to wander around and have a look at all the snazzy upgrades. All Nick could think, as he noticed the obvious multi-millions spent on such a facility, was that the Falcons better kick butt this year. If they didn't, the population of Atlanta, in general, wasn't going to appreciate their hard-earned tax dollars being spent on such an over-the-top display when there was a perfectly good stadium sitting right next door that was about to be imploded.

There were plans for the old Georgia Dome space, which would be turned into a green space and parking area to be used for tailgating on game days, and as a culture, arts, and music venue during other times. Nick hate to see the dome go, but hopefully, the city would do all they promised to make good use of the area once it was demolished.

Atlanta was his city, and he cared what happened here.

"Wow. This place is amazing. I hate to admit it, but it's even more impressive than the Superdome in New Orleans, even after they re-did it after Katrina."

"Now, *that* is a hostile fan environment."

She ignored that. "How did you manage to get tickets on the fifty-yard line in the new stadium?"

Nick shrugged. He would save her the gory details. "I saved a guy's life. He appreciated it."

"Now that sounds like a story."

"Let's just say, he didn't have much of a chance at surviving a gunshot wound when he came into the emergency room. We gave him our best efforts, and he made it. Now, I have some sweet seats to this game."

"Sounds like a lot of excitement, and maybe a little danger here," she said.

"The danger is usually over by the time we get them. We deal with the consequences of whatever bad decisions and poor choices people make that brings them to us. Sometimes our patients are just in the wrong place at the wrong time or wind up in terrible circumstances, like traffic accidents. Lots of traffic in Atlanta. And lots of trauma from the accidents."

"Have you missed the pace? The excitement of wondering what might come crashing through the door at any moment?" Rachel asked.

Nick hadn't really thought about that. "No. I guess I don't. I've enjoyed the reduced stress. Not losing patients daily to senseless tragedy has been a relief, quite frankly, and very easy to get used to."

They purchased their game dogs and fries, along with two giant drinks, then found their seats. "These are incredible seats."

"Yeah. They're sold out for the season already if you look on the website. I think these are the kind of season tickets you can't get unless somebody dies and you inherit them," he said.

She nodded. "My dad had those kind of season tickets at the Superdome when I was growing up. Being a political bigwig, we were always able to get tickets to anything anywhere. That's one of the few things I miss about that lifestyle. We were recognized almost anywhere we went because of my dad, so he and Mom always knew what we were up to. I don't miss that."

"Where's your dad now?"

"He bought a house on the shore in Orange Beach. Cammie asked me the other day if we had invited him for Christmas. I felt somewhat guilty because I hadn't given it a thought."

"I know what you mean by feeling guilty about discounting someone for Christmas. I'll be in Ministry, and I don't have any intention of coming home during the holidays, even if I get a day or two off at Christmas. I just can't stomach the idea of going back for one of those family dinners where we all dress up, speak politely and pass the potatoes. Mom pretends the entire time there's a camera in the room recording us. It's her way of proving to herself that we can all behave properly, and that she did a good job as a mother raising us."

"Holidays are a lot more fun now that we live in Ministry. All that formality fell right off us as if we never lived in a household like that. And we *did* live in a household like that, though my mother never expected us to behave perfectly or stiffly, even when we dressed up and trotted out the good china every Sunday at the dining room table."

"We did too. And we went to church at the enormous Methodist Church on Peachtree Street so the neighbors would see us there and my mother could tell everyone we did," Nick said.

"For us, the relief of living in Ministry is like unbuttoning the top button on your pants under the table when you eat too much. It's comfortable and casual, and the tight bounds of propriety aren't so constricting. Certainly, people live by a code of decency and manners, which is refreshing and nothing less than one hopes for in a community."

Nick nodded. "Seeing patients who aren't on the verge of life and death is a similar feeling for me. I don't have to guard myself for what's to come every time someone comes through the door at the hospital like I do here."

He realized now why he didn't stop by the hospital. Nick was avoiding it. If he went back, would he want to stay? Right now, he was content to continue what he'd been doing these past weeks. So, far, this trip had been fun, but it didn't make him miss the city. He couldn't wait to get back to Alabama, quite frankly.

The noise all around them grew as the stadium filled in with fans finding their seats, and now the teams were warming up on the field. It was hard to talk in a normal volume without nearly yelling to hear one another.

Rachel stood up, waved and whistled through her teeth when Drew Brees ran out and waved toward their section, where they were only about ten rows up from the field. He made eye contact with her, mouthed her name, and blew her a kiss.

"You're kidding. You know Drew Brees?" Nick was astounded.

"I told you my dad got us into every game from the time we were kids. He knows my family. The inner circle of New Orleans is surprisingly small."

Nick shook his head. "I'm surprised you don't want to spend more time there."

Rachel leaned over so he could hear her. "It was a fun way to grow up, but my dad pretty much ruined it for us by being arrested and convicted, then going to prison."

"Ouch. I guess that makes sense. So, are you going to invite him to Ministry for Christmas?"

"I'm going to speak with my mom and sister about it. Not sure yet," she nearly yelled.

Then, the players on the field went to the center of the field for the coin toss, and there wasn't any more conversation possible. Only cheering and football.

It was almost midnight when the game ended, and the only happy person in the Mercedes-Benz Dome in Atlanta was likely Rachel. She now wore her jacket on top of her jersey after getting several aggressive and nasty comments thrown at her on the way out of the arena.

"I didn't even think to ask where we're staying tonight," she said, as they got to the car.

"I made a reservation at the Omni for tonight, if that works for you," he said.

"That's fine with me, but if you want to drive back tonight, I'm okay with it," she said.

He looked at her then. "Are you sure?" It was about a three-hour car ride home to Ministry. He'd had the same thought earlier about just heading back tonight.

"I would almost prefer going home, if that's okay with you. I can drive if you don't feel like it. We can grab a cup of coffee, and I'm good to go."

"The reservation is refundable at the Omni, so let's do it," Nick said.

They stopped for a coffee before leaving the downtown area, and then hopped on I-20 heading out of Atlanta. "Thanks for doing this. I'm so glad we made the trip, and the game was amazing, but there's just something about going home to Ministry that gives me peace."

He had to agree. It was as if that tiny Alabama town had become his home as well, even as he left the only home he'd ever known.

>>>><<<<

THEY ARRIVED BACK home just before four a.m., and tried hard to be as quiet as possible so as not to disturb Mrs. Wiggins.

Rachel was exhausted, and wanted nothing more than to fall into bed and sleep for twelve hours undisturbed.

They carried their bags upstairs to their respective apartments. Rachel was uncertain if Nick planned to come back to her place and say good night, or if he wanted to stay with her since they'd planned to spend tonight together at the hotel. It was one of those uncharted moments where she didn't know whether to extend an invitation or just let the situation lie.

As she placed her camera bag next to her desk, a noise at her door made her look up. Nick was standing there. "Hey, there," she said.

"I wanted to tell you that I had a great time. I also wanted to apologize for what happened at my parents' house. I'll get to the bottom of how it happened with my mother." He'd walked closer to where she was and now pulled her against his big, hard body.

She sighed. He was so warm and sexy. "I had fun. Let's not worry about that other stuff right now. I'm really tired, and you've got to work tomorrow."

He kissed her gently. "Want to snuggle?"

She giggled and led him by the hand to her bedroom. "Sure. Let's snuggle."

By the time Rachel had brushed her teeth and re-entered her bedroom, Nick was sound asleep under the covers in her big bed. He'd taken off his shirt, so she was able to appreciate his smooth, muscled arms and shoulders, visible above the coverlet. He really was a gorgeous hunk of a man.

Rachel pushed away any misgivings about what had happened with his ex earlier and went to lock her apartment door. She then crawled into bed wearing her favorite giant LSU sleep shirt, and snuggled against his large, warm body. He pulled her against him in his sleep and sighed, grunting softly, which made her smile.

Nick really did seem to like Ministry, which was surprising after hearing how he was manipulated by his company into coming to work here. Was there any chance that he might consider making it his permanent home? From an outsider's perspective, Atlanta appeared to be a far better place for an up-and-coming surgeon, with its large hospitals, prestigious job titles and opportunity for career advancement. Could he sacrifice all that for a life here? With her? That didn't even seem like a slight possibility. More like a ridiculous dream.

For the moment, she would enjoy his arms around her. That's likely all that would come of this, and it's all she could count on or expect. Rachel should keep in mind all the letdowns her mother had endured at her father's hands, and her sister's entire first marriage. Why did she think things would go better for her? Maybe because she'd seen such recovery and improvement in Sabine and Mom's second-time-arounds. Surely, it could go that way the first time for some folks.

As Rachel relaxed and her thoughts began to meander, her dad came to mind, and she decided she would definitely discuss inviting him here for Christmas with Mom and Sabine. He could stay with Sabine and Ben, and if not, she would make room for him here. Her sectional made into a comfy bed, if needed. Mom wouldn't be terribly excited about the idea, but she understood that family was in short supply for Dad these days, and now that Mom had found someone, she wasn't likely to begrudge him time at the holidays with his daughters and granddaughter.

Truth was, Rachel missed her daddy. And while he'd done a lot of truly awful things, she hadn't stopped loving him. He was still the same person she'd spent her entire childhood loving with her whole heart. It had been a long journey to admit that she could still care about him and reconcile that he could be both men, the one who'd loved and raised her, and the one who'd let them all down so terribly, and in such a public and humiliating way.

It was also easier to feel a little more generous while she lay here wrapped in warm, and what felt like loving arms.

Love? Did she love Nick Sullivan? How did vulnerable thoughts about her dad lead her to such a sudden and shocking possibility? And what did her father have to do with it? She must really be punch-drunk.

Rachel needed to speak with Sabine. Her sister was the only person who could help her make sense from this terrible conundrum. But that meant Rachel would have to fess up to the fake dating and to her very real and scary feelings that were swirling in her mind and body regarding Nick. Daddy issues were obviously the cause of so much of Rachel's misgivings when it came to making good decisions about men. This was too important to trust to her own questionable judgement.

Could one know enough about another person in this short a time to even consider such a relationship? Rachel understood that sex for women, especially, was very emotionally confusing and connecting. Maybe it was that damn oxytocin hormonal thing. There was some kind of study she'd read about a "loving" feeling after sex. Is that what was currently muddying her waters with all this sappy stuff? No. It had been slowly building since day one. Rachel had ignored her own warnings. Nick checked all her boxes, and slipped through the safety net she'd erected to protect her heart.

But then again, she couldn't blame him if he didn't want to stay in Ministry, which meant changing the entire path of his career and his life. And she really had no idea how he felt about her. He may be viewing this as a fun fling until it was time to resume his life in Georgia.

It might be helpful to know more before she accidentally spilled her tender guts to him and he took off for the hills.

Then, it occurred to her that he *could* think she was the bomb, but imagine the two of them living in a fancy house in his childhood neighborhood in Atlanta. Because, well, what woman in her sane mind wouldn't want that?

Rachel. Rachel didn't want that. In fact, as fun as their trip together to Atlanta had been, she couldn't stomach the idea of even staying the night. She'd wanted so badly to get back to her sweet little town where almost all the people in the world she loved were. Rachel wanted to be here, with them all. And Nick. She wanted to be here with Nick too. It was an idyllic life. The pace was slower, sure, but now that she'd made the adjustment, there wasn't any other place in the world she wanted to create a family. She thought about the giant Christmas tree in the square, and all the lights adorning the storefronts just outside her windows.

Would Rachel give up a person she could potentially love to stay here and roll around in such comfort and joy? She just hoped there was a chance she wouldn't need to.

⫸⫷

NICK WOKE IN Rachel's bed without her in it. His phone alarm was beeping on the bedside table, so he grabbed it and silenced the obnoxious sound.

He made his way in to her living area, and saw that she was sitting at her desk, hard at work already on her computer. "Hey there. Sorry I fell asleep on you."

"It was four in the morning, so I guess I can forgive you." She smiled, a mug in her hand.

"There's coffee." She motioned toward the kitchen.

He ran a hand through his hair, which was likely standing on end in all directions. "Thanks." He grabbed a cup and noticed her staring at him.

"Oh, sorry." He was clad only in his boxer briefs, his usual straight-out-of-bed attire, but perhaps it was a tiny bit unusual for her to see him like that.

"Don't mind me. I'm enjoying the show."

"I wish I had time to put on a better show for you, but I've got to shower and get to the hospital." He went to where she was sitting at her desk and knelt next to her. "Can I have a raincheck until tonight?"

Rachel raised a brow. "Sounds like it might be worth the wait, so, the answer is yes. I'll look forward to it."

He stood and kissed her forehead. "See you tonight."

"Are you forgetting something?" Rachel asked, and motioned to his naked chest.

"Oh, you mean my clothes? Yeah, I'll just go get those." He turned to go and mooned her.

She let out a howl of laughter and held up her fingers. "Eight. I give it an eight."

"Harsh, woman." He grinned, then went to grab his jeans and Falcons sweatshirt from her bedroom. When he came back out, dressed, he said, "Tonight, you will amend that. I'll be shooting for a solid ten, so suit up, girlfriend, and prepare yourself."

"Looking forward to it." She waved as he exited.

He stepped out into the hallway and nearly bulldozed Mrs. Wiggins, who was just coming down the corridor, a feather duster in her hand. "Oh, good morning."

"Well, hello there, Nick. Glad the two of you made it home safely from Atlanta. How was the game?" The tiny woman's expression was pleasant, and revealed nothing resembling judgement.

"The game was close, but the Saints won, so Rachel was happier with the outcome than I was." Nick realized how this must look to her, but he would be late if he didn't get a move on. "But we had a nice trip, even though it was quick. I'm headed to the hospital this morning. I need to shower and get to work."

"Well, I'm just doing a little cleaning this morning, so don't let me keep you. Have a lovely day, my dear."

"Thanks, Mrs. Wiggins. You too."

Nice. Nick had done the walk of shame right in front of his elderly landlady. At least he'd put on his pants first.

⇥⇤

"HOW DO YOU both feel about Dad coming for Christmas?" Rachel asked Sabine and her mother later in the day. Sabine was only working half days on Thursdays and Fridays now that she was getting farther along in her third trimester.

"I guess it was bound to happen sooner or later," Mom said, but didn't sound especially happy about it. They were having lunch at Sabine's house while Janie napped.

"I'm proud of you, Rachel. I thought about asking him to drive up from the beach, but I was waiting until it was your idea. Dad hurt you most because the two of you were closest. I'm okay with having him here for Christmas if Mom is."

"Like I said, it won't be comfortable, especially now that I'm with Norman, but I guess we'd best go ahead and take the bull by the horns here. Your father won't like that I've found someone else," Mom said.

"No, he won't. But he's the one who got us where we are now. Not that it's a bad place, but it's certainly not where we all envisioned ourselves. His actions had consequences for all of us. He'll deal or he won't visit," Sabine said, all wise and counselor-like.

Rachel gave a snort. "Yeah, who would have thought we'd all end up here instead of living in New Orleans? But I have to say, it's a pretty sweet alternative."

The other two women nodded. "No arguments here. It's like finding one of those little towns in a movie that you wish existed in real life—and then it does," Mom said. "I mean, just look at this house."

"I do love my house." Sabine looked around and sighed. "Yes, things *are* pretty sweet here."

"It's funny, because I love my little apartment too. It

feels like home here," Rachel said.

"So, you'll give Dad a call tonight and invite him?" Sabine asked Rachel.

"Yeah. I'll call him. Can he stay with you and Ben at your house?"

Sabine frowned just a little. "I hadn't thought of where he would stay. I guess he can stay with us. I'm sure Ben won't mind. It's just that he's got such a *big* personality. I've never had him as a guest before. He's always been the man in charge of the household. Hopefully it will go well."

"If he acts up, you can kick him to the Ministry Inn. It seems to be a nice place now that the Balfour-Monroe family has come back to claim it." The inn was recently renovated and re-opened after being shut down for years. The historic old building took a lot of time and care to restore, and Grey Harrison's company had worked on it for nearly two years now. The inn was open for business and was booking for the season, but the official grand re-opening would coincide with the Christmas parade.

"You might want to go ahead and book him with Ivy at the inn to avoid any awkwardness for Sabine. He would like it there, Rachel. It's right up his alley. He would rather be someplace where he doesn't have to mind his p's and q's so much. You know how he is. He's best when he can meet you for dinner and then leave."

Rachel and Sabine shared a glance. "You might be right. I'll suggest it as the first option and see how he responds."

Ivy Balfour-Monroe was also new in town, and one of the single friends Rachel had made since coming to Ministry, though Ivy kept to herself mostly. The two women met at the grocery store the first time when Ivy had slipped on a broken egg in the dairy aisle and Rachel had helped her up. They'd struck up a conversation and been friendly ever since. But Ivy was shy and no one in town seemed to know her very well. But she and her daddy had done a bang-up job on the inn's renovation.

Sabine nodded. "Okay. We'll take him if he gets offended at the idea of staying someplace besides with one of us. I'll warn Ivy ahead of time if he chooses to stay at the inn."

"Has anyone told him about Norman?" Mom asked.

Rachel and Sabine both shook their heads.

"So, how do we want to handle that?" Mom asked.

"I'll tell him. I'll throw some Freudian lingo at him and then a heavy dose of guilt, which he so deserves, and he'll wonder what hit him."

"Great idea. And tell him if he behaves nasty to me I won't come near him," Mom said.

"I'll tell him, but the two of you do need to talk, Mom. There's so much history between you, and you do share two daughters. That's not going to change. So, it's time to make peace if you can. At least you can try."

Mom seemed to consider that for a moment. "Okay. I'll agree to speak with him, but if he starts that bullying behavior or trying to boss me around like he did when we were married, I'm going to tell him to go screw himself."

"*Mom!*" Rachel was shocked at her mother's continued anger toward her father.

"Sorry, girls. Just remembering how he used to treat me still gets my back up," Mom said.

"Mom, I get it. When I think about Richard and what he put me through, I still sometimes wish I could get my hands around his neck; the anger for the years of my life he took from me threatens to overshadow the incredible life I have now. But it's over. We can't get back what they took from us; we can, however, pity them for what they lost, and celebrate our new lives and freedom from the past."

"Yes. We can. And that's why I won't kill your father when I see him. So, you can thank me for that. Any other kindnesses will be baby steps, okay?" Mom downed the rest of her iced tea as if it was a neat bourbon.

They all laughed.

Chapter Thirteen

RACHEL SPENT THE morning editing headshots of contestants for the newspaper article on the upcoming Christmas pageant. Emma asked that all the shots be taken with the same background so no one went rogue to a fancy photography studio to try and one-up another pageant contestant. Not all the contestants were Emma's students, but since Emma was the pageant coordinator, she made certain no claims of preferential treatment could be made.

The photos of the girls made Rachel smile. Some of them were "pageant pretty" with their hair and makeup done to perfection, but many of these girls weren't classically beautiful, and Rachel saw such hope and promise in their eyes. It was refreshing to see a somewhat diverse group, mostly white and black, and a few Latina, as there weren't as many races represented here in Ministry as Rachel was accustomed to in New Orleans.

Every face held a story. Rachel would do her best to write the stories to represent each one in the short biographies filled out by the contestants.

She had invited Emma to stop by and give her opinion of how it was progressing thus far. Emma put her reputation on the line by heading up the pageants, along with the committee, so she oversaw every aspect with the careful eye of experience she'd gained through years in the business.

Rachel had seen Emma in action and respected her dedication to putting on a high-quality production where both the entrants and their parents felt confident in allowing their children to participate in something with Emma Laroux's name associated with it. Of course, she was Emma Laroux Pope now, and she was very large with two squiggly little ones just waiting to pop right out after the holidays.

"These shots are amazing, Rachel. We're so lucky to have your talent here in Ministry. And *I'm* thrilled that you came here to live, and now I can hire you to do my photography. Do you know how hard it was before, having to hire all this out to someone who didn't have your vision?"

"Now you're making me blush."

"Well, my mother feels the same way. She relies on your work to make the events at Evangeline House shine in perpetuity. The way clients feel about their wedding photos after their wedding is over is the one thing that keeps the memory of the event alive. If they aren't thrilled with the photos, the memory of the event is less wonderful."

"I hadn't really thought of it like that. It's the one tangible thing, besides the video, they can hold in their hands and relive the memories through. They can actually see their beautiful flowers, the venue, and how vivid the surroundings were where they made memories."

"Exactly. So, you see how incredibly important the work you do is for this community, don't you?"

"I know that I love what I do, and I'm happy it brings to life over and over something in the past. I can't wait to get my studio up and running so I can do more on-site studio work. With lighting, lenses, and cameras, I'll be so much better at my work. I feel like a hack right now compared to what I know I'm capable of."

"Well, I get it because I've seen the magic my husband works when he goes into his studio. He makes magic every day, sometimes just photographing food for promos. But every shot he takes has his stamp on it, and he takes pride in what comes from his production team."

"Like Matthew said to me a few days ago, he's an artist. I never really felt that way about what I do before, but I'm finally starting to, thanks to everyone's appreciation of my work," Rachel said.

"Good. Now, I'll let you do your magic here so you can get this to the newspaper," Emma said, and grabbed her purse and scarf from the table.

Rachel stood from where she'd been sitting at the desk to walk Emma out. "So, how are you feeling? You look like it's time to have those twinsers," Rachel motioned toward the tall blonde's very large and protruding belly.

"They are playing doubles right now. I swear they aren't planning to wait full term. My doctor says I'm doing well, and that all is normal with the pregnancy, but sometimes I worry."

"Are you not feeling well?" Rachel was suddenly concerned. She believed that women intrinsically knew their own bodies.

"No." She wiped a small trickle of a tear before it fell all the way. "It's just that we tried so hard to get pregnant, and it took longer than we expected. I feel like all my eggs are quite literally in one great big basket here. They just have to be okay. I guess I'm just a little scared is all."

"I totally understand how that must be when everybody else waves away your concerns and tells you you're fine. Even if you are, you still worry," Rachel said.

"Thanks for that, for understanding. Everyone else just says I'm being silly."

"I know it can't be easy right now. Sabine is struggling with only one little football player in there. I know she can't even imagine two."

Emma smiled and nodded. "Please give Sabine my best. I'll see you at the pageant next week for sure."

Rachel checked the time and realized she had to get over to where Santa would be waiting for the first group of eager lap-sitters, ready to tell him all their Christmas wishes. And it would be Rachel's job to record that special moment for the future.

She grabbed her camera bag and extra battery pack from where it was charging in the wall socket. No doubt, she would need fresh juice before the day was out.

On her way to the gift shop where Santa was currently stationed, she noticed the Christmas tree in the square was showing progress, though it was mostly covered up by the scaffolding surrounding it. It appeared as if the colored lights were completed and the ornaments were placed about halfway down the tree. There were sparkling crystal-like clear ornaments, which were most likely a heavy-duty molded melamine plastic, that reflected the colorful lights. The effect was brilliant.

Rachel couldn't wait until she was able to take photos of the tree completely lit and decorated. Santa would move outdoors on nice days near the tree in the square for photos as soon as possible. It was all coming together now and the feeling downtown was festive, especially now that the shops were all putting their finishing touches inside their windows and all around.

Rachel neared the inn and remembered that she needed to speak with Ivy regarding a reservation for Dad, so she popped inside since she still had a little time before she was due at the gift shop.

Bells jingled on the front door as she opened it, a throwback to an earlier time. "Nice touch," Rachel said more to herself than anyone else, eyeing the aged brass. She would remember brass bells when it came time to open her own studio.

Rachel hadn't been inside since the place had been open to the public. Ivy had shown her around before, but now that the furniture for the seating area was in place, the damask curtains hung, and the marble floors shined, the place was stunning.

"Hey there, friend. What brings you in?" Ivy stood behind the beautifully restored aged wood counter. Everything in the lobby of the inn had been meticulously refurbished to its former glory.

"Wow. I'm amazed, Ivy. The inn looks fabulous." Rachel tried to keep her mouth from hanging open. Then she realized Ivy stood waiting for her to answer a question. "Oh, I'm here to pencil in my dad for a few days at Christmas if you have any openings. I left him a message to call me back, but I didn't want to wait in case you're getting close to filling up."

"Good idea. In the last couple hours, we've had a ton of calls. It's getting close all of a sudden, so let's see what I have left. When do you think he'll arrive?"

"I'm not exactly sure, but I would guess by the twenty-third, and then leave the day after Christmas."

Ivy was so efficient. She was a throwback to like, the sixties, in her dress. She always wore lipstick to match her nail polish, and such fun clothes, but never trashy. "Okay, I'll have to put him either in a suite or a smaller room. Which do you think he would prefer?"

Rachel honestly didn't know. With her father's penchant for luxury, and the ability to pay for it, she figured she ought to book the suite. But since he'd been in prison, maybe he'd changed his lifestyle somewhat? Who knew? "Can I let you know? He's going to call me back later today, and I'll find out. Just so you know, he's a bit of a character. I think I've filled you in a little on my family history."

"Ah, yes. I remember you telling me about your dad. Okay. I'll hold both rooms until midnight. But if we fill up, I'll need to call for an answer. I hope you understand."

"Of course. Sorry to be so indecisive. I honestly don't know which room he would prefer at this point."

"Got it. Sorry we couldn't make Thanksgiving with the Larouxs. Dad called Miss Maureen after. We ran into a major plumbing issue and had to stay here all day until the guys handled it. Couldn't take the chance they wouldn't rush it on a holiday." Ivy's makeup was perfect, and Rachel just knew she wore black patent leather pumps behind the counter. Her dress had a white background with large black polka dots, and a wide black belt. She was trim and had the most gorgeous dark red hair. How she'd remained single until now was a mystery to Rachel.

"Oh, no problem. Of course, you missed some awesome food and lots of kids and dogs running amok."

"I hear you and the new cute doctor are dating. That was quick work, sister."

Rachel laughed, picturing Nick in his boxers, hair sticking up, so amazingly sexy this morning, and she thought about his promise for later, and felt heat rise in her cheeks. "Well, he is my neighbor, so the proximity probably helped things along."

"You're blushing like an old maid. Must be a pretty hot memory to bring that kind of red to your cheeks."

Rachel was *not* sharing that particular memory with Ivy, so she said, "Well, I've got to go take some Santa pictures or there's gonna be sad, disappointed kiddos in town. I'll let you know about the room later when I hear from Dad."

"Fine. Don't throw a lonely old maid a bone."

"Old maid, my ass. Girl, you could have any man you snapped your fingers at."

"As if. I don't see any men swarming around here. Do you?"

"Just wait."

Rachel gave her a little wave. "Tell Mr. Mason I said hi."

＞＞＞＜＜＜

RACHEL TOOK PICTURES of what seemed like a whole county's worth of children with Santa. Poor Santa appeared ready to rip the beard off, though the man spent months growing it to this length leading up to the season. The requests from the children ranged anywhere from domination of the universe to *please cure my brother's cancer for Christmas.* That one sent them all reaching for a tissue. What happened to dolls, little red wagons and BB guns? For every photo, an online form with payment had to be filled out, since the photos were digital, and would be edited and sent directly to the family. It was a lot of work, but the sheer volume was financially feasible. Rachel was on a single-minded path to studio-ownership.

She wanted to buy a storefront and grow her business. But she didn't want to do it alone. Rachel saw herself turning over an "out for lunch" sign and meeting someone for a quick bite, and heading home at the end of the day to share dinner and stories about clients—and patients?

As she left the gift shop, Rachel couldn't shake the thoughts that rambled in her head from last night as she'd fallen asleep in Nick's arms. *Was* she falling in love with him?

Instead of heading back upstairs to her apartment, she decided to head over to Sabine's house. Yes, she really did need to bounce some of this off her sister's psychologist brain. Sabine would tell her if she was behaving like an idiot.

Sabine and Ben lived a couple miles out of town on a piece of land with a barn, animals, and several acres, so she gave her sister a quick call to let her know she was coming.

Sabine was home, resting with her swollen feet up. "Come on over. You might have to chase Janie around while we talk, but I'm dying to hear all about it," Sabine said.

Great. Nick would likely get home in about two hours, so it gave her just enough time to speak with her sister and get back in time to freshen up for *the show*.

When she was just out of town, Rachel's phone rang. She

answered on speaker.

"Hey there, honey, it's your daddy. I got your message about Christmas."

"Oh, hey, Dad. What do you think? Would you like to come?"

"I'd love to see my best girls, but what does your mother say about it?"

"Well, she's agreed that you should spend some time with me and Sabine. I don't know how much she'll be around, but we've cleared it with her."

He got quiet on the line for a minute, then said, "I'd like to sit down and have a talk with your mom if she'll agree to it."

"Probably best to take this one step at a time." Rachel could tell her father was impatient to mend fences with Mom. Best to just dive right in. "Dad, you know Mom has moved on, right?"

"Moved on? What do you mean? Is there another man?" Rachel could feel his disbelief all the way from the Gulf Shores.

"Dad, she's dating someone here in town. He's a really nice man."

"She's my wife." His outrage was obvious.

"No, she's not. And you know it. The double standard here is too ridiculous for even you to deny. Really, Dad?" This was the kind of behavior that made her never want to resume this relationship or date a man again.

As Rachel pulled into Sabine's driveway, she texted her sister. *Can you come out to the car? I'm in your driveway and I've got Dad on speaker. I spilled the beans that Mom is dating someone. He's not taking it well.*

Sabine's answer was immediate. *Ben's here, so I'm on my way.*

"I know we're divorced, but I hoped Elizabeth would forgive my mistakes now that she's had some time to calm down."

Sabine slid into the car. "Hi Dad, it's Sabine. I just joined the conversation."

"Hey there, honey. I hear your momma has taken up with some man up there. I was telling Rachel that I still consider her my wife and I don't accept the idea of her being with someone else."

Sabine and Rachel shared an eye-roll. "Well, Dad, you don't have a say in this. Mom isn't your wife anymore, and you drew first blood there. In other words, you cheated, you lied, and you tore up your marriage and family with your actions."

They heard his sharp intake of breath. Rachel was shocked at Sabine's unusually honest and straightforward statement. "Well, I guess that about says it all, doesn't it?" Dad said, his tone quiet and calm now.

"Dad, you don't get your way this time. It's over between you and Mom. The best you can hope for is that she agrees to be in the same room with you without ripping out your throat," Sabine said.

"Wow. That's harsh, Sabine. I doubt your mother is as unreasonable as you make her sound."

Both Sabine and Rachel snorted. "Are you kidding? Mom's anger toward you is deep and endless. She's found a little happiness now. Don't come up here and try to ruin that. If that's your plan, we're rescinding the invitation. You didn't see Mom when Janie was born because we made sure of it. This is a bit of a test. Hopefully, the first visit with your granddaughter here since she's old enough to remember you will go well for everyone."

"Well, girls, I'm flummoxed. I really don't know what to say." Dad's fight was all gone.

Rachel spoke up then. "Say you'll come. I've made a reservation for you at the Ministry Inn for Saturday the twenty-third, until the day after Christmas. All you have to do is call and tell them whether you want the small room or the suite and give them your credit card number."

"Okay, darling. I'll do it, and I'll do my best not to kill your mother's lover."

"Seriously, Dad. You have to behave. We live here, so no complaining about the food to the owners of the restaurants and such. In other words, don't make a stink in town while you're here." Rachel sounded like somebody's mother, even to her own ears.

"Rachel, I've changed. I'm not the same man I was in New Orleans. After all, I'm not the man in charge of things

anymore. I'm an ex-con who's learned a lot of hard lessons."
He sounded sincere.

"We'll take your word on that," Sabine said. "We look
forward to seeing you, Daddy."

"Yeah, Daddy. Which room are you planning to take? I
told Ivy I would let her know by the end of the day, so she
could let the other one go."

"Why, I'll take the suite, of course."

"Don't you want to know how much it costs before you
decide?"

He laughed, deep and full. "Don't you girls know that
money isn't an issue? I've offered time and again to help you
if you need it. To give you a monthly allowance, even."

Rachel had been so offended in the past by Dad's offer to
support her. She never, ever wanted to know where the
endless money came from because the source was likely a
deep, deep well drawn from his past filled with corruption
and political favors. "Thanks, Dad, but I'm good."

"My husband and my career pay for my lifestyle, so, no
thanks," Sabine said.

"What about your mother? Is she alright with the divorce
settlement? I made sure she had enough to retire on. But I
can do more if she needs it."

"She's fine, Dad. I've never heard her express a need for
anything since she's been on her own."

"I know you girls believe the money comes from a bad
source, but it doesn't. Your grandparents were obscenely

wealthy, you know. Nothing I ever did was for the money. You girls have trust funds you've never even touched. You know y'all aren't like normal kids."

Rachel knew that both she and Sabine had some sort of trust fund set aside from their grandparents, but since she'd never really had to struggle, Rachel hadn't ever asked her parents about the money. She'd just assumed that money was for the future and her own children's futures. It was hardly even mentioned.

"I've never really needed the money, so it hasn't been something I've spent time thinking about. Plus, you and Mom never really talked about the trust funds."

"Well, you're old enough now, and if there's something you want to use it for, there's plenty of money in it to supplement your lifestyle or help you buy your first house, or whatever you might need."

"Well, I'm planning to keep the money in trust for my children," Sabine said.

"It's there if you need it, girls. I want to you know that it became available to you at age twenty-five. It's in the Whitney Bank in New Orleans."

"I'll let Ivy at the Ministry Inn know you want the suite. Call her with your credit card tomorrow, okay?" Rachel said.

"I'll do it. Thanks, girls. Please give your mother my best."

"Bye, Daddy," they said in unison.

They hung up.

Still sitting in the car, they were silent for a few minutes.

"So, what did you want to discuss?" Sabine asked.

"The conversation with Dad just exhausted me."

"Obviously, you need to talk. So, talk," Sabine said.

Rachel took a deep breath and let it out. "I think I'm in love with Nick."

Sabine's eyes grew huge. "Get out!"

"That's not the therapist's reaction I expected."

"That was my sister response." Sabine grinned at her. "Holy crap, girl. You're in love?"

"I said, *I think,* which is why I wanted to talk to you about it."

"Do you believe I would be able to tell you if you really are?"

"I wanted to be sure. How can I be sure? I think about him all the time. He's a really good person from what I've seen, besides the fact that he's a Falcons fan."

"Ooh, strike one."

"Very funny. Anyway, he's so cute and sexy. And we're, um, very compatible, if you know what I mean."

"You've *slept* with Doctor McHottie?"

"Yes. I have. I know you think I've been around a lot more than I have, but I really haven't been with many guys."

"I know that, silly. You were all talk."

"How did you know? I was away for all that time."

"I knew."

"Well, anyway, I can *see* myself with him, like, in the future. Having dinner at the end of the day, bathing our kids. Stuff like that. But I see him here with me in Ministry. I don't see myself moving away to Atlanta and living the lifestyle of a bigshot trauma surgeon's wife."

"Are you more interested in being here or being with him, no matter where that might be?" Sabine asked in her therapy voice.

Rachel thought about it. Could she be happy here without Nick? Or, could she be happy someplace else with Nick?

"I guess if you really love someone, you do whatever it takes to work out a life together, huh?" Rachel asked, but it was more like an answer.

"No. You don't give up your dreams, and you don't settle for something less than you deserve. One person doesn't get everything they want. There must be compromise. But both people have to be willing to go as far as necessary."

Rachel nodded. Was she willing to make changes to be with Nick? She could still have a photography studio in suburban Atlanta, and she didn't have to be in the middle of town in the fanciest area. If she really loved him, she would.

If he wanted to be with her, he could help her by adjusting how and where they lived within the Atlanta area, couldn't he? The wouldn't have to live in the same neighborhood as his parents. Rachel figured there had to be some less urban areas nearby with a more rural feel. She couldn't ask him to give up such a promising career and insist he move here, but after living in Ministry, Rachel didn't think she could go back to true in-town living.

"I think I care about him enough to make big changes. I do," Rachel said.

"Then, you know your heart, Sister. Don't let this guy slip away without letting him know how you feel just because the obstacles appear too far beyond your ability to solve them."

"You know, you're worth every penny."

Sabine laughed. "I'd better get inside and feed my crew before I run out of gas." She shifted her excessive girth and made to exit the car.

"Thanks again. I'll keep you posted. We've got a stay-home date tonight."

Sabine opened the door, a wistful and faraway look in her eye. "Sounds like something Ben and I used to do before we started pro-creating."

"You'll get there again. Baking these nieces and nephews inside your body for me is pretty important, you know."

"Yeah, and I look forward to a day very soon when you're growing your own little humans. Then, you'll understand."

"Thanks for everything, Sabine, including making me an aunt."

"If I were you, I'd stop by the store and pick up some food and wine if you plan to spend the evening having a heart-to-heart with a man. You'll need to feed him first, and a little liquor won't hurt either one of you."

"Gotcha. Go feed your family. They're probably think-ing I took you away since we've been out here so long."

"Good luck tonight. Let me know how it goes."

"Don't worry, you'll hear about it either way."

Chapter Fourteen

❧

NICK WAS CONFRONTED at work by an attractive single female patient with a suspiciously mild case of poison ivy. "It *reeaally* itches."

"Poison ivy can spread, so be careful to wash your hands thoroughly and try to avoid scratching as much as possible. I'm prescribing over the counter calamine lotion and Benadryl every six hours. It might make you sleepy, so take care while driving."

The pretty girl with the light brown hair narrowed her eyes as if he weren't telling her what she wanted to hear. "Over the counter, huh? You mean I could have saved my fifty-dollar co-pay and gone to the Walgreens?"

He nodded. "Yes. This isn't serious. I'm sorry you wasted your time and money. But be sure and don't rub it in your eye, because you will end up here with a real problem then. And you'll be very uncomfortable with a much larger issue."

"So, thanks for nothing, I guess. I heard you were really hot and single. You're hot, but you're not looking at me like a single man would, so I'm assuming you're with someone."

"I work here; I don't date here, or discuss my personal life," Nick said, put off by the young woman's manner.

"He's dating someone," Georgie said, as she showed their patient out. "It's our town photographer, Rachel Prudhomme. You might know her." Georgie's tone was pure honey, but Nick had now known his nurse long enough to read between her sticky sweet words. It would go something like, *Get out, Stanky, and leave our guy alone.*

Nick had to smile. In the short time he'd been working at Ministry General, the staff had shown an inordinate amount of loyalty to him in many small ways, which let him know they cared, and that he'd been accepted here. When he thought about some of the catty, backbiting things that went on in some of the departments during his rotations, and his time working as a doctor on staff at his most recent position, this was such a refreshing environment.

Nick had done some serious soul-searching, and met with George Granger. George's meeting with the board a few days ago when Nick had met Rachel for lunch was related to that same situation.

Nick was looking forward to his evening with Rachel, so as soon as he got off work, he stopped by the market to pick up a few items.

As Nick perused the aisles in the small specialty market looking for just the right items, a shrill voice cut into his concentration. "Somebody help us!"

Nick turned to see the woman who he'd last seen in a really bad reindeer sweater leaned over a man prone on the floor. He immediately left his cart to lend a hand.

"Oh, thank God. Please help my daddy."

The man wore his sheriff's uniform, complete with badge and radio clipped to his shoulder. Nick checked for a pulse and respiration. There was none. So, he told, Angie, was it? "Call 9-1-1." Then, he began CPR.

A small crowd formed around them. Angie cried. And the sheriff coughed and came to, thank the Lord. His color wasn't great at first, but at least he seemed coherent. The paramedic arrived shortly after that, and administered oxygen and started an IV.

Sheriff Davis was weak, but conscious, and looking better by the minute. He grabbed Nick's wrist. "I want to thank you, son."

"Don't try to speak. You're welcome. Dr. Granger is on duty at the hospital, and I'll call and check on you in a little while."

He nodded. "Granger's a good man." The paramedics nodded to Nick as they rolled the gurney away.

Angie came over then, and threw her arms around Nick's neck. "Thank you for saving Daddy's life. I don't know what I would have done if you hadn't been standing there." She was sobbing, now, mascara running in black rivers down her face.

"I'm glad I was here to help. He's speaking coherently, so

that's a good sign." He patted her arm briefly, then broke contact.

"I'm so sorry for the way I behaved the other day. I was bitchy and hateful, and I was wrong." She hung her head.

Nick smiled at the woman, who was obviously ashamed. "Hey, no worries. Go on with your dad now. He needs you."

She waved as she ran to catch up with her father as they put him in the ambulance.

Nick exhaled, relieved the sheriff would likely be okay, depending on the condition of his heart. He didn't show any outward signed of a stroke, so that was good.

Several shoppers still loitered nearby, discussing what they'd just witnessed in whispered tones, which made Nick slightly uncomfortable, so he smiled and gave a quick wave, just before he turned to retrieve his shopping cart a little farther down the frozen food aisle.

"Doctor Sullivan, is it?" a woman, maybe in her fifties, asked.

"Yes, I'm Nick Sullivan."

"We just wanted to tell you that we've never seen anything like that before, and well, you saved the sheriff's *life*. Thank you. It's so nice to know you're living among us and that you're willing to step out and be a good citizen and all." The woman stepped up and hugged him.

He was surprised. Did she think he *wouldn't* do everything possible to save a dying man's life? "Uh. Of course." He returned her hug, although not quite as enthusiastically, because that would be uncomfortable—for him.

Another woman, who was likely around eighty, stepped forward then. "Young man, we hear you'll be leaving us in a few weeks, and I for one would just like to say that I wish you'd give our little town a shot. We're not as backward as we seem to those on the outside. Ministry has a lot to offer. We could use a good man like you—and another good doctor—among us."

Nick smiled then. "I'll think about it."

As he resumed his shopping, Nick's heart sang. Surely what just happened was a sign. There had been quite a few signs lately.

He picked up a dozen red roses in the floral department. "You know red roses mean love, don't you?" the tiny elderly woman at the counter, who was arranging a mixed bouquet asked, as he spent a moment finding the freshest and loveliest roses.

He kind of thought everyone knew that, but just nodded his head instead of saying so.

"If you give a woman red roses, you'd better mean what they say."

"Don't worry; I do." He winked at the wide-eyed little busy-body.

She blushed and turned back to handling her own flowers.

RACHEL HAD COOKED a meal, though she wouldn't likely admit that to her family. They didn't know she was perfectly capable of doing such. And she'd not shown them her skills or talents because so long as they believed her inept in the kitchen, they took care to send her meals prepared in their kitchens.

This was a special evening, and if she were going to spill her guts to Nick, she planned to ply him with food and wine first, as Sabine suggested. The scampi sauce was perfect. She'd combined butter, lemon, garlic, with a hint of white wine. She'd seasoned that with coarse black pepper and salt. She would add the shrimp at the same time as she put the angel hair pasta on to boil. The water was already boiling in a large stock pot, and the garlic bread was ready to pop into the oven just as soon as she heard Nick arrive home next door from work.

Now, while the sauce simmered, Rachel would put a little effort into her appearance, which she could honestly say she'd not done much since she and Nick had met. Their time together had been mostly casual and unplanned, so, besides their quick trip to Atlanta, where she'd worn a football jersey, he'd never seen her "date ready." Thanksgiving didn't count because it had also been a casual dinner, and she'd intentionally not gussied up for him.

So, putting on makeup, a sexy, yet still casual dress, and perfume felt odd, but more than a little exciting. Rachel hadn't gotten to the ripe age of twenty-six without realizing her appeal to males, especially when she put a little effort into it. For the most part, she'd been disinterested and somewhat oblivious, but not completely ignorant of being attractive to men. Now, it mattered. Nick had made his interest in her very clear. But she wanted to solidify that interest into something more. Going the extra mile with her appearance wouldn't make a difference if he didn't feel the same about her emotionally, but they were still in such a fresh and exciting discovery stage of one another. It couldn't hurt.

She finally heard the door shut next door. She checked the time on the clock next to her bed. It was a little later than he normally returned home.

Her phone rang, and she saw it was Nick. An explosion of tiny butterflies swirled in her tummy. Lord help her, she was textbook swoony. "Hello there."

"Hi. I just got home. You still up for some company after I shower off the day?" he asked.

Okay. This was ridiculous. Now she was swoony at the sound of his voice over the phone. "You bet. I made dinner."

A pause. "Should I be concerned?"

She laughed. "Only if you're allergic to shellfish or garlic."

"I thought I smelled something cooking when I came down the hall. I'm starving. I'll be there in fifteen minutes with wine."

"Great. See you soon."

As Rachel moved into the kitchen to finish the meal, she got a text from Sabine. *Sending my love. Hope your evening goes well.* Rachel smiled. She'd been blessed with a wonderful big sister and mother. She guessed she would deal with her daddy issues along the way.

There was a short knock at the door, then Nick walked in. It seemed they'd had similar ideas for this evening. He was wearing a sport coat and button-down shirt with dark jeans and loafers. He was holding a large bouquet of red roses and a bottle of wine. And some sort of dessert.

"Wow, you look fantastic. Can we skip dinner?" He kissed her on the cheek and nuzzled her neck.

A little thrill shot through Rachel. "Umm. That sounds tempting, but I've spent a considerable amount of time on the preparation, so let's enjoy all of it. We've got all night."

"Okay, dinner does smell amazing. Can I do anything to help?"

"You can pour us a glass of that nice wine." She turned her attention back to what he was holding. *Red roses?* Hmm…Best to not read too much into it yet. But, red roses. The first time he'd brought her flowers, they weren't red roses. "Wow, those are gorgeous. Thanks." She took them from him and laid them on the counter while she grabbed a vase from up in the cabinet.

"I know you like roses," he said, and though his eyes were making her insides mushy, she didn't pick up on anything more.

She motioned to the dessert. "That looks delicious. What is it?"

"I was told it was some sort of trifle by the pastry chef at the dessert counter at the market. I'm still amazed that a town this size carries such specific items."

The market in town wasn't an average grocery store—anymore. It had begun as a deli that did catering. They carried specialty hand-sliced meats, fresh fish and shellfish, daily-made desserts, breads, and they had a killer wine and cheese selection. "We're a picky bunch, and now that Jenna Martin has taken over the family business, she's really gotten the pulse of what people want. A couple years ago, she completely renovated, expanded, and revamped the place and it's been a hugely successful endeavor."

"Smart ideas. With all the cooking shows, recipes passed around on social media, and focus on food intolerances and allergies, it makes sense to give people what they want and need." Spoken like a true medical man.

"Everybody loves to eat. Well, I guess not everybody, but here in the South, so much of what we do is centered around food. Might as well be healthy and happy."

"Speaking of food, I think your pasta's about to boil over, and it would make me very happy to help you drain it while you finish the scampi."

She nudged him in the ribs and handed him the strainer. "Fine. I'm turning off the sauce. The shrimp are ready. I'll get the fresh Reggiano Parmesan from the fridge.

"I smell the bread. My mom always burned the bread." He wrinkled his nose.

"Don't worry. I have the timer set."

"A woman after my heart." He dramatically laid a hand over his chest in that general region.

If he only knew where tonight's conversation was headed on her end. The oven timer sounded.

He grabbed the potholders that were sitting on the counter. "I've got this."

The pasta was in the strainer, so Rachel transferred it to a large glass bowl and took it over to the table.

She kept the scampi in the pan and placed it on top of a trivet in the center of the table.

"You're pretty good at this for someone who never let on you could cook."

"Shhh. Don't tell my family I learned all their secrets. They think I'm all but useless in the kitchen, and I prefer it that way. If they think I'm over here starving, they'll share their food with me and I don't have to cook for one."

"I know. It just doesn't seem to be worth the time and effort. It's a lot more fun to share a meal." They'd placed everything on the table now and sat down together. "I could get used to this."

That's what Rachel was thinking. She held up her wineglass. "Here's to not eating alone."

They toasted their togetherness and dug into the scampi.

"I can't believe you've kept your cooking skills a secret

this long. Holy cow, this is delicious."

"It's my mother's recipe. She's a fantastic cook, and has tons of old New Orleans recipes stashed in a great big box. At some point, I need to help her scan them all onto the computer. I'd love to print out the pages, laminate, and organize them by food groups. Create a family cookbook of sorts." Rachel hadn't really developed this idea until now. She'd only considered trying to save the recipes from getting lost or destroyed.

"That would be a fantastic birthday or Christmas gift. Most of our mothers are in the same situation. They haven't ever let go of their stained and torn favorites. Mom likes to cook, but she's kind of lost her passion for it the last few years since she and Dad are alone in the house."

"Wouldn't it be fun to gather everyone's moms' recipe boxes and make cookbooks for them next year?" Rachel asked, suddenly enthusiastic about the project. She was thinking about Maureen Laroux, her mom, maybe Matthew's mom, and Nick's mom.

Then she realized what she'd said aloud. Next year. Where would they be next year? Her lip trembled, dammit. *No. She would not cry. She wasn't a crier.*

"You okay?" he asked and put his fork down.

Rachel pressed her lips together, hard, and nodded. But without her permission a single tear slipped out her left eye and down her cheek. All the way down and plopped right into her scampi.

Nick's expression suddenly grew troubled. "Rachel, please tell me what is happening."

"I'm going to miss you. I'm not seeing my immediate future without you in it." She just blew it. The thing she was going to bring up so gently, he would hardly have seen it coming.

His face grew stern, as if he was trying to control his own emotions. "I've been giving it a lot of thought too."

"I like you being here—with me. I swore to myself I could do this, that I wouldn't get attached." Her face crumpled into a full-blown hiccupping sob. "I'm attached."

He dumped his chair backward and pulled her from her chair into his arms. He held her for a moment while she sniffled a little in his embrace. Then, he maneuvered them both to the sofa. *Oh, the horror of the ugly cry.*

"Rachel, all I've been thinking about lately is a way for this to work—to give us a real shot, because I've gotten attached to you too." He gently touched her cheek. "I didn't mean to, but here we are."

"Yes, here we are and you're leaving in a few weeks," she said.

"I know your family is here, and that this is where you want to make a home and raise your family someday."

Rachel nodded, and placed her hand on his. "I just got here and settled in. I've been wandering around freelancing since college, and this is the first place I've begun to put down roots since my dad broke up our family. It's not that

I'm unwilling to move, I just don't think I'm ready to leave my mom and Sabine again, yet. This is so hard."

"Atlanta's not that far from Ministry. Not so far that we couldn't try to figure this out for a little while until we know what it is we both want."

Rachel fought the urge to cry buckets now. She'd had some stupid idea deep down that he'd be willing to just give up Atlanta for Ministry because she'd become attached to him. How stupid was she?

"Okay. Well, I guess weekends wouldn't be so terrible," she said in a very small voice. He would pine for her here in Alabama; wouldn't he? *That was sad and pathetic, wasn't it?*

"Rachel, I've got commitments I need to see through in the short-term. But I want to be with you."

"I understand. I mean, who would just give up an entire career for some girl they just met in a podunk town in Alabama?" That sounded so uselessly needy. *Who has she become?*

He stared at her with the saddest expression. "I wish I could right now."

"Well, let's get on with that show you promised me. Or, have you changed your mind?" Rachel put on her happy face. The one she pulled out when things got tough.

"Rachel, I—" He tried to pull her to him.

She stood then, and went to pour another glass of wine. "Would you like some?" she asked.

He shook his head, his face a mask of worry. "I can go if

you want."

She came back over to where he was sitting. "No. I don't want you to go. I don't blame you, you know? It's just such an impossible situation. Stay with me tonight. Let's make our time together the best we can while you're still here."

Rachel stood in front of him now, still holding her wineglass in one hand. She reached out for his hand with the other. He smiled, still with a sadness in his eyes, though he took her hand and rose. "I hope you know, there's no place I'd rather be than here with you."

"Good thing, because that's where you are. Now, on with the show, big boy," she teased and led him to her bedroom. "I hope you brought a pile of those little wrappers."

"Don't worry. If I'm with you, they're with me."

"Smart man."

>>><<<

RACHEL DECIDED A distraction was needed today. As she meandered down the street and approached the deserted retail space on the corner she'd been eyeing since she'd moved to Ministry, she wiped off a spot on the dusty front glass and attempted to peer inside. Sadly, the interior windows were covered with butcher paper, so it was impossible to see anything. She'd not had the courage to research who the space belonged to, yet. There wasn't a sign declaring the empty storefront for rent or for sale. Her grand idea for a studio had been mostly talk and dreaming, thus far. Very few people even knew her plans.

Rachel had convinced herself these plans were in the future, at some as-yet-to-be-determined date and year. Maybe it was time to determine when that was. Her father's mention of the trust money had got her thinking about things. She could inquire about her trust any time she wanted. Or, at least broach the subject with her mother. Mom never really spoke of it, so maybe it was time to bring it up.

But first, she wanted to find out who owned this little slice of heaven that was sure to be her future studio. Especially now that Nick had all but told her he wasn't planning to change his life for her anytime soon. Well, that wasn't exactly what he'd said. But Rachel decided not to get her hopes up, and to concentrate on moving forward with her plans for her own future.

Last night had been amazing, considering the emotional nature of their conversation earlier in the evening. They were so physically compatible, and at ease together in both intimate or casual situations. Rachel looked forward to watching football with Nick almost as much as having mind-blowing sex with him.

She understood what a rare thing that was, and because it was so important they both felt the same way, and were willing to go to the same lengths for a long-term relationship, Rachel decided to let Nick work out whatever he needed to. She'd made it pretty clear she was willing to make big changes to be together, at least eventually.

"Hi there. Window shopping?"

Rachel nearly jumped out of her skin. "You scared me to death, Ivy."

Ivy laughed. Today she wore a long-sleeved black jumpsuit with white piping and a wide white belt and black, shiny high-heeled boots. Her hair was in some sort of a chignon. At least she thought that was what women called the throwback updo hairstyle.

"Don't you look adorable? Aren't you chilly?" Rachel wore a heavy sweater layer over a collared plaid button-down with jeans and boots.

"I sacrifice comfort for fashion on a regular basis. But, this oddity is warmer than it looks." She motioned to her outfit. "So, what are you doing trying to see through windows?"

"I'm interested in opening a photography studio, and I've had my eye on this space for ages. Do you know who owns it?"

"I do. We own most of the block, though most folks don't know it. We've been renting retail spaces here for years with the local realty company as property manager. They handle the upkeep and repairs, and keep the Balfour name somewhat quiet as the name on the deed. It keeps us out of the papers, though now that Daddy and I are back and publically running the inn, it doesn't matter so much anymore."

"Why didn't you want your name out in the open before?" Rachel asked.

"When you're not around to answer people's questions, they have a way of creating their own reality about you. It was our way of keeping a low profile knowing we planned to return someday to restore the inn and live here again. If the stories and speculation had gotten too out of hand in our absence, it would have been hard to come back."

Rachel nodded, thinking about ever going back to New Orleans after her father's public debacle. "I understand. My daddy left a trail of trash for endless tales to be told about our family back in New Orleans. Most would likely be true, of course, but there's no one left to set the record straight when they become too fantastic."

Ivy winced. "I guess you do get it. We didn't have scandal, so much as people wondering why my parents left the town and never came back. Speculation in a small town is so much fun."

"So, this space—is it for sale?" Rachel asked.

Ivy made a face. "I've never considered selling property on Main Street. Renting, yes, but not selling. It's my family's legacy."

"What about a long-term lease with improvements?"

"I'd be willing to discuss restoring the space to your needs and leasing it," Ivy said. "Let me talk to Daddy about it. We've been so busy with the inn, we haven't made plans for the few empty storefronts here."

It wasn't exactly what Rachel was hoping for, but it might work. Ivy was a business woman above all else, and leasing the space would allow Rachel to buy equipment without having to come up with money to buy the building.

"Okay. Thanks so much. Let me know what you and Mr. Mason come up with."

"What about your hottie doctor?" Ivy asked.

"Nick? What about him?" Rachel instantly became defensive.

"Why do I think this has something to do with him? Did you break up?"

"No, we didn't break up. This studio has been my dream for a long time. Nick is here temporarily, and I can't stop my life while he figures his out."

"That sounds a little angry. Are you sure you don't want to give him a little time before you jump into a long-term commitment to opening and running a business?"

Rachel shrugged. "We're going to try the long-distance thing for a little while. I don't want to sit around hoping he decides I'm what or who he wants."

"Still, Rachel, love has a way of derailing plans and re-routing our dreams. Just look at my parents. My mom would never have left Ministry. Her family owned half the town. But she followed my dad to Atlanta because that's where their future took them." Ivy placed a hand on Rachel's shoulder. "They were happy, Rach. For all those years together. Sure, my mom wanted to come back here to retire and restore the inn, but she got sick before they had the chance. Don't take the chance of losing Nick to pride."

Rachel thought about that. "It's so early in our relationship, Ivy. I just don't want to get stuck with my heart broken and left with nothing. If I have my studio, at least I still have my dream."

"Tell you what, I'll talk to my dad, and we can draw up the plans together. You can have a look, and let us know what you want, and give us some idea of what you're thinking. That should buy you some time with Nick."

"Thanks, Ivy. Please don't tell anyone how bad I've got it for him."

"Are you kidding? My lips are sealed. We're friends, aren't we? And I'm thrilled to get this storefront moving in the right direction. We're doing our part to beautify this town."

"Y'all are doing a great job."

The two women hugged, and Rachel continued toward the giant tree in the square. Today, she planned to photograph the downtown area, all gussied up for Christmas. The storefronts were pure perfection, complete with lights, garland, and small lit and decorated trees set out front under the overhangs during business hours. After hours, the trees were placed just inside the plate glass windows, and the nighttime effect was stunning. The oversized ornaments had been hung between shops, just at the rooflines. High enough to be out of children's reach, but low enough to be seen and admired throughout the holidays.

The children's tree decorating was scheduled for this evening. Every family in town, or even outside of town, was invited to bring a hand-made ornament to hang on the tree. Of course, Rachel would be there to take photos during the event as well.

As much as Rachel might like to have indulged today in a bout of self-pity, her schedule didn't allow it. So, she settled for internal fretting and muttering from time to time when she thought about the embarrassment of being the one who was willing to make the most changes. It was never good to be the one who loved the most in a relationship. Just ask Mom.

Speaking of Mom, Rachel would make time in the next few days to have a conversation with her about money.

As Rachel continued finding new ways to showcase Ministry through her lens, she muttered and grumbled, likely appearing somewhat troubled to a passing bystander.

When the tiny pinging sounded on her phone indicating she'd received a text message, Rachel debated whether to check it. But since her sister was obscenely and beautifully pregnant right now, she decided to take the risk to her heart. *Last night was amazing.*

Rachel didn't want to smile, but his words made her think about last night, and she grinned despite herself. Last night was amazing. But she would wait ten minutes before answering. He deserved that for the angst she was experiencing today.

She clicked a shot of a tiny resident reaching up on his tiptoes to touch the bottom branch of the ginormous tree. Rachel managed to capture the awe in his expression. Her heart flipped. The perspective on this one was so compelling in an elementally human way. Rachel decided to do this one black and white. It was magazine-worthy. It was perfection.

She approached the little guy's mother, who'd been just a few feet away and showed her the photo.

Tears filled the woman's eyes upon seeing it and Rachel offered to send it to her.

"It's incredible. Oh, thank you. Are you a professional? Can I get you to take JJ's picture?"

"I'll be taking Santa photos all week. But please don't feel obliged. I just wanted you to see it and have a copy. Some shots are special. Your son is adorable, by the way." Rachel winked at the toddler, who waved at her with his chubby fingers.

"I don't feel obliged. I want more. He's growing so fast, and I was just told I can't have any more children. He's going to be my only one." The woman teared up again. "I want to remember every moment. The picture you took today is special, and always will be. Thank you."

"My name's Rachel Prudhomme. I work in town and do school photos, and freelance. Here's my card." Rachel handed over her business card.

"I'm Lydia. Thank you. I can't wait to set something up.

We need family photos taken too. We've been planning to do them for awhile now. It's great to know who to call. Do you have a studio or do you go wherever your clients want?"

"I have a studio I can use for now, but I also do outdoor sittings and can come into your home if you prefer."

"Oh, that's wonderful. I'll call you soon." Lydia carefully placed Rachel's card into her wallet.

"Great, Lydia It was nice meeting you both. I look forward to hearing from you," Rachel said. "Bye, JJ."

Rachel sent JJ's photo to the email address Lydia had given her before she forgot. When she did so, she noticed the text from Nick again. *Last night was amazing.*

What if she was told she couldn't have children? Nick's babies? She was heartbroken for Lydia, who she'd only just met.

Rachel looked down at her phone and answered the text. *How about we try it again tonight?*

His response was immediate. *I get off at six. See you then. I'm cooking tonight.*

Then she remembered the event this evening. *Tree decorating starts at six. I'm taking pictures. After?*

I'll meet you there. We can grab pizza after. I'll walk you home.

It's a date.

So, it didn't sound like he wasn't interested in pursuing a relationship, but she'd offered to make changes, which meant to possibly relocate. She hadn't been especially enthusiastic about that, but she'd offered. He hadn't jumped on that,

SUSAN SANDS

which made her think that maybe he wasn't sure about his feelings yet. Then again, it hadn't even been a month. She really should reel it in a little bit and adjust her expectations here.

But he said he wanted to be with her.

They really *should* take this one day—one night—at a time.

Her mood lightened then, as she moved through town snapping away, finding people and things to shoot. Ministry at Christmastime was so much more that its decorations, but the lovely décor created a stunning backdrop for everything else it had to offer.

Chapter Fifteen

THE DAYS FLEW by in a blur for Nick. Fortunately for his patients he was good at his job, and no one noticed how distracted he'd been, even when he was on duty at the hospital. His overwhelming goal was how to make his relationship with Rachel work out—permanently. He was completely in love with her. Not just saying words kind of in love. The kind of heartsick, fourteen-year-old boy kind of love whose every moment is saturated with the girl of his dreams.

If one of his childhood friends could see him now, they'd tell him how totally whipped he was, and Nick would likely just nod and agree with a big ole goofy grin.

Nick had absolutely no pride right now where Rachel was concerned. She didn't seem to realize how completely smitten he was. If she had any idea what heaven and earth he'd been moving in the past two weeks to make their paths the same journey, she might understand. But he wasn't quite done aligning things yet. Just a couple more details until he was ready.

Tomorrow was exactly one week until Christmas. He and Rachel had hit every single scheduled Christmas event Ministry had to offer so far. They'd done the tour of homes, run the 5k together, and tonight they were attending the Christmas beauty pageant for all ages. Normally, this wasn't his kind of gig, but he'd been recruited to help carry equipment and act as photographer's assistant, along with her paid assistant, Chloe, for the evening.

He wore a red sweater with black slacks. Hopefully a photographer's assistant could opt for a pop of color for a Christmas event. This was a pretty swanky event, so he hoped he wasn't under dressed.

He was sitting in her living room watching football when she came out of the bedroom. She was wearing a black button down shirt with black slacks, her normal attire when photographing an event. "You look festive," she said.

"Is it too much?" he asked.

"Nope. It's just right. Photographers try to be as invisible as possible, so we don't have to dress like the guests, thank goodness. I can't see myself squatting with my camera in front of the stage in a little black dress."

"I wouldn't mind you giving it a try." He wiggled his eyebrows.

"Ha. Not a chance. Now, help me get this stuff loaded up, sexy packhorse."

"You want me for my strong back. I see how it is."

"I'll let you show me how strong your back is later. This stuff isn't very heavy." She winked at him and handed him her somewhat heavy camera bag.

"I'll be your slave, woman, for a kiss."

She giggled at his antics, and showed mercy by leaning in for a slow, soft kiss that promised all sorts of fun later.

"You're killing me." He smiled at her, taking another bag of equipment from her.

"Matthew has his camera set up with most of the big lighting and umbrellas for studio photos, so I'm thankful I don't have to cover both."

"I'm surprised he still does normal photography, considering his current position."

"Matthew still loves to take photos. He's a magician behind the lens, so when he has time and Emma can get him, everybody's lucky. I learn so much every time I watch him work."

"How are you going to catch everything?" Nick asked.

"Matthew's going to take the studio shots and video, and I'll be doing the on-stage shots of the girls as they are walking and performing. There are private photographers some parents have hired as well, but they have instructions to keep their distance from Matthew and me, and not to block any of our shots. Emma included it as a clause in the pageant paperwork."

They'd made it to her car, where she already had a few things loaded.

"I can't thank you enough for helping me tonight. This is a big job for just me and my assistant, and it's a busy evening, so if I don't get a chance to speak to you again before the pageant is over, please know that I wanted to."

He smiled at her, and said, "I like watching you work. It's as if you forget the world around you and focus only on finding the artistry in every shot you take. It's fascinating for someone on the outside. Plus, I just like to watch you in a kind of creepy way."

"Weirdo. But that was a nice thing to say. And I give you permission to creep on me just a little while I work."

⋙⋘

RACHEL REALLY WAS grateful to have Nick with her tonight. Lately, he'd been behaving a bit oddly. Almost like a teenage boy. Kind of silly and sweet, and happy to hang out with her no matter what Ministry Christmas event she'd dragged him to over the past week or so.

They drove to the old Ministry Theater a mile away where the pageant was being held. The theater had been updated and restored several years ago, according to Miss Maureen. Events too large to be held at Evangeline House that required a stage and audience were often housed at the theater. They'd held the Little Miss Pecan Pageant at Evangeline House until last year, but they'd also moved it to the theater this year, since its gain in popularity statewide.

"I've heard there's a huge winter storm heading toward

the deep South. Like, one of those hundred-year super-storms, and it might dump snow here on Christmas," Nick said as they pulled up in front of the gorgeous old theater.

"Oh? I hadn't heard about it. Being from New Orleans, hurricanes are our nemesis, not usually winter storms," she said, almost dismissively. The theater was dressed up for Christmas like the rest of Ministry, which made Rachel itch to get out and take tons of photos of the theater itself. But she had a lot of hard work to do tonight.

As they unloaded equipment, he said, "They're saying this storm has the potential to do some real damage and restrict travel for the holidays."

She turned her attention from the theater to the weather then. She really was a bit of a freak when it came to weather. "Oh, dear. I'll tell my dad to head on up early if it starts to look threatening," she said. A hundred-year storm wasn't something she wanted to think about.

"We'll turn on the weather channel when we get back tonight and have a look. It's still a week out, so forecasts change. I just thought it was worth mentioning."

She nodded, now concerned about this weather event. "Definitely."

Rachel had lined up a local college student home on her break to help with a few of the events during the Christmas season. So, Chloe met them at the car to help unload and organize equipment for their evening.

Rachel had parked in a space designated for her by Emma, so once things were unloaded, they were able to go inside without having to worry about moving the car again. *Thanks, Emma.*

Inside the theater, the madness had begun. Mommies and girls of every age were not bringing out the best in one another during last-minute preparations before the ceremonies began. Rachel had a strong desire to pull out her camera and take candids of this backstage behavior. The mother-daughter dynamic in the theater was a perfect storm of hormones, anxiety, and straight-up female competitive spirit mixed with a heavy cloud of Aqua Net. She hoped no one lit a match or the whole place might go up like a torch.

Nick's eyes were wide and maybe a little scared, if Rachel was reading his expression right. She realized he grew up with only a brother. This pre-pageant situation likely horrified him. As horrific as it might seem, things would improve once the show began. Or, maybe once it was over. Rachel had to giggle just a little at his shell-shocked look.

Matthew approached and noticed it as well. "Dude, you should chill. One day you're going to have a daughter of your own and you'll have all this to look forward to." Matthew slapped Nick on the back.

"I've seen some really terrible things in my life being a doctor, but I have to say, this ranks right up there with a bus collision with massive casualties." He didn't appear to be joking.

"Right, doctor humor," Matthew said.

"This is just wrong." He shook his head.

Rachel looked over to where a mom was gluing long, black spiderish fake eyelashes onto a little girl who appeared to be around six years old. "Ah. The lashes. Yes, those are very wrong."

"Hey guys. Are you all set?" Emma approached, large and sparkly in her dress made for three.

"Wow, you look amazing," Rachel said. She was stunning, no matter the size of her belly. Tall and blonde, with flawless skin and gorgeous light blue eyes, Emma could give any of these gals a run for their money up on stage.

Emma snorted. "They might crown me Miz Bovine Alabama at this point."

"You're beautiful. Now, let's get through this thing without your going into labor," Matthew said, and then kissed the tip of his lovely wife's nose. It was obvious how much they adored one another, and it made Rachel happy and uncomfortable at the same time because Nick was also standing there beside her.

She wanted with Nick what they had so badly. Could Nick feel her yearning? She dared a glance at him and saw in his eyes the same emotion, or was she just mirroring it? He smiled at her then and winked.

The moment ended abruptly as Matthew turned to Rachel after Emma left to check something with the sound guy, and asked if she needed anything. "I'm set up in the corner of the foyer. As soon as the girls are ready, they come to me for a studio shot. My assistant is handling checking them in and making sure they get to me. I guess Emma showed you your tape marks on the floor where the contestants will stop and pose for the judges, which is when you'll take photos."

"Yes, we met earlier in the week and went over everything. Thanks for double-checking." They were now standing in front of the stage.

"I have my team coordinating video in the booth upstairs. We've got cameras in several places filming. Of course, we'll edit later. We can also do some stills if we want to pull anything off video," Matthew said.

"I have so much to learn from you," Rachel said.

"You are a fantastic photographer. You've got an eye for your subjects that most people never develop. It can't be taught, and it's far more important than any kind of studio or special equipment."

"Thanks, Matthew. I appreciate your support."

He nodded and winked at her. "Well, it looks like it's time to get this show on the road."

They moved to their respective places and Rachel did several test shots, using Nick as her subject.

Once the lights went down and Emma stepped out into the spotlight, there wasn't a moment to take a breath. Rachel's camera flashed non-stop, and the contestants dazzled.

The music was loud, the lights bright, and the applause thunderous. Winners and runners-up were crowned, there were tears, and the entire evening was an unquestionable success.

"Wow. What a night," Nick said as they were loading up.

"Yes, it was a fantastic event. I take it you aren't still as horrified as when we arrived?"

He shook his head. "No. Not so much. I must admit it was baptism by fire for sure. But once I saw the product of all the preparation, I saw how much of it was nerves beforehand."

"It was fun—a lot of work—but fun."

"Yes, let's get you home."

≫≫≪≪

RACHEL AND NICK flipped on the weather channel once they were in their jammies with a glass of wine curled up on Rachel's sofa. "Holy cow. You weren't kidding about this storm system. It's huge."

Nick's experience with terrible weather as it related to being an emergency room doctor and trauma surgeon meant car accidents and people with horrific injuries. Southerners lost their minds on the roads in winter weather, mainly because the roads weren't prepared, the cars often weren't equipped for it, the people didn't have much experience driving in it. Ice wasn't meant for anyone to drive on, even a four-wheel-drive vehicle. People just refused to stay home and off the roads.

"I think I'm going to call my dad and ask him to come a day sooner. The weather isn't expected to move in until Christmas Eve, but Daddy is scheduled to come the twenty-third.

"That might not be a bad idea. Chances are, the inn won't be booked up earlier than that."

Rachel nodded. "Do you mind if I call him now?"

"Of course not. While you do that, I'm going to give my parents a call and check in. I haven't spoken to my mother since our unfortunate visit over a week ago." He made to leave and give her privacy.

"I wondered if the two of you had a chance to clear the air yet. I'll just go into the bedroom and you can call your parents from in here. This shouldn't take long."

"I hope I can say the same thing." He rolled his eyes. He dialed the house phone, which was a habit, since Mom still believed cell phones were for emergencies.

"Hello? Nick is that you? Let me go in the other room. I can hardly hear anything in here—your father's got the TV turned up so loud."

"I called because we haven't spoken since Rachel and I stopped by the other day."

"I didn't have much to say, really. I couldn't believe you brought her here without asking," Mom said.

"Mom, you need to switch teams now. *Right now.*" Nick had made up his mind about Mom's lack of allegiance to him, no matter whom he dated. "You should support *me,*

Mom. Not the girl you think I should be dating. *Me.* If I tell you I've fallen head-over-ass with somebody else, you should be happy for me."

"Language, Nicholas."

"No. I'm a full-grown man, and you don't get to tell me how to speak. I'm not profane, though I do respect your feelings as much as possible. You need to respect mine. I'm in love with Rachel Prudhomme. Did you hear her name? It's important that you get it right. P-r-u-d-h-o-m-m-e. Get used to the fact that Monica won't be your daughter-in-law. I'm sorry if that hurts her or you."

Silence.

"I did everything I could to be kind to her. I didn't just break up with her, we had problems, Mom. I didn't tell you how she behaved because I didn't want you to be unkind to her or for your feelings to change toward her. She was obsessive and jealous for no reason, and her behavior wasn't something I could live with. Ask her if you don't believe me."

"I knew. I just wanted to believe she could change. The two of you seemed so perfect together, at first."

"And yet, you allowed that drama at the house to happen and Monica to cause such a scene?"

"I'm sorry, Son. She showed up and I didn't know what to do. I haven't even met your Rachel Prudhomme. I had to choose sides on the spot."

"Wait. Did you just apologize and admit you were

wrong?" And snow was in the forecast for Alabama. Nick had to sit down. The world was now officially spinning off its axis. Perhaps hell would freeze over now.

"Yes. I did. And I meant it. Your being gone has made me realize, what's the point?"

"What do you mean, what's the point?" What an odd thing for her to say.

"Of living to be old? I love you boys more than anything. Your father hates me, and if I don't have grandchildren to love and spoil, so what's the point? Obviously, I'm difficult and nobody wants to deal with me. You're the only one who will even talk to me, and now you hate me too. Your brother laughs at me like I'm a joke."

"I don't hate you, and you're not a joke, Mom, but you are difficult. And Dad wouldn't behave the way he does toward you if you would cut him some slack. You're a hard-ass, Mom. You need to chill."

"Chill?" She actually laughed. "I guess I do need to chill just a bit." But he also heard her voice crack a little.

Nick heard her father yell in the background, "Amen to that, Son."

"*Leo,* this isn't your conversation."

"Let's just say I'm invested," Dad said loud enough for Nick to hear. "Chill, woman." Then dad hooted with laughter.

"I'll try, okay? To chill. But you all have to be patient with me." Then she clearly turned to Dad. "You too, Leo."

"That's fine, but you have to be open to us reminding you to chill."

"Okay. And you've got to stop bullying Dad."

"I don't think you've got to worry about that anymore. He's doing a happy dance all over the house. I've lost all control now, I'm afraid." But she had a smile in her voice that Nick hadn't heard in years.

"Say, Mom, why don't you and Dad come for Christmas? There's a nice inn here in Ministry right in the middle of town, and it might be nice for the two of you to have a little road trip."

"Well, I don't know if your father would want to leave for the holidays—"

"We'll pack up and leave day-after-tomorrow, Son. Gotta batten down the hatches before we leave. Big storm coming," Dad called through the phone.

"Yes. I was going to mention the storm if you didn't know about it. Tell Dad I'll call about a reservation at the inn in the morning," Nick said.

"You know he's been glued to the weather channel ever since they spotted the storm," Mom said. Nick imagined her rolling her eyes.

"I figured. Well, if it hits, we can all be snowed in together. All these historical buildings have wood-burning fireplaces, and there's plenty of firewood for sale."

"Should I ask Chuck to come?" she asked.

"Sure. He can stay at my place," Nick said. It would be

nice to all be together here instead of around their usual starchy dining room table.

Rachel had slipped into the room at some point and was sitting at her computer loading photos from tonight's pageant. Nick hoped he hadn't overstepped by inviting his family here for Christmas while they were spending their last days together.

He also wondered how much she'd heard.

Hi mother was speaking again. "Well, this conversation has been odd, to say the least, Son. I guess I'd better hang up and deal with your father. I do look forward to seeing you and meeting your Rachel."

"I know she's looking forward to meeting you too, Mom. Good night." He ended the call and came over to where Rachel was staring at him with a puzzled expression.

"How did you effect that kind of change in your mother's perspective? Is there something about your mother's mental status you haven't told me? She doesn't have multiple personalities, does she? Because last I heard, she had big plans for you to spend your life with Monica."

He shook his head, laughing softly. "She only has one personality, and we're working on that one, but I've convinced her to be on Team Nick, no matter what."

"I'd root for that team," she said with a grin.

"You're on that team." He stood up and moved the short distance to her desk, gently grasped her wrist, and pulled her into his arms. "Star player, if you know what I mean."

꧁꧂

"JUST PUT THOSE bags in my room. No, don't set it on the *ground.* That's extremely expensive luggage."

It was Tuesday morning, the second day of filming in the square, and Matthew called Rachel in to see if she could take some publicity photos for the show now that Jessica Greene had arrived. The woman wasn't scheduled to appear on camera until Wednesday, but the studio wanted to do some last-minute online promotion. Rachel wasn't certain exactly how they planned to place it, but apparently Matthew and his team had their hands full doing their job.

"Hi, Ms. Greene, I'm Rachel Prudhomme. I'm here to take some promotional shots for the network."

"Oh, hello, dearie. Have you come to interview me for a national spot?"

"No, I'm here to take photos for the show."

The woman's face fell. It was clear she was hoping for much more than getting her picture taken. "Well, I want a softening lens and full makeup."

"There's a makeup artist on set, so once you get settled, you can check in with her. The software I use can soften any imperfections on the shots."

Ms. Greene narrowed her already heavily made-up eyes at Rachel. "Just make sure I don't look like somebody's mother." The waddle under her chin was going to make that particular request a challenge. Rachel wasn't a magician.

"Got it." Rachel smiled sweetly at her, and moved to

speak with Ivy.

"Good Lord, that woman is a piece of work," Ivy said. Ivy, who was normally able to handle most folks without getting ruffled, appeared ready to go for Jessica Greene's throat.

"Have your sweet-talking daddy deal with her," Rachel said.

"There's an idea." Ivy grinned mischievously.

Rachel asked, "Do you think it would be okay for my dad to drive up today and check in? I know he wasn't scheduled for a couple days, but there's a big storm moving this way and I would feel better if he was here before the traffic and the bad weather."

Ivy pulled up the reservation on her screen. "Yeah. Sure. I'll just change the booking. We've already had some cancellations, so we're not as tightly booked as before. And while we've got a pretty full house because of all the events, we don't really book up until later in the week."

"Okay. He's only a few hours away, so I'll let him know." Then she asked, "When are Nick's parents scheduled to arrive?"

"They should be arriving sometime this afternoon. Sounds like this might get pretty interesting," Ivy said, her big brown eyes alight with interest.

Rachel nodded. "It might. I'll keep you posted."

"Good luck taking pictures of Mimi over there."

"Mimi?" Rachel didn't follow.

"Don't you remember that character on the Drew Carey show when we were kids? She was mean and nasty and wore tons of makeup? That's who Jessica Greene reminds me of…Mimi."

Rachel pictured the large woman in a mumu with loads of blue eyeshadow and a perma-scowl. This caused her to burst out laughing in a way that made her very glad she hadn't just taken a sip of a very hot or cold beverage just then.

The two giggled like teens for another moment before getting it together. "How am I supposed to keep a straight face while doing my job now?" Rachel demanded of Ivy.

Ivy shrugged. "Good luck, sister. I'm rooting for you." Then she snorted again.

"Bah. Some friend you are," Rachel muttered and picked up her bag. She headed toward the set where Cammie was hard at work filming. They'd located the set far enough away from the Christmas tree so that residents and visitors could still enjoy taking photos and move freely, but close enough that the tree formed a perfect backdrop for their temporary location.

The point wasn't to keep people away, but show the town as it was now: filled with the spirit of Christmas. For some, that meant the deeply religious spirit, depicted in the life-sized classic manger on one side of the square. Others observed the holiday in a more decorative and commercial way that included trees, Santa, and gift-giving. Rachel loved everything about Christmas, spiritual and all. Even the most commercial parts of Christmas brought families together to share time, meals, magical moments and memories. While some would argue that wasn't the meaning of Christmas, Rachel figured it was still special and holy—and certainly better than nothing.

Rachel saw that Jessica Greene was sitting in the temporary tent having her hair and makeup tended to. Hopefully, the photos wouldn't take too long and she could be available when both her father and Nick's parents arrived.

She watched Matthew as he directed the segment. Cammie was making banana bread pudding with praline sauce. Rachel took note of the way each member of the production team moved in tandem as they adjusted lighting, tweaked items on the set, and made small sound adjustments as needed. They were a well-oiled machine. Those who'd gathered to watch, stood behind the barriers, and were obviously just as impressed, judging by their awed expressions.

Rachel realized that Cammie was a well-known celebrity, but having gotten to know her so well, Rachel often forgot just how famous Cammie was. Her weekday cooking show held the top spot on the food channel.

A bell rang indicating the filming segment was complete, and there was a commercial break. Normal noise levels could resume within a certain proximity until the red light appeared and the *Quiet on the Set, Please* sign came on again.

"She used to be my grunt, you know." Jessica Greene had approached while Rachel was watching Cammie and the crew.

Rachel had no good response to the woman's rudeness, so instead, she said, "Are you ready?"

Jessica narrowed her eyes at Rachel, probably for not engaging. "Fine, where do you want to start?"

"Right this way." Rachel had to give it to the makeup artist. She had some serious skills with those products and brushes, which made Rachel's task immeasurably less difficult.

"Will Cammie join us when she'd done?" Jessica asked.

"She's supposed to. I need to take some shots of the two of you together. So, we'll stay close to the square while we work. Let's get a few next to the tree to start."

"Fine," she said.

NICK HAD RECEIVED a text from Chuck that he'd made it to Ministry with Mom and Dad. He and his most recent girlfriend, Stacey, had broken up right after Thanksgiving, so thankfully, that wouldn't be an issue with Mom, since Stacey hadn't been her favorite.

Nick hoped that one day Chuck would find what he had with Rachel. Though he couldn't officially announce his plans, Nick hoped that by Christmas, or at least by New Year's, he would have definitive plans set for big changes in his future—ones that included Rachel. Unless he went big, Rachel wouldn't truly believe or trust in his intentions.

He'd picked up on her deep distrust of men, based mostly on her father's actions. Her dad had been the only man she'd truly loved up 'til now, and it was time Rachel understood that what he had done to her mother wasn't the norm. Sabine's first husband also had a role in how trustworthy Rachel perceived the men in her life at an extremely vulnerable age.

Even though Sabine was now very happy and settled, and their mother was as well, what had stuck with Rachel was the initial experiences during her formative years. And the deep distrust and anger that followed when they'd let her down.

So, Nick realized he had to do this right. Where he left no doubt for her that she was his one and only, and that he was in this for real.

Today, though, he'd been especially busy at work getting ahead of this storm.

The hospital had gone into crisis mode, and was preparing for the worst, just in case. They'd ordered additional supplies for treating hypothermia and a multitude of other cold weather-related conditions. The staff was also preparing for the rise in weather-related accidents, so today, they'd created a surplus of trauma kits for stitching up, casting, and treating injuries sustained in falls, minor and major traffic accidents, and other possible traumas.

His background as a trauma and emergency room physician in a large hospital came in especially useful at times like this. "It's hard to believe we're going to need all this," Georgie said, as she wrapped up another sterile tray.

"Hopefully we won't, but if this storm is as bad as they're predicting, we don't want to be caught without enough supplies."

Then he spotted Suzette, who was carrying several sets of crutches to the supply closet. "Suzette, do we have another portable x-ray we could move down here from another department during the storm?" Nick asked.

Suzette thought a minute. "Let me check with oncology. They aren't full right now and might be willing to part with one."

"Thanks. Tell them it's temporary."

Dr. Granger approached. "You got the ship ready, son?"

"I think she'll float, sir." Granger was a navy man, and his references to running a hospital were most often comparable to running a tight ship.

"Good. I'm relieved at having all the additional trauma kits ready. Good thinking. Bringing down the extra sterilization units was a good idea. It takes too long to run those instruments through a full cycle if you wait too long."

"You're right about that. Anything we can have on hand down here to treat minor injuries quickly, the more efficient we'll be. I hope the main power doesn't go out, but it's more likely to happen if there's ice on the lines. Then, we're in for a whole other set of issues. We've got back-up generators, but they don't provide the same level of power long-term."

Nick hoped they'd fueled the generators up completely, because it was likely they would need the alternative power source. He didn't want to ask because Dr. Granger was overseeing the facilities and personnel. Nick had his specific tasks. "I'm going to call the mayor and send over some basic common sense safety and medical info for residents. We so rarely have this kind of weather, and people tend to lose their minds. There are things they might not know or have forgotten. I'll send it to you first and you can add anything you want before I send it to Ben," Dr. Granger said.

"Sounds like a great idea. Information is the best way to keep people from making poor choices," Nick said.

"Son, I understand your parents are due to arrive today. Go on and spend some time with your family while you can. When the weather arrives, it's gonna be all hands on deck around here. I'll cover here. Your shift's almost over any-way."

"Thanks, sir. I owe you."

"That's not how it works around here. We do what we can for each other. You saved my friend's life over at the market the other day."

"Don't mention it. It's what we do."

Dr. Granger nodded.

"Go on, now, and see your folks."

Chapter Sixteen

"HEY THERE, DARLIN'." Rachel turned at hearing the voice of her childhood. *Daddy's here!* She had to temper her initial reaction of pure love and excitement. Because she remembered she wasn't supposed to feel that way about him anymore. He hadn't changed. He'd gained the weight he'd lost since being released from prison, and was now back to his healthy-looking old self.

"Hey, Daddy. I'm so glad you made it." She stepped into his hug. What else could she do? He stood there with his arms wide open and waiting. He smelled like men's Dior, just the same as he had since her earliest memories of him. He pulled her in a big exuberant bear hug, nearly lifting her off her feet.

She'd missed him. *Oh, how she'd missed him.*

"So, where's your sister and her little angel?" he asked.

"She should be on her way as soon as Janie wakes up from her nap. I've just finished up from doing some promo shots with Jessica Greene and Cammie Laroux. Have you checked into the inn yet?"

"Not yet. I saw you over here, so I came right over. You look fantastic, sweetheart."

"Thanks. Looks like the beach agrees with you. Why don't we head over and get you checked in? Nick's parents should be arriving any time now too. I would like to say hello and make sure they get settled in too."

"Nick? Who's Nick?"

Rachel blushed under his scrutiny. "He's, uh, someone I've been seeing. A doctor from Atlanta who's filling in at the hospital."

Her father frowned. "What do you know about this *Nick*?"

Rachel's eyes narrowed. "Enough. So, don't come here and get all protective. You don't get to do that."

"Fine. But I want to know more about him."

"He should be here soon. You can ask him all the questions you want. But you must be very polite to his parents. It's their first visit here as well."

As they walked toward the entrance of the inn, Rachel noticed Nick approaching from down the street. She sighed with relief. Reinforcement would be a very good thing right now. She just hoped her father would be polite.

She waved to Nick as he approached. Daddy wasn't looking just then, and instead was focused on rolling in his suitcase through the front door as Mr. Monroe held it open. There were quite a few people in and around the inn now. It seemed the town was indeed filling up early in anticipation of the storm. Rachel thought it was a little odd that people would leave home at all with a storm coming. Maybe being here in Ministry during a storm was better than someplace else for these folks. Who knew how long a storm like this might last?

"Wow, it looks like everyone's here early for Christmas. I can't believe they didn't cancel," Nick said. He leaned down and kissed her cheek and gave her a quick squeeze.

"I was just thinking the same thing." She stopped just before going inside. "Be warned. My dad just arrived."

"Well, I got a text about a half-hour ago that my parents and brother were here. Have you met them yet?"

She shook her head. "Looks like the party's started."

"Might as well get through the introductions." He started to pull open the door, and Mason Monroe took over the task.

"Hello, you two. Welcome to the Ministry Inn. I do believe your relatives are right inside."

"Thanks, Mr. Mason," Rachel said.

As her eyes adjusted to the dimmer light in the foyer of the inn, Rachel spotted her father instantly. He was smack-dab in the middle of a ruckus at the front counter. With Jessica Greene. The woman's volume was turned up way too loud for a public venue. As Rachel hurried over, she heard Jessica say, "I don't know who the devil you think you are, but there's no way in hell you're taking my room."

"Dad, what's going on here?" Rachel asked.

Her father opened his mouth to answer, but Jessica Greene piped up, again, with her outside voice blaring. "This *man* thinks he's going to steal my suite."

"My good woman, I have no intention of *stealing* anything. I'm certain there's a reasonable explanation that our room keys share the same number."

The young woman at the desk appeared flustered. Rachel feared she would bolt should this continue. "Hi there, is Ivy or Mr. Monroe available?"

The girl, Daisy, her name tag said, smiled, sensing an empathetic voice. "Ivy will be back shortly, and Mr. Mason is helping the bellmen with luggage. We have so many guests checking in at once, it's taking all of us to handle things."

"Can you tell me why both parties have the same room numbers on their keys?" Rachel asked carefully, so as not to scare her.

Daisy leaned in so as not to be overheard. "Well, best I can tell, it's just a mix-up. They're meant to be in suites next door to one-another, but the keys got switched. Before I could explain this, Ms. Greene started yelling."

"So, there's no problem with the room?"

Daisy shook her head. "The keys they both have are meant to be for Mr. Prudhomme's room. I have Ms. Greene's right here."

"I'm Mr. Prudhomme's daughter, Rachel, and a good friend of Ivy's. Could you give me her room keys and I'll sort it out?"

"I've seen you in here with Ivy several times, so I know who you are," Daisy said. "Thank you for doing this. She didn't want to listen to what I had to say." Daisy motioned toward Jessica.

Rachel took the key and nodded. She then turned to where she heard her father suggesting he and Jessica Greene share the suite. Rachel sucked in a horrified breath. But Jessica Greene's response was worse.

"Well, you sly devil, you. What say we get this worked out and you can buy me dinner?"

Oh, Gross. "It looks like there was just a small key mix-up," Rachel said, trying not to gag at the idea of the two of them getting cozy.

They both turned toward Rachel, who held up the small envelope with the room keys for Jessica. "These are for Ms. Greene's suite. The other key there—" she pointed to the one in Jessica's pudgy hand—"is Dad's second key."

"Looks like the problem is solved. May I buy you dinner tomorrow night?" he asked Jessica. "I've just arrived and have family commitments this evening."

She blushed full-on. "I would be delighted."

Good God, that was quick work.

"Until tomorrow then. Unless I see you between now and then. It's a very small town." He bowed slightly.

Once they were out of hearing range, Rachel turned to her father. "What in the world was *that*?"

"A little harmless flirtation to cool the angry little woman's sails, *non*?" He grinned.

"Well, from where I stood, it was pretty disgusting. Best stay as far away from that bag of wind as possible."

Dad appeared thoughtful for a moment. "I think she's misunderstood, perhaps."

Before Rachel could reply, Nick approached with an older couple and a younger version of himself.

"Rachel, I'd like for you to meet my parents, Leonard and Beverly Sullivan, and my brother, Chuck Sullivan."

"Hello, there. It's so nice to meet you all." Rachel put her hand out to Nick's mom first.

The woman pulled her in for a hug. This was completely unexpected. "Please call me Bev, dear." They separated, and Rachel read a sincerity in her eyes that eased her fears.

"Hello, there Rachel. I'm Leo. Nobody calls me Leonard except my mother, God rest her soul, and my banker. It's wonderful to meet you." He didn't hug her, instead he kissed her cheek, and smiled warmly. She noticed he had Nick's same dimple.

"It's wonderful to meet you both," Rachel said.

"I'm Chuck. I'd tell you my nickname, but my mom is standing right here," he said, and leaned down to kiss her on the cheek, the same as his dad had done. This was a mischievous young man.

"It's great to meet you, Chuck. My imagination is running wild now." She could only guess at the many rhyming phrases for Chuck.

"You have *no* idea," Chuck said. "It's a popular drinking game among my friends."

She'd almost forgotten about her father standing there until he'd spoken. "Well, hello. I'm Jean-Claude Prudhomme, Rachel's father. She's somewhat ashamed of me. Ex-con, you know."

Bev's eyes widened at her father's comment, and she placed her hand over her chest as if there was a risk of a cardiac episode at her father's announcement.

"Don't worry, it was all white-collar stuff. I'm totally non-violent." He winked at Bev, whose eyes widened even further.

Leo seemed nonplussed and stuck his hand out to shake Dad's. "Nice to meet you, Jean-Claude."

"Pleasure to meet you both," Dad replied.

"Dad, this is Nick Sullivan. Dad, Nick."

Rachel tried to determine from her father's expression if he was going to cause trouble. "So, this is Nick? It's a pleasure, son."

"It's great to finally meet you, sir."

Whew. Crisis averted for now. So glad that was over. At least Dad hadn't tried to out-squeeze his hand or do a chest bump, stare-down, or some alpha nonsense. She wouldn't have put it past him. It was bad enough he'd made the ex-con joke and freaked out Bev.

"Hear there's a big storm headed our way," Dad said to

the group.

The men all grunted and nodded. Nothing brought a bunch of males together like the weather report.

"We've been preparing for the worst all day at the hospital," Nick said. "Hoping we won't need half of it."

"Well, I, for one, am glad to be here with all my boys. This place looks like it's stood the test of time. I don't think a little ice and snow is going to take it down. Just look at that gigantic fireplace. I hope they've got plenty of wood in case the power goes out."

"This town is one of the most prepared places for pretty much everything I've seen so far," Nick said.

Rachel glanced over at him, wondering if he realized how proud he sounded of Ministry as he spoke of it. Like it was his town. Not the place he was leaving in a week or two. She still didn't know exactly when he was scheduled to go back to Atlanta. They'd avoided that discussion lately, instead focusing on spending and enjoying as much time together as possible.

She figured they would take things as they came.

A tiny shriek sounded, and soft little bands closed around her legs. "*Wachel!*" Janie giggled when Rachel picked her up high and covered her tiny cheeks with kisses.

"Sorry about that. She got away from me when she saw you. Wild little hooligan," Sabine said, slightly out of breath from chasing her daughter.

"Hi, honey." Dad turned to Sabine and hugged her

tight. "Is this my granddaughter?" His eyes had turned so soft and tender that it was all Rachel could do not to tear up.

Sabine saw it too and her reaction showed in her expression as well. "Yes, Dad, this is Janie. Janie this is your grandpa."

"*Gampa?*" Janie repeated, a tiny frown between her perfect baby brows.

Daddy dropped down on one knee, so Rachel did the same. "I'm your grandpa. Can you give a high-five?"

Janie stood in the circle of Rachel's arms still, uncertain. Rachel nodded and smiled, showing Janie it was okay. "It's okay. Look, Auntie Rachel will give Grandpa a high-five first."

After that, Janie decided that *gampas* were big fun.

"Sabine, she's the most wonderful thing ever. And you're about to have another. When?" Daddy asked.

"January fifteenth is my due date. I hope this little football player waits that long."

"Well this is all very exciting. She's just adorable, Sabine," Bev said. "I look forward to having grandchildren one day. I'm Bev, and this is Leo and our son, Chuck. We're Nick's family."

"Oh, I'm so sorry. There's so much going on right now. I should have already introduced you," Rachel apologized.

"I should have," Nick said, clearly trying to take the responsibility off Rachel's shoulders.

Sabine shook their hands. "Welcome to Ministry. It's so

great to meet you all, and wonderful that you've come for Christmas. We love having family all around during the holidays."

"Your town is beautiful and all dressed up for Christmas. Of course, I've been here many times in the past, I've never seen it quite so festive. I have some family here."

"That's right, Rachel says you're kin to Judith and Jamie. I know they'll be thrilled to see you all," Sabine said.

Bev made a doubtful face then. "Well, we'll see about that. I haven't always been their favorite person in the family."

"But it's Christmas, so we're going to roll with the holiday spirit and assume things will go well. Right dear?" Leo said.

"We'll all do our best, won't we?" she answered.

Rachel tried not to smile. There was a story here, she was certain.

Sabine cleared her throat. "I hope it's okay that I've taken the liberty to make dinner arrangements. As soon as I found out everyone was arriving today, I figured we'd all want to gather and eat together to get to know one another."

The group all looked at each other and nodded their assent. "Thanks, Sabine. What did you have in mind?" Rachel asked.

"Is everyone okay with Evangeline House?" Sabine asked.

Rachel explained, "It's Sabine's husband's family home. They cater events and parties."

"My husband is the mayor, and I know he will want to meet everyone tonight at dinner. Right now, he's in a meeting with city officials doing storm preparations for the roads and such."

"That sounds nice. Thanks for including us. Is this the Laroux family you had Thanksgiving dinner with, Son?" Bev asked Nick.

He nodded. "Yes, it is, Mom. I can't wait for you to meet Mrs. Laroux. The two of you will like one another."

"Okay. Great. Everyone can get settled in their rooms, and Rachel and Nick will meet you in front of the hotel at six-forty-five since they both live just across the street."

"Sounds good, sweetie," her father said.

"I'll go and make sure everything is set for our dinner later. My mother-in-law is an amazing cook, so we are in for a treat, I'm certain."

"Please thank her for doing this," Bev said.

"Yes. I know it couldn't have been easy to pull this together on such short notice," Rachel said. Of course, if anyone could do it with relative ease and grace, it would be Miss Maureen. Hopefully, everyone would mesh well around a dinner table.

"Well, I, for one could use this time to freshen up and unpack, so I think I'll head upstairs." Bev hooked her arm with Leo's and gave him a meaningful look that clearly meant he was to accompany her.

"See you all later," he said.

"We'll meet you both down here in a little while," Nick said, then turned to Chuck. "You can come with us and I'll show you where I've been staying."

Chuck grabbed his bag, and said, "Lead the way, Brother."

Everyone else went their separate ways, agreeing to meet up at the specified place and time.

"So, Chuck, how's school?" Nick asked his brother as they made their way across the street toward Mrs. Wiggins's big old house.

"Ah, it's school, you know." Chuck looked around. "Dude, this place is awesome. I've never seen so much Christmas in my life."

"Yeah. It's pretty awesome," Nick said.

⭆⭅

DINNER REMINDED NICK of a stage play. The meeting of different families from different cultures trying to learn about one another, but also trying not to offend, while offending.

"So, Bev, how long have you lived in Atlanta?" Maureen Laroux asked politely.

"Oh, gosh, we've been there for ages. I wouldn't want to live anywhere else," she said. Then, she realized her mistake and tried to back-pedal. "But I'm sure it's nice here too. I mean, just look at your lovely town."

Maureen smiled serenely. "Yes, we do love it here."

Nick cringed inwardly. He guessed this was bound to

happen eventually.

Rachel's mom had agreed at the last minute to attend the dinner party, but not without Norman, which put a considerable strain on things. Her father sat stiffly, an angry tight expression on his face.

"Elizabeth, it's good to see you looking well," Jean-Claude remarked.

"Why, thank you, Jean-Claude. I hope your trip was pleasant," Elizabeth said.

They were icy cold to one another, and it made Rachel and Sabine shift in their chairs and dart eye-rolls back and forth.

"I know Rachel and Sabine are glad you could make it for Christmas, Mr. Prudhomme, and I hope you are finding the Ministry Inn comfortable," Ben said, obviously trying to smooth the tension in the room.

And Nick was worried about his parents causing a scene. Not that they were out of the woods yet in that particular area, but having other distractions made Bev and Leo appear less conspicuous in their starchiness.

"The food is delicious, Miss Maureen. Thanks for hosting us all on such short notice," Nick said.

"Nonsense, son. This is the kind of thing we do. Wouldn't have it any other way." Howard, Maureen's husband spoke up, as he covered his wife's hand with his and beamed. "Maureen's the best hostess and cook in three counties. I think she might have a magic wand someplace, but so far I haven't found it."

Everyone laughed at that. Nick had met Howard at the diner his first evening here, and from what Nick understood, nobody knew much about his clandestine past, so he was a mysterious character, to be sure, but he was certainly engaging.

"You are very welcome, Nick. It's been lovely meeting your parents and brother. I do hope you'll all join us for Christmas dinner."

"Oh, no, we wouldn't think of barging in on your family Christmas dinner." Bev was horrified at the very idea.

Maureen laughed and waived away her protests. "Nonsense. We find family wherever we can. If we need more tables, we add more. There's always plenty of food here, and we'll not hear any more about it. Plus, we might get snowed in. Here is the best place to be in a snowstorm. My Howard is always prepared for any emergency." She winked then.

The rest of the evening went along, with several edgy comments flung back and forth between Rachel and Sabine's parents. The bottom line between them was that Jean-Claude saw red that Elizabeth brought her new boyfriend to dinner.

Elizabeth made it clear that was tough shit due to Jean-Claude's past insults to her and their family.

"So, you see why I wasn't sure about inviting my father here for Christmas?" Rachel asked Nick when they finally got back to her apartment once all the parents had been returned to their lodgings. Chuck was next door at Nick's place on the phone with a girl.

Nick nodded. "I get it. Truth is, I was relieved that my parents weren't the ones making the scene tonight," he said. "Because, on a different day at another dinner table, I can guarantee you they will."

She laughed. "Thanks for making me feel better about it. Daddy is so frustrating. He refuses to see this is all his making. And Mom should *not* have brought Norman to fling in his face. Especially when we were all just meeting your parents. It wasn't the time to air our dirty laundry."

"No harm done. My mother will be fine. I think my dad was entertained by it all, truth be told."

"Did you know that tomorrow is cookie baking day?"

"Huh?"

"The cookie bake-off and swap. I'm helping Mrs. Wiggins with it. She's been heading it up. I haven't done much, but tomorrow, we're going to get up really early and bake. Then, we'll go to the square and set up the judging and swapping area."

"Sounds like somebody might get their feelings hurt," he said with a snicker.

"Oh, you mean if their recipe doesn't win?" she asked.

"Yup. Sounds like a contest of pride to me."

"Pride and prize. The winner gets to hold the trophy until next year and lord the bragging rights over her competitors for the next three-hundred and sixty-four days."

"Oh, good heavens. I think I might skip this one. Sounds like an opportunity for trouble."

Rachel nodded. "Might be. But the cookie bake-off is almost as anticipated around here as the pecan pie contest, though not as official and regulated. You don't have to bake your cookies in front of anyone or prove rights to your recipe for this one like the pecan pie contest."

"Wow, that sounds a little over the top."

"Maybe. But folks around here take their baking seriously, especially when it comes to being crowned number one."

"I guess we've all got to have goals, huh?" Nick said.

They were sitting together on the sofa, and Rachel was leaning against Nick's shoulder. Only a few more days until Christmas. She was missing him already. "So, we haven't had much chance to talk about what happens next."

"No, we haven't," Nick said. "But please understand how much I want to be with you."

She snuggled against his hard, warm chest. "And I'm going to do my best to make this work." He kissed her on top of her head. "I can't believe it's all coming to an end so quickly."

"Nothing is ending, Rachel. It's all just beginning for us."

Rachel hoped he was right. She wanted so badly to believe his words. Why would he say them if they weren't true?

Chapter Seventeen

RACHEL MET MRS. Wiggins, her feline companion, Spags, and her stuffed cats downstairs at seven a.m. sharp. The woman amazed Rachel with her energy. She'd already baked two batches of shortbread cookies, and was working on another variety of raspberry-filled ones.

The two women were baking to provide treats for spectators. Yes, there was a competition, but afterwards, there would be a cookie and candy swap between participants, then the public would be invited to partake in refreshments as well. So, Mrs. Wiggins wanted to make certain there were plenty of extras to go around.

"What can I do to help?" Rachel asked.

"You can tell me what's going on between you and your hot doctor while you put those cookies in the tins over there."

Rachel understood Mrs. Wiggins would require an update on Nick and her relationship, but it was difficult to describe at this point. "Well, he's leaving soon. And we're going to try dating long-distance for a while to see how it works out. I'm not sure beyond that."

"You're sad about this, aren't you?" she asked, nailing Rachel with a bespectacled stare.

Rachel nodded.

"Well, I don't blame you. This thing the two of you have had going on—" Mrs. W motioned her hands covered with potholders—"it's been a pretty wonderful and dreamy whirlwind romance."

Rachel smiled. "Yes, I guess it has. I'll be sorry to see it change or end. I really do care about Nick." Rachel used the spatula to transfer the shortbread cookies into the tins, creating layers separated by pre-cut rounds of wax paper.

"Sounds like an understatement to me. You're sorry in love with that man is what you are. But it's okay, because I've seen the way he looks at you, and he's got it just as bad."

"I can't ask him to give up his career and stay here with me. It's too early in our relationship. What if it didn't work out?"

"What if it didn't? Do you think he couldn't get a job just because the two of you broke up?" Mrs. Wiggins asked.

"No. I just don't want him to get off track from where he planned."

"Then, you're just too nice. Love is giving up everything and expecting everything in return. If you are both willing to do those things, then it will work out."

"That just doesn't seem practical," Rachel said.

"Love rarely is."

Rachel remembered the story of Cammie Laroux Harrison and Grey Harrison as she'd been told. Cammie was offered her own cooking show in New York but she'd turned it down, unbeknownst to Grey. Grey was willing to pull up roots and move to New York, leaving everything behind to start a new life with her and Samantha. The network had called and offered to film here in Ministry as a counter-offer, so Cammie would agree to do the show. Both had been willing to give everything up for the other—or at least try to adapt to a new life.

Rachel could see the parallels between Nick and her situation. Of course they didn't share the same kind of history Cammie and Grey had, but Rachel understood the idea of taking that leap of faith for something as important as the chance for a life with someone that might be so worth it. Before she'd met Nick, that concept of blindly trusting in an uncertain future with a man would have been laughable considering her anger and distrust. But lately, Rachel had opened her eyes to those around her who hadn't given up, and their stories made it all seem worth the risk.

Nick made it worth the risk. Oh, she hoped he was.

She and Mrs. Wiggins worked for a couple more hours, and accumulated what seemed like several hundred cookies, though it was closer to several dozen.

Moving all those baked goods downstairs and out to where the tables were being set up took almost as much time as the actual baking. Maybe not, but Rachel got a workout making the many trips back and forth. A large banner was displayed announcing the event in the square. And there was no shortage of people, mostly women, beginning to arrive. Tins and containers of every kind were carried to the tables. There were several categories for entry, so cards with names had to be filled out, declaring whether the item was a savory, candy, or cookie entry.

After the judging, anyone who entered could bring a plate or empty tin and "swap" goodies by taking several items of their choice from others' containers. Once the participants had taken goodies, then the public was invited to sample the treats. There would be hot cocoa and coffee served. Carolers were singing in the square as well to add to the ambiance.

The wind had picked up overnight and the temperature had already dropped several degrees, so it was beginning to feel wintery today. The storm was approaching and showing no signs of slowing.

The states in its path were reporting record snowfall, power outages, and ice on their roads. Rachel hoped the town, and the entire state, was indeed ready for this kind of weather.

For now, they had a cookie competition and swap to manage. The judges had arrived and were waiting until the entry deadline to begin their important work. This was becoming a deluge of women in winter coats placing their treats strategically in front of others as if that might help them win the coveted prize.

Rachel and Mrs. Wiggins were fielding questions and managing the five-dollar entry fees and handing out entry cards and pens. Finally, as time was ticking down to the start, they had one last entrant who wouldn't leave.

"How can we be certain this will be judged fairly? What if a judge doesn't like pineapple?" Bettie Jo Kemp challenged, just before she set her container down.

Rachel had heard the stories about BJ Kemp, and what those unfortunate initials stood for, but wisely kept *that* to herself. "Hi Bettie Jo. We have three judges who will judge on a variety of standards. Your entry won't be discriminated against for any ingredient, I assure you."

"This recipe was my great-grandmomma's, and it's *always* everybody's favorite at church, just so y'all know." The woman arched her brows, encompassing Mrs. Wiggins and the judges, who were getting ready to do their thing. It was a blatant attempt at intimidation.

Rachel overtly checked the time. "The entry deadline has officially ended. Judging may begin."

"What? No. Here. Here's mine," BJ plopped her tin down.

"Have you filled out your paperwork and paid your fee?" Mrs. Wiggins asked.

"Yes. Yes, I have," the woman replied, somewhat frantic.

"Then move on and let the judges work," Mrs. Wiggins

suggested.

"I wasn't trying to suggest that my pineapple bar cookies should win. I just—"

"We'll see you later. Thanks for your entry, BJ," Rachel said.

"*Nobody* calls me that anymore." The woman stalked off.

One of the judges snickered. "I went to high school with that girl. She hasn't changed."

It seemed that where there were so many good people and great things to recommend the town of Ministry, there was no escaping the handful of rotten apples, who, for whatever reason never seemed to learn their lessons.

Which made Rachel think of Cammie, who was filming her show with Jessica Greene today just on the other side of the square. Rachel hadn't gone over to see how *that* was going, and wasn't certain she wanted to. Hopefully, the woman was on her best behavior and wouldn't do anything to cause Cammie to want to set her hair on fire again. Of course, that was the story of the two women's history together, according to Jessica Greene.

Rachel couldn't believe her father had made a dinner date with the woman, of all people.

As the day wore on, and the judging was completed, the square filled up with interested attendees waiting for the results. The clouds moved in and the wind was icy. Hot chocolate and hot spiced cider was served as the carolers began singing. The winter weather didn't seem to detract from the Christmas spirit or the crowd.

The hundreds of cookies, fudge, and other treats were opened at last and served to the public. Rachel was amazed by the sheer amount of variety and quantity they'd taken in and were able to supply to the folks who'd come out. It was early evening now, and with the overcast skies, the lights in town were all turned on. Large space heaters had been brought in at some point during the day. Apparently, they'd been in storage for some time in anticipation of the Christmas festival, but hadn't been needed due to unseasonably warm temps the last couple of years.

Rachel had worn a ski jacket and thermal pants today that she'd dug out of her closet, having hung on to them from a ski trip taken years before, she'd been thankful they'd traveled with her all this time.

She hoped Nick had brought some cold weather gear from Atlanta. The weather wasn't usually super cold here, but Rachel knew it got that way every few years without much warning. They'd had a couple mild winters in the South, so they were due for some pretty chilly weather.

The clean-up volunteers had arrived, so that meant her and Mrs. Wiggins's shift was over. Rachel offered to help Mrs. W back up to the house, but the woman shook her head. "My friend, Ted, here has offered to escort me to dinner and back home." She nodded toward an elderly gentleman, who appeared to be sleeping at first glance, but then Mrs. Wiggins gave him an elbow to the ribs and he perked right up, and introduced himself.

"Hello, dear. I'm Theodore Rosenstein. So happy to make your acquaintance."

Rachel smiled then. She took his bony hand in hers and said, "It's wonderful to meet you, Mr. Rosenstein. Please don't keep Mrs. Wiggins out too late. I worry, you know."

His rusty laughed warmed her heart. "I'll keep that in mind, young lady."

He put his arm out to Mrs. W then. "Shall we, my dear?"

Mrs. W winked at Rachel and muttered in her ear as she passed, "Don't wait up."

Rachel laughed and picked up her purse and camera, preparing to head toward the hotel to see if she could meet up with her father, or see if Nick's parents were around or needed anything.

≫≫≪≪

NICK HAD JUST received the most amazing news, and he couldn't wait to have a minute alone with Rachel to share it. But it would require their having an important conversation. So, it wasn't something he could just whisper in her ear.

Just as he took off his lab coat to put on a warmer winter one to head home, a call came in on the radio that there was an accident an hour away with multiple traumas.

"Dr. Sullivan, they're asking if you can take a Life Flight to the scene. They'll send a helicopter for you. They need a trauma surgeon, and you're the only one in the area who can get there in time. There are two critical patients who will have to be stabilized on site before they can be moved. It's a mother and young daughter."

"How soon can the helicopter be here?" he asked.

"Twenty minutes. Their surgical team will be on the flight. They are short-staffed with the weather."

He nodded. After hearing further details, he said, "Make sure we have enough supplies for both surgeries, in case we've got to do them on scene. And lots of blood." Nothing about this sounded good. One victim was trapped under a vehicle, and the other had been thrown through the windshield and was somehow compromised with a tree branch puncture.

He texted Rachel to let her know what was happening without going into much detail. His good news would have to wait.

Nick had been relieved when he'd learned that Ministry General had a helicopter pad on top of the building and worked with a Life Flight service that allowed surgeons and physicians from all specialties to work together in saving critical patients in smaller hospitals where there weren't as many resources. This sometimes meant traveling on short notice to other places with lower populations. He'd never had to fly to a crash site before, but if it meant saving lives, well, he'd been trained to do that. Ministry was a small town, but they were rated a level III trauma center and were well equipped for most emergency general surgeries and other crises. The hospital itself was one of the larger ones in the neighboring counties, and Nick's advanced surgical training made him more sought after when something like today's accident occurred.

He grabbed a pair of all-weather boots from the closet in his office, and as soon as the 'copter landed, he dressed in a flight suit one of the team handed over to him. Part of his trauma rotation had been working with the Life Flight transport teams. The supplies were loaded from the helipad and they wasted no time getting off the ground.

Introductions were made. "Nick Sullivan." They shook hands. There were four of them total, besides Nick. Buzz, a retired navy corpsman and now a surgical nurse, Jeff, a former air force combat medic, and the pilot, Wes, also a former navy guy.

"I'm Vanessa," the female transport team member said. She pulled out notes on a clipboard and handed it to him along with a set of headphones. Nick clicked his harness on and she filled him in on the victims of the crash.

The pilot spoke a few minutes later. "Hang on. We've got wind gusts, and it's going to be tricky landing. There's ice on the ground, so be careful trying to get to the patients."

They discussed stabilization, and the possibility of on-site surgery procedures if the patients were too unstable. "We've got plenty of blood and supplies. The temps are just below freezing, so keeping the patients warm enough but the field sterile will be a challenge out in the open. We'll need to create a small space surrounding the patients, and keep onlookers away."

The woman said, "The state police are on the scene, and have created a barrier surrounding the crash victims. It's on a major highway, so there are people around, but they're trying to get the traffic flowing. The challenge is that the temps dropped quickly while it was raining, and the county didn't have time to treat the roads. This storm has blasted in earlier and stronger than anyone anticipated, so there's ice and it's causing a hell of a mess."

The helicopter tipped alarmingly as the pilot tried to land. "Hang on, y'all." The pilot's terse voice came through the headset.

A huge gust of wind sent the 'copter sideways, and threw them all back against their seats. The cars below had come way too close for comfort that time. Nick had experienced rough flights in the past, but nothing that had made him gut-sick quite like this. His heartbeat had risen, and sweat broke out on his brow. The others appeared equally alarmed.

"Okay, gang, let's try this again. Hang on." This time the pilot managed to lower them down onto the side of the busy highway. They landed with a thud, but at least they were down safely.

Vanessa scrambled out, taking Nick's hand as he helped her down from the helicopter. She was a tall, pretty, African American woman who appeared to be in her thirties. Of course, he gave a hand down to the others too. It's what one did to prevent ankle sprains.

They quickly unloaded the cases and headed to where the police were directing them as quickly as the icy patches allowed. No one would be served by one of them breaking an ankle.

The state police captain Johnson, as denoted by his badge and name tag, addressed them, "Female, Caucasian, age thirty-one. Pinned under the vehicle. Extent of injuries unknown. Her name is Julie. She's conscious and asking about her little girl."

"Tell me about the child," Nick said.

Captain Johnson's face became grim. "Becca, female, age four. Thrown from the vehicle and landed on a tree branch. She's currently impaled and conscious. Looks bad, Doc. I sure hope you can help them."

⇛⇚

RACHEL READ NICK'S text again. He wasn't coming home now, and she had no idea when he would finish up wherever he was.

"So, has anyone heard from Nick today? I can't imagine what's kept him this late."

"I got a text around the time he was supposed to get off work that said he'd had an emergency call and had to take a Life Flight helicopter to a car accident scene and that he would be in touch as soon as possible."

"In this weather? I hope everybody's okay. I hate to see anyone flying anywhere in a helicopter with this wind," Leo said.

Rachel had the exact same thought. She'd had a weight in the pit of her stomach ever since she'd received his text.

"Well, I suppose we should find ourselves some dinner. Anybody got a suggestion?" Leo asked.

Rachel wasn't especially hungry after all the treats she'd been exposed to today, but she figured they had to eat. "There's a good pizza place just a couple doors down. It's close enough that we can walk."

Bev had been somewhat quiet since the talk of helicopters and car crashes. "We might as well give it a try. I'm a little worried about Nick, truth be told, so I'd like to stick nearby."

Rachel gave Bev a quick sympathetic squeeze around her shoulders because she felt the same. "I've been a little off-kilter since I got the text too. I'll let you know the second I hear from him."

Bev tightened up just a little. "You'd think he would have contacted his family first."

Uh-oh. Here she was, this stiff mother Nick always spoke about. The one who gave him crap about his doing everything the wrong way. He'd texted his very new girlfriend important information and left her, his own mother, out of the loop. Rachel understood why that wouldn't be smart, she really did.

"He should have. If I ever have a son or daughter, they'd better contact me before anyone else if things go haywire. But if I do hear from him, I will let you know because I realize you're worried about him."

Bev smiled a little then. "I did give birth to the ungrateful child."

"You should remind him of it next time you see him," Rachel said.

"Then, he'll give me another lecture about how I should be less irritating and that I should chill."

"We get it that you worry. It's your job. If you didn't worry, there would be something wrong with you," Chuck said. He hugged his mom and added, "Slick Nick will be fine. And whomever he decides to inform of that fact will share it with the rest of us."

Bev sniffed a little, clearly not certain whether to be insulted or to chill.

They weren't the only group who'd decided pizza was a good idea. The place was packed and it took almost an hour to get seated, which did nothing for Bev's humor. Not hearing anything from Nick didn't help the situation, Rachel was certain.

Rachel said hello to several people she knew who all asked where Nick was. She decided to avoid any details for now, other than to say he was working. Any gossip regarding his situation could spark speculation and spread gossip like a wildfire. She simply didn't have enough information to say what was happening yet.

"Well, ruffle my feathers and call me a chicken! It's Uncle Leo and Aunt Bev as we live and breathe, Jamie."

Rachel turned to see Judith and Jamie standing next to their table. She'd almost forgotten about their connection to the Sullivans.

"Well hello there, girls. We were hoping we'd see you while we're here." Leo stood and hugged them both. He seemed genuinely thrilled to see his nieces.

Bev smiled at them as well, but with far less excitement. "Judith. Jamie. What a lovely surprise." She kind of air hugged them both.

Chuck, not to be ignored, made his presence known to his older cousins. "Hey cousins. It's me, Chuck." He grinned at them both.

"You're shitting me," Judith said to Chuck, then turned to Jamie. "He's shitting us."

"No way. You were just a grubby little kid last time we saw you," Jamie said.

They both greeted Chuck with genuine enthusiasm.

"We were just on our way out, but do give a call before you leave town. Maybe we can meet up again before you head back to Atlanta. Hopefully this storm will pass without too much trouble."

They said goodbye and promised to stay in touch.

"Those gals have grown up fine. Just fine," Leo said, smiling.

Bev kept her voice controlled. "They're fine, I guess. Better than they used to be."

Leo leaned toward Rachel and said, "Bev looks down her nose at my family. She thinks they're lower class since they're from the country."

Bev's face flamed. "I do no such thing."

Chuck laughed and reminded his mother, "You call them, *your father's people.*"

"Well, it's their lack of propriety more than anything else. And it's unkind of you both to make fun of me like this in front of Rachel. What will she think of me?"

Rachel felt sorry for the woman, even though she likely deserved her serving of humble pie. "I won't think anything, Bev. And I think they're ganging up on you."

"Well, I *try* not to be snobby. I know that's what they're saying about me. I was just raised—differently." Bev's face pinched up and she stopped talking.

Rachel had nothing to say to that.

By the time they'd finished dinner and exited the restaurant, there was still no word from Nick. It had been dark now for a couple of hours, being winter, and sunset happening so early now. Rachel had zipped her coat all the way up around her neck. It was well below freezing now, and the wind was icy and blowing.

"Storm's coming in. Should be here by morning," Leo said. They'd just entered the lobby of the inn.

"Let's share cell numbers so we're all connected," Rachel

said.

At this point, Bev didn't make any snide comments. Her worry for Nick was obvious. "Is there anyone we can check with about Nick?" she asked Rachel.

"I'll call the hospital and find out what they know," Rachel said. She had been thinking the same thing. It was unusual that he hadn't been in contact with anyone since he left. That had been hours ago.

Rachel separated from the group and looked up the number. She hated to be the worried girlfriend calling to check up on Nick at work, but this weather situation was truly scary.

"Ministry General, how may I help you?"

"Hi, this is Rachel Prudhomme. I was hoping to get some information on Nick Sullivan. He went out on an emergency earlier and we haven't heard from him. We're getting a little worried now with the storm moving in."

"Oh, yeah. I've heard some chatter about that. Let me see if I can connect you with someone who has information about that. Hold just a moment, please."

"Thanks."

Rachel waited what seemed like forever before someone came back on the line.

"Hi there, Rachel, is it? This is Dr. Granger in the emergency department. Nick is still out at the crash site. It's a rather serious situation, and the weather's not helping, I'm afraid. They can't take off yet because of the wind, and the roads are iced over now. There's a cell tower down in the area, so they don't have service. Give me your number and if we hear anything someone will give you a call."

"So, is he alright?"

"Last I heard, they were still trying to stabilize the victims and stay warm. I'm sorry I can't offer more information, young lady. I understand his family is here in town. Please give them my best and know we're doing everything we can to bring him home safe and sound."

"Thank you, Dr. Granger."

Bev, Leo and Chuck now stood in front of Rachel listening to her end of the conversation. Waiting.

Rachel couldn't believe what she'd just heard. "The cell tower there is down, and they're still working to save the victims. The helicopter isn't meant to fly in this kind of weather, and can't take off now because the wind is too strong, and the roads are iced over."

Bev's intake of breath was followed by a sob. "How will they stay warm?"

"They have ambulances and still have fuel, so right now, they have heat," Rachel said. But she understood that fuel would run out sooner or later.

"I'm sure they have thermal blankets and such as well. People don't freeze to death these days, Mom." Chuck tried to reassure Bev, but it almost sounded like he was trying to make himself feel better about the situation.

How would they stay warm out in this weather without

any reinforcements? What kind of supplies *did* they have? Were there any other vehicles where they could take shelter and crank up the heat, at least for short periods? Rachel tried not to roll over into panic mode. "Yes, I'm certain the police are there and well-prepared for this storm."

"Hey there, honey. Geez, who died?" Jean-Claude Prudhomme approached unnoticed, and took in their grim faces.

How typical that her father would say such a thing at such a time. She took him by the arm and pulled him away from the group. She quickly explained the situation and how serious it was.

He immediately apologized, first to Bev, then to both Leo and Chuck.

"Thank you, Jean-Claude. There was no way you could have known what was happening," Leo said.

Rachel remembered then that Daddy was supposed to have dined this evening with Jessica Greene. "Did you have a date?"

"As a matter of fact, I did, and it was lovely." He smiled.

"Well, where is she?" Rachel asked, not because she wanted to know, but because it gave her something to talk about besides Nick's situation.

"She's an early-to-bed girl, and asked to be escorted home right after dinner."

"Smart woman," Bev muttered beside her where her father couldn't hear.

Rachel suppressed a grin. "Well, I think I'm going to head home now. Chuck, did you want to come up to the apartment or stay here?" she asked Nick's brother.

Chuck addressed his parents, but mostly Bev, "Mom, do you need me to hang here with you and Dad or should I go up and wait for Nick at his place?"

"Your mother and I will wait here together. You go on with Rachel. If anyone hears any news, we'll all be in touch," Leo answered for Bev, who appeared suddenly exhausted.

"Please try and get some rest. The storm will likely be here by morning, so if the cell service goes out, we still have a landline at Mrs. Wiggins's place. She made me enter the number in my phone, so I'll text you that number as well and you can make a note of it when you get to your room. The inn has a landline, so we should still be able to stay in touch."

"Thank you, dear. I apologize for being rude earlier. I'm afraid it's my go-to when things aren't going my way," Bev said to Rachel.

"I get cranky sometimes, too. We're all human, so we'll do well to remember it." Rachel gave Bev and her dad a hug and wished them a good night.

"Dad, you know I live in that big old house across the street, right? Number 227, Apartment A, upstairs." She brought him to the large window of the inn and pointed across and down to the right. "Just there." Mrs. Wiggins old mansion could be seen sitting just down from the shops on the corner.

"Beautiful old place. I saw you head there the other day, but didn't know which apartment. Now I do. Stay warm, sweetie. Your Nick will come back to you."

She hugged him again, feeling his support and the security of having her father with her. "Thanks for coming, Daddy."

She noticed his eyes fill. "I love you, Rachel. I know I've been a screw-up as a dad, but I'll always be here for you."

Rachel nodded and turned toward Chuck, who was waiting a few steps away. She and Chuck zipped up their jackets and headed out into the cold, windy, night. The colorful lights and Christmas decorations still appeared so cheerful, as if nothing odd was happening, as if there was no beastly storm bearing down on this nearly-perfect town.

When they arrived at the house, Rachel knocked on Mrs. Wiggins's door. She wanted to make certain the elderly woman had made it home safely after her dinner out with Mr. Rosenstein.

Mrs. Wiggins answered after the second knock, but she wasn't alone. "Well, hello, Rachel. Is everything alright?" *Was Mr. Rosenstein in his undershirt back there?*

"Uh, I was checking to be sure you'd made it home alright," Rachel said.

"How sweet. Well, as you can see, I have a guest, so we can talk tomorrow. Bye, now." Then, she shut the door in Rachel's face.

Rachel figured the woman didn't need to know anything about Nick. Right now, there wasn't anything to know anyway.

"She was in a hurry," Chuck said from behind her.

"Yeah. I think she was in the process of getting lucky."

They both made a face.

Chapter Eighteen

"AM I GOING to see angels when I go to heaven?" four-year-old Becca asked Nick. The tiny child was shivering from cold, and barely conscious. She'd been nearly hysterical when they'd approached earlier to find her supported by officers where she'd been impaled through her midsection by a three-inch diameter tree branch. She'd been facing the tree, hanging about two feet above the ground. At first, she wasn't aware of her circumstance. Shock had kept her from feeling pain.

But the cold had settled into her little body, and she'd begun to shiver intensely. The officers had tried desperately to keep her warm while a saw was brought in to cut the branch in front of her and at least get her away from the tree so they could work on removing it. But the emotional and physical trauma of her facing the tree while trying to cut the branch was tricky. Shielding her from what was happening was impossible.

"Becca, honey, you might see angels when you go to

heaven, but right now, we plan to keep you here with us so your mommy and daddy can watch you grow up," Nick told her as he tried to determine what, if any, organs had been damaged by the limb.

A large light shone on the area where they worked. Nick decided they should try a different tactic. "This saw is too big and will be too loud. The branch isn't any harder or bigger than a bone. Let's try the bone saw instead."

Most often, bone saws weren't part of medical supplies brought along in such situations, but he'd suggested one after hearing about Becca's mom being pinned under the car. Terrible things had been done in the name of saving lives. One couldn't always save limbs as well.

"Buzz, here is going to cover your eyes, okay? This is going to make a loud noise, but not as loud as the other one did. We're going to put your headphones back on so it won't be scary, okay? Vanessa's going to get you another blanket so you'll be warmer." They'd brought a pair of the helicopter's headphones out so the noises wouldn't be so jarring.

The little girl nodded. Lord, he hoped she survived this ordeal. "Okay, here we go." Nick wore protective eye gear, but the sharp pieces of the tree branch splintered everywhere in what seemed like a million pieces. One of the officers held up a piece of tarp to try and protect everyone as much as possible.

The high-pitched whine of the saw was awful and loud, and it was likely that no one would ever forget this moment.

Finally, the branch was severed in two, and Becca's weight was absorbed by the many pairs of hands and arms who'd worked so hard to support her these last hours. Of course, there was still a tree branch in her middle. For now, it was still protruding in front about three inches. The sharp stick came out her back about a foot.

"You did great, Becca. Now, we're going to bring you to the ambulance where we can keep you warm."

They carried the little girl, branch and all to the medical van that had been at the ready for hours. He'd had the team prepare in case an onsite life-saving surgery was necessary. That was still to-be determined. The first rule of impalement was: *never remove the object.*

Becca's mom, Julie, was critical, but stable, after the emergency response team managed to use a winch to unpin her from her position in the overturned vehicle they'd been traveling in. Becca was four, and that meant she'd been in her car seat, but she'd recently learned to unbuckle herself, and according to Julie, she'd turned just for a second, begging Becca to snap the buckle back together, when they'd hit a patch of black ice. The car had left the roadway and things had gone horribly wrong from there.

Julie was in a separate ambulance with broken ribs and a collapsed lung. She had a compound fracture to her left tibia/fibula. It was a nasty injury, but if they could get them both to a level I trauma center within the next few hours, Nick was hopeful. If not, he hated to think about possible consequences of the combined injuries.

The immediate problem they faced was this blasted storm. There was no getting out now.

"Let's get Becca on her left side and try to make her comfortable. Take the pressure off by elevating the gurney to about a forty-five-degree angle. If that doesn't work, try the other side. Give me an update on her vitals once you get her hooked up. Let's hang a unit of O neg. and give IV Zosyn 2g, piggyback. I'm going to see your mommy now, Becca. She will want to know how you're doing."

Becca's breathing was fast and shallow, and she was very pale, a sure sign that shock had fully set in. She nodded slightly, but her eyes were glassy and she wasn't engaged. At least they could warm her up fully in here. For now. Until they ran out of gas. He preferred not to think about that.

Nick had warmed up considerably inside, but pulled up the hood on his jacket to make his way to the other ambulance where Julie waited. She was in and out of consciousness, mostly due to the large amounts of morphine they'd had to give her for the excruciating pain she was in due to the leg fracture.

"Hi there, Julie. Good news. We've gotten Becca inside now. She's resting comfortably now in the ambulance right next door. We're getting her all warmed up and taking great care of her." Nick noticed a tear track down the side of Julie's face. "She's stable, Julie. We're going to get out of here. This wasn't your fault."

Nick hadn't ever felt more helpless.

"I'll come back in a few minutes and check on you." He patted her hand. It was cold, despite the warmth inside the van.

Nick's eyes met Jeff's, and they shared a worried moment. *How were they going to get out of this?*

"I've been in worse circumstances, Doctor. We're going to get through this."

"I'll bet you have, Jeff. That gives me confidence." Jeff was a combat medic. He'd seen terrible things in places Nick could only imagine. "Thanks."

"It would be nice to have one of the big birds here like we fly on our missions. That would get us out," Jeff said. "This tiny chopper isn't meant for rescues, only for transporting patients from hospital to hospital in normal conditions."

⟫⟪

RACHEL WASN'T SATISFIED to sit and wait to hear from Nick. This storm was coming, but before it did, she was going to do everything she could to bring Nick and the people he was with home safely.

"Chuck, how do you feel about going someplace with me?" she asked.

"Um, sure. I have a feeling this has something to do with my brother."

"You are right. Did I notice you've got a four-wheel-drive truck?"

"Yes. I insisted we take it because of the weather. Mom had a hard time climbing inside, but we got her there."

"Great. Then, I'll let you drive. We should be fine to get to the hospital and back before the roads ice."

"Let's go." He led her to his late-model black pick-up, which was indeed a challenge to climb inside for a regular person. It was a guy truck, to be sure.

They drove to Ministry General without a problem. There were a few snow flurries, but the roads were clear. Rachel showed Chuck where to park outside the emergency department and they went inside.

She spoke to the same girl, Candy, at the information desk when she'd called earlier. Candy called Dr. Granger up immediately.

"Nice to see you, Rachel. We're getting concerned about Nick over there. He's not able to move his patients due to icy and windy weather. They're sitting right in the worst of it and things are becoming critical for all, I'm afraid."

Dr. Granger's words were like a punch to the gut for Rachel, but she had an idea. Maybe a crazy one, but it was worth a shot. "Dr. Granger, do you know Howard Jessup? He's Maureen Laroux's husband."

"Why, yes. I think everybody in town at least knows of him. Got some secret spy background, but nobody really knows the extent of it. Or, so I'm told."

"Right. He has high-level government clearance and has

access to all kinds of planes and such. Special military-type equipment. Could we use one of those big rescue-type helicopters in this kind of weather?"

Dr. Granger appeared thoughtful for a moment. "Those types of machines rescue folks from mountaintops in snow-storms. I don't see why they couldn't be used in this kind of situation so long as there was a place to land the thing. Do you think Howard would be able to get us something like that at a moment's notice?"

Rachel thought back to when Sabine and Ben had been in a pinch last year in New Orleans. Howard had come to their rescue by calling in favors well above any local law enforcement or political pull Rachel had ever seen. Even with her father's influence, Howard had but to pick up the phone and *big* things happened.

"I think he's our best shot at getting those people help and bringing Nick home."

"How can I help?"

"I need to know exactly where they are. Like, coordinates you would use in the military. I'm going to call Miss Maureen now, before the weather gets too bad here."

"I'll get on it," Dr. Granger said and headed toward the back.

Chuck hadn't said a word. He just stared at her. "Who is Howard?"

"That's what we would all like to know. If he keeps using his powers for good, I think we can wait to find out. Let's just see if he can help Nick now."

She dialed Miss Maureen's phone number. It rang three times.

"Hello?"

"Hi, this is Rachel. I wondered if I could speak with Howard."

"Of course, dear. He's right here."

"This is Howard."

Rachel quickly explained the situation and asked the important question, "Is this something you could help with?"

"Of course. I'll just need the exact location where the pickup should take place. I assume you'll want this to happen within the hour?"

"Oh, Howard, thank you."

"This is a small thing. One day, somebody's going to ask me to do something challenging. Okay dear, where are Nick and our victims?"

Dr. Granger was now standing in front of Rachel holding a piece of paper. "I'm going to let Dr. Granger here at Ministry General give you that information."

She handed the phone to the waiting doctor, who gave Howard all the pertinent information.

"Sounds like they're all set," Dr. Granger said as he handed Rachel's phone back to her.

"I'm going to call my parents and let them know what's happening," Chuck said, and stepped over to the small waiting area.

Rachel had tears of relief in her eyes.

"I hope you don't mind my sticking my old nose in your business, but our boy, Nick is really excited about making this change. I'd never have taken him for a small-towner at first with all his big-city training and such."

His words took a minute to penetrate her brain. "What change?"

"Just today he got the final word. He's free and clear of all his commitments in Atlanta. He signed a contract as the head of Ministry General's general surgery department. We'll be able to offer so many more kinds of surgical options right here instead of sending them to Birmingham or Huntsville."

Rachel was flummoxed. "I—didn't know." Nick had been working behind the scenes to be with her. What if he didn't make it back? He'd made all the changes—met her more than halfway. She'd done nothing for him except say that someday she might consider moving to Atlanta. But not right now. He really must love her.

She nearly melted to the floor. "Whoa, there. Let's let you sit down. This has been a stressful day. Let's put some faith in Howard and the Lord. We're gonna have that boy home for Christmas."

Chuck came over to where she was sitting. "You okay?"

She shrugged. "Did you know he was giving up his career in Atlanta to come here?"

Chuck nodded. "Of course he was. He loves you, Rachel. I've never seen him this happy or content about any decision in his life. And I've known him his *whole* life. He loves Ministry. When Nick first got word he was coming here, he hated the idea of leaving Atlanta, but you wouldn't believe how impressed he was with the hospital and the whole town. It was like he'd come home the minute he stepped foot here. Now that I'm here, I totally get it."

She smiled a little then. "Atlanta's his home. How will your parents react?"

"Unfortunately for the two of you, I'm looking for them to follow Nick here. The mere mention of grandchildren throws my mom into a new reason for living tizzy."

She exhaled then. *Just let him come home to me.*

Rachel noticed the Christmas tree in the waiting room, its lights twinkling brightly. She prayed then. For the safety of the family in the crash, the first responders and their families, and for all the people who'd gotten caught up in the storm. *Please let them all come home for Christmas.*

"We'd better get back home in case the roads get bad," Chuck suggested.

"Yes."

They said goodbye to Dr. Granger and headed back to her apartment. Chuck decided to stay on her couch in case they heard something. Rachel was relieved because she didn't want to be alone. She hadn't called Sabine or her mother because she didn't want to worry anyone.

Fuel was low in both ambulances after keeping them running most of the night to keep the patients warm, IVs charged, and machines operational. Unfortunately, something had to give soon. The roads had cleared of most cars by now, as they'd slowly made their way to safety. The sleet had fallen for a couple hours, completely coating the highway and cutting off any chance travel by roads. The temperatures had dropped by another fifteen degrees and the wind still blew.

Several highway patrol vehicles were still on the scene and the officers were now loaded together in one car, saving the gasoline in the other vehicles. They were sharing warmth by staying inside together. Nick and the transport team were evenly split between the ambulance with Julie and the one with Becca inside.

The patients' conditions were declining, and they all knew it. Nick understood the risk of infection for both increased with every passing moment they remained in an unsterile environment and without the desperately needed surgeries they required.

As the last of the fuel burned out in the medical vehicles, the team began to feel the effects of the day. One at a time, they began to nod off. Nick had set his watch timer to check on his patient. Vanessa was in the other vehicle and had done the same.

They'd better get a few minutes rest while they were able. The steady beeping of Becca's heart monitor lulled Nick

SUSAN SANDS

into nodding off, but a deafening bumping and whooshing sound from outside startled Nick into standing position. *What the hell?*

He pulled on his jacket, zipped it, and ran outside to see spotlights. The others had also come outside as soon as they'd heard and seen it. Nick placed his hand over his eyes to shield them from the wind and bright lights so he could see what was happening. It looked like two huge military choppers with the medical cross on the side had landed on the highway.

Two or three figures were headed toward them with two gurneys. Somebody had come to the rescue.

The noise was too loud to communicate much until they were inside. Lots of hand motions and one-word commands made do. The teams and the police worked together and loaded Julie and Becca. The state police officers were also loaded on the other chopper and told they were to be dropped off at their local headquarters.

There was still no word on who these people were until Nick was sitting beside Becca checking her IV bag.

"How's she doing?" One of the men sat down beside Nick.

"If we get her to a level I trauma hospital soon, I think we can save them both," Nick said. "Thanks for getting us all out of there."

The man grinned. "It's the least we could do for Howard."

Nick frowned. "Howard?"

"Yes. Howard Jessup. He called this rescue in. Says to tell you that Rachel is looking forward to having you home soon."

Nick shook his head and laughed. "How does Howard do something like this?"

"You don't know much about Howard, do you?" Clearly that was a rhetorical question.

He answered it anyway. "No, but I'm going to thank him just as soon as I see him."

"We're heading to Birmingham with the patients. I assume you'll want to consult with the surgeons there, then we can get you home. The weather's about to hit pretty hard, so time is tight."

"Wow, this is full-service, isn't it? Yes, I do need to let the hospital know what care we've given them up until now. We were able to get medical histories before Julie lost consciousness."

❧❦❧

RACHEL FELL ASLEEP waiting to hear something from Nick. She nearly jumped out of her skin when a warm pair of lips found her cheek in the lamp light of her bedroom. She hadn't even turned out the light.

"Nick. Oh, my God. You're back." She reached out and pulled him down onto the bed. She shook with relief.

"Rachel," he whispered.

She pulled back and got a good look at him. She wanted to cry with relief, but mostly hold onto him and never let go.

"I'm home, Rachel. This is my home."

"Dr. Granger told me what you did. That you took a permanent job here. Why didn't you tell me?"

He held her softly and stroked her hair. "I love you. I owed it to you to be sure it would all work out before I said anything. I didn't want to let you down."

"But I didn't do anything for you. You did it all."

"But you did. You trusted me."

"How is that anything?"

"Are you kidding? It's the biggest thing. You guard your heart like no one I've seen. I recognize that and I understand what a risk you've taken in letting that guard down with me. I had to prove to you that I was in this for real and that I wouldn't go home to Atlanta and break your heart. So, here I am. Home with you to stay, if you'll have me."

She thought she might just burst with love for him, then it occurred to her that she hadn't even said the words. "Nick, I love you—the real, forever kind of love people feel when they meet the person they think they'll die without. Tonight, when I heard you were in danger, I had to find a way to bring you home to me. Then Dr. Granger told me what you'd done and I realized you felt the same. I was so afraid for you." She squeezed him tight around his abdomen.

"My biggest fear was not getting home to you to let you know how much I love you. So, thanks for contacting

Howard. What does he *do,* by the way?"

"We may never know all of Howard Jessup's secrets, but he's been there when anyone in town has needed him, so I won't ask."

"Remind me to thank him in person when I get the chance."

She laughed.

"So, we've got a whopper of a storm moving in. We'd better get some sleep," Nick said.

"In a minute," she said, and wrapped her arms around him, showing him why they should wait.

Much later, Nick said, "You were right. Sleep is overrated." They were curled together like a couple of kittens.

"Told you so." Rachel hadn't ever been this happy and relieved. Nick had made it back to her safely. The weather outside was truly frightful, with the wind blowing in great icy gusts. The power had gone out while they'd slept.

"We should probably start a fire so we don't get cold."

"In a minute. I have to tell you something."

He propped up behind her on one elbow. "Oh? What's that?"

"It's important that you know how much love you. I love you for doing all the work. You knew I didn't want to leave my family or this place, so you made the sacrifices for both of us."

She felt the rumble in his chest. *Was he laughing at her?* "You're wrong, you know?" He pulled her to him. "I was being at least fifty-percent selfish in making those changes. The living I'll provide for you will be roughly half the money, and I'm okay with that. I figure it costs about half as much to live here. The selfish part of it is that I don't have to worry so much every day. When I arrived here, I figured out almost immediately that this is an easier way of life, and one I much prefer."

"So you copped out?"

"In many ways, I did. I'm a different person here, with you. A better person. I'm not as driven or competitive. My wants are different. In Atlanta, I thought I wanted an expensive lifestyle and a cool car. Here, I only want what I have. I'm completely content working at Ministry General doing what I've been doing."

"For how long? Will it continue to be enough?" This worried Rachel.

"With you by my side, how could it not? Here, I'm helping people live their lives, not keeping them alive and sending them away. I can walk into the grocery store in Ministry and see my patients living and thriving every day. Their happiness and quality of life matters to me, I realize. Their humanity matters."

Rachel understood then and nodded. "You are more than you were. That's how I feel about this town. It's made me better. Made me care about things in a way I hadn't before in a deeper and richer way."

"Yes. You do get it. So my wanting to stay was no sacrifice. I get you and I get a new home where I can breathe deeply and thrive, and where I'm a real help to others, and a part of something."

A tear tracked down her cheek. Her relief was so incredibly profound that he hadn't given up his life for her.

"I love you and want to marry you, Rachel. I want to have babies with you, I want to see your dreams realized."

"Marry me?" she echoed.

"Yes. Will you marry me?" His expression was fathomless.

Rachel just stared at him as if he'd asked her to dance naked in the snow.

"We can wait if you want."

"*No!* I just—yes, of course I'll marry you. I adore you, Nick Sullivan."

Epilogue

One Year Later

RACHEL FLIPPED THE sign on her studio window to *Closed for Christmas*. Finally. The bells jingled merrily as she shut and locked the glass and heavy wooden door. Ivy and Mason had done a fantastic job renovating and building out her vision. Rachel hadn't expected such support from the community as she'd worked toward her dream this year.

Matthew had gifted her with a couple of exquisite pieces of photography equipment that she would only have been able to dream of acquiring years from now. Miss Maureen had some of her best work framed for the walls of the studio. Emma gifted her with several portrait props. She'd said it was selfish, and it would help her with her pageant portrait needs in the future. Ivy had negotiated a hundred-year lease, or as long as Rachel wanted the space with no rent increase.

Things in Rachel's life had come full-circle since last Christmas. She was meeting Nick, his parents, and Chuck at the inn to grab a sweet spot for the Christmas parade. Ivy planned to join them for dinner after the parade. Rachel wasn't sure, but she sensed an odd vibe going down between Chuck and Ivy, despite a couple years' age difference. Chuck was due to graduate with his master's degree from UGA in the spring.

Tomorrow was Christmas Eve, and Daddy and Jessica were scheduled to arrive. It was hard to believe the two of them had actually made a go of their relationship. It had taken awhile for Rachel and Sabine to accept the odd and loud woman as someone who would be around, perhaps indefinitely, and possibly as a permanent fixture in their father's life. The idea of it made Mom laugh like crazy every time the subject came up. The divine providence of Jean-Claude Prudhomme stuck with Jessica Greene, even at his own choosing, was too richly deserved in her mind.

The baby portrait business in Ministry was booming. Sabine and Ben's baby boy, Daniel, would celebrate his first birthday on New Year's Day. Janie was totally devoted to her baby brother, besides wishing he'd been a sister. She simply had to be reminded not to put bows in his hair from time to time. Emma's twins were hale and hearty, and had just learned to walk, an adjustment for the new parents, to be certain. Cammie's had been a Valentine baby last year, so she and Grey had their hands full.

The snow-blower was cranked up to maximum output this year, working hard to create a white Christmas, at least for the duration of the parade. At just under sixty degrees, the machine had much work to do.

The crowds were thick, as usual this year, and the inn was packed. The giant tree rivaled last year's and may even have a foot or two bragging rights. Rachel no longer covered all the newspaper stories, thankfully, because they'd hired a real reporter over at the paper, so Rachel was able to focus on what she loved: making magic through her lens. And making a home with her handsome husband. They had just put in an offer on a home near Evangeline House.

Since last year's parade had been canceled due to the snowstorm, this one was doubly anticipated. Santa would ride on a float with his elves and throw candy canes. Ben and Sabine had plans to ride on a family mayoral float this year instead of the requisite convertible to smile and wave from.

"Hi there, Wife." Nick kissed Rachel's cheek and nuzzled her neck for a second before greeting his family. Bev and Leo were seriously considering a move to Ministry. Rachel appreciated that they were taking it slow.

A woman's voice cut into Rachel's greeting her husband. "Excuse me, are you Dr. Nick Sullivan?"

Nick turned toward the early-thirties woman, who was holding a young girl's hand of maybe five. A dark-haired man stood with them.

Rachel saw recognition in his expression. "Yes. Hi. I recognize you both from the accident last year."

"Yes, I'm Julie, and this is Becca. We never got a chance to thank you for what you did. You saved our lives." She hugged Nick as tears welled in her eyes.

Nick squatted down and spoke to the little girl, Becca. "Hey there, Becca."

She grinned at him shyly. "You took the tree out of my tummy. Thank you."

Rachel watched him melt. "You were so brave. You're welcome." Oh how she wished she had her camera.

Becca suddenly raised her dress and showed him her tummy. "See my scar?"

He traced the round and rough scar with his finger and then tickled her tummy. She giggled. "That is a very nice-looking scar."

The father extended his hand. "We call you Saint Nick in our house. Thanks for saving my two best girls."

"It was a tough day, but they were some of the bravest patients I've ever had. Thank you all for coming here. This means so much to me to know you are both doing well."

"It's been a tough year of therapy on my leg, but I don't even have a limp anymore," Julie said.

"That's truly wonderful." Nick seemed overwhelmed. "Saint Nick, huh?"

"Always and forever to us."

"I would like to introduce you to my wife, Rachel."

They all shook hands and said hello. Then Rachel had an idea. "My photography studio is just over there. I would love to take some shots of your family with Nick, if you would be willing." Nick thanked her with his eyes. She understood how much this reunion meant to him, and having some photos together would be special.

Julie's eyes lit up. "Oh, that would be wonderful. Thank you, Rachel." Then, she turned to Nick and said, "I was hoping to thank a man named Howard while we were in town. I kept hearing his name while we were on the helicopter."

"I'm sure we could give him a call," Nick said.

Nick was her Christmas miracle every day, for a year and counting.

The End

More by Susan Sands

The Alabama series

If you loved Forever, Alabama,
don't miss the rest of the Alabama stories.

Again, Alabama
Cammie Laroux and Grey Harrison's story

Love, Alabama
Emma Laroux and Matthew Pope's story

Forever, Alabama
Sabine O'Connor and Ben Laroux's story

Christmas, Alabama
Nicholas Sullivan and Rachel Prudhomme's story

Available now at your favorite online retailer!

About the Author

Susan Sands grew up in a real life Southern Footloose town, complete with her senior class hosting the first ever prom in the history of their tiny public school. Is it any wonder she writes Southern small town stories full of porch swings, fun and romance?

Susan lives in suburban Atlanta surrounded by her husband, three young adult kiddos and lots of material for her next book.

Visit her website at SusanSands.com

Thank you for reading

Christmas, Alabama

If you enjoyed this book, you can find more from all our great authors at TulePublishing.com, or from your favorite online retailer.

CPSIA information can be obtained
at www.ICGtesting.com
Printed in the USA
LVHW04s2045270718
585150LV00002B/349/P